ARTICLES OF FAITH

ARTICLES OF FAITH

MICHAEL CANNON

**FREIGHT
BOOKS**

First published May 2014

Freight Books
49-53 Virginia Street
Glasgow, G1 1TS
www.freightbooks.co.uk

A CIP catalogue reference for this book is available from the British Library

ISBN 978-1-908754-50-9
eISBN 978-1-908754-51-6

Typeset by Freight in Garamond
Printed and bound by Bell and Bain, Glasgow

the publisher acknowledges investment from
Creative Scotland toward the publication of this book

For my mother

Michael Cannon was born and brought up in the West of Scotland and worked variously as an apprentice engineer, tax officer, various temporary occupations and oil worker before returning to higher education to study literature. He now works for the University of Strathclyde. His debut novel *The Borough* was published in 1995 and *A Conspiracy of Hope* followed in 1996, both published by Serpent's Tail. His novel *Lachlan's War* was published in 2006 by Viking to much acclaim. His fourth novel *Four New Words for Love* was published in 2013 by Freight Books. He lives on the south side of Glasgow with his wife and daughter.

ONE

When he was three years old Michael Neavie was treated to the optical illusion of a ship sailing down a street. Thirty thousand tons of blunt keel and angular superstructure slides across his vision, interrupted by skeletal cranes and gingerbread tenements. He sits, balanced on his mother's jutting hip. She, with one arm around him, the other braced against the sandstone for purchase, stands in the pose of a capital K, buttressing the block. Her skirt is pulled taut against her splayed calves in a ladder of horizontal folds like corrugated tin. The hand against the wall intermittently detaches itself and flattens in a casual salute, as she shades her eyes against the mid-morning glare. She's standing at the close entrance to the terrace which slopes steeply, perpendicular to the river. Her block is one of a number, like clay furrows, the red sandstone drinking in the morning light, windows flashing in a string of descending suns to merge with the glare at the foot of the hill. Alternately bracing herself and shading her eyes, Deborah Neavie follows the ship's path as it glides on the scarcely glimpsed river, a streak of molten tin behind the intervening buildings.

Waves of sound float up from the launch: the indistinct fog horn of a distantly amplified voice; the detonation of the bottle against the hull, more imagined than felt; the roar; the displacement of metal and dragging chains.

Dotted at close entrances down the street other young mothers, similarly burdened, hold their children up. The women point, exhort, explain. They know this is one of the calibrations in their allotted history.

In her classroom above the tenement terraces, aloof from the beano, Miss Herne sits with a pile of corrections. She's putting the solitude to good use. Mr Gilchrist, the Headmaster, with what Miss Herne would consider questionable judgement, has subscribed to the local propaganda and permitted the children to bear witness to their history. Postponing her distain, Miss Herne watched her children file out in the company of the delegated assistant. From her window she watched the buoyant crocodile, scarves flying, join the tributaries of other classes as the mass of the school tramped down the hill in an air of infectious hilarity. At the first outrolling of sound Miss Herne's lips twitch, and again, and again, until she becomes more irritated at herself for this repeated spasm than at its cause. A boom, that sounds more like artillery, causes the glass to creak. She puts down her pen and gazes into the vacant sky and wonders at the herd mentality that compels them to club together and exalt over an iron hulk obeying the laws of gravity. To see the activity would require her to stand up, cross the room and gaze down the hill. But she won't. This voyeurism is a kind of participation. Secular crowds disturb her. Church congregations above a certain size also give her a sense of disquiet, the silent cacophony of all those felt intentions, wanting and wanting, like a clamorous butcher's queue, compromising her intimacy with God.

Miss Herne has eschewed the launch just as, in two years from now, she will eschew the safety of the Anderson shelter, as the Luftwaffe tries to level Clydebank. That piece of allotted history will find her kneeling on the floor of her first floor tenement, blackout blinds agape to admit the pulsed light of the incendiary bombs. While others cower she will kneel before the crucifix, praying with fierce joy, steepled fingers at right angles to horizontal forearms, bony elbows gleaming in concert with the rapt attention of liquid eyes as phosphorescent flashes illuminate the room. This young-old woman gazing up in adoration at the tortured sagging body, the sibilance of her whispered prayers drowned out by the maelstrom beyond the window; an old-young woman, worshipping His pain, daring the detonations as they approach.

But the day of the launch holds no clues for the happy crowd of the inferno that will one day be visited on them. Shading her eyes again, Deborah turns to look at Michael. His eyes swivel, as if trying to locate the source of the sound. Finding the task beyond him he buries his face in her neck. She strokes the fine filaments of his silky hair, murmurs to him, returns her hand for purchase and turns her head to stare down the hill. She wonders how much, if anything, he will retain of this moment, interleaved in history like a pressed flower. He won't know himself until, many years later, approaching Suez, he's confronted with the majestic passage of superstructure between sand dunes and casts back to a half-grasped image of a descending terrace, sliding bulk and a sense of euphoria, billowing, like smoke, up from the river.

Looking at him she decides his age won't disqualify him in future. He will join the school, balanced on her hip or his father's shoulders, watching the Clyde spawn giants. And in fact he's there at the next launch, and the one after that, and the one after that, until he confuses sequence with consequence. 'Heavy,' he says to his father, imitating the gesture of smashing the bottle, and his father grasps his meaning and laughs.

'Heavy,' his father repeats, and repeats the gesture.

Stephen Neavie is delighted with the error, and repeats it among his workmates, in the lee of these hulks. He fosters it, embroiders it, so it will become the stuff of family folklore: the bottle that moves the ship. He comes home from work with stories of the vigilance of him and his workmates, to preserve this precarious equilibrium. Imagine the disaster of an accidental launch. What if someone were to lean against the hull?

Stephen is a man who, as far as Michael can tell, descends the hill every morning to spend his day among metal and smoke, and comes back every night smelling of both. What about an inopportune flock of starlings? Stephen's amused by his own invention. What about a particularly violent sneeze? His good-humoured baritone laugh resounds off the kitchen pans. Michael seeks Deborah's skirts and hears her chide Stephen in a voice on the edge of laughter.

Compared to others they have space, but it's still a cramped household, destined to become more so, and Michael is used to the muffled sound of their strident coupling before he ever understands what it is.

In this bright sunny morning, staring down the hill, Deborah Neavie can never conceive of any of this ever coming to an end. The shipyards will ring and flash. When necessity demands they will glow in the dark, and these hallmarked works of pride will sail down the estuary into posterity. Clyde Built. Her eyes film in uncharacteristic nostalgia, for a time not yet gone, and she's caught up in the euphoria of the moment. Even the boy feels it. A mote swims into the corner of her eye. She wipes it with a pulled sleeve and watches it resolve into the figure of Father Delaney making his arthritic progress up the hill. Even at this distance his complexion is visible. He's a series of unresolved dots, topped and tailed by the dark smudge of a suit and trilby, his florid face a purple wobble balanced on the white speck of his dog collar. The gradient is testing, as is his habit. There are rumours about Father Delaney in the parish. There are rumours about everything in the parish. Stephen, exposed to brutalities at work she can only guess at, has taught her to suspend her judgement. 'Fucking women,' she has heard him breathe, believing himself out of earshot. He never swears in her presence.

The persuasion of the women Father Delaney passes can be guessed at. Mrs MacGregor, a devout Episcopalian, greets him civilly.

Mrs Beith, an inflexible Calvinist, nods to him with the glacial condescension of one of the elect. As he puffs past her, each comforts themselves in their separate ways. He reminds himself to pray for Mrs Beith in her error. It's one of these numerous mental notes he makes a dozen times a day, consigned immediately to the oblivion of trivial intentions. She reflects that he will have an eternity of regret in which to contemplate the error of his choice. The Catholics are more effusive. Each relaxes as he passes, grateful not to be the subject of his attentions. Deborah knows her odds are narrowing. He didn't haul his liver up this gradient in the windy sunshine to enjoy the view. She shades her eyes once more and affects not to see him until he passes at the base of her steps, bowed, one hand on the iron railings, their greeting delayed by the fit of tartarean coughing that subsides as he gradually cranks himself erect. He raises his hat. The wind catches his hair, scant and unruly, and lifts it like a lid until he forces the brim down on it.

'Deborah.'

'Father Delaney.'

'And how is young...' he waives his hand in a rolling gesture, as if flicking out benedictions '... Peter?'

'And who might he be, Father Delaney?' The hand continues to roll until she's obliged to supply 'Michael'.

'Young Michael?'

'He's grand, Father.' He's buried his face in his mother's neck at the prospect of this dark figure standing at the bottom of their stairs. She's contemplating her meagre quota of biscuits. 'Would you like to come in for a cup of tea?'

'Very kind, Deborah, but I can't just now.'

She does her best not to look relieved. Another roar from the river brings a welcome distraction.

'You were at the launch then, Father, blessing the ship perhaps?'

'Launch?' He looks momentarily perplexed. She is now re-evaluating the situation. This isn't, as she hoped, co-incidental. He's not wandered up from the church and the river buoyed by an excess of good will. 'Yes the launch.' He sketches another casual benediction in the direction of the river. 'There were other clergy...' She's thinking the more the merrier, some ecumenical blessing that covers all contingencies, when he suddenly stops in his distracted movements and looks directly at her. His colour has begun to subside, with the exception of his nose, a roseate blob in the centre of his face. If she half closes her eyes, as she used to do during bored moments at church, it becomes the sole distinguishing feature in his face, a conical red jelly in the vague pastry flan above the dark mouth, droning out orthodoxies. She's half minded to try it again, after all this time, when she realises she's not according him the respect his office demands.

'Will your husband be in tomorrow evening?'

'We're in most evenings, Father.'

'Is eight o'clock convenient?'

No one from the parish has ever refused him. No one ever would. He knows this and is showing unusual circumspection. Eight o'clock will give them time to get the tea out the way and make preparations.

'Eight o'clock would be fine, Father.'

TWO

Standing at the blackboard Miss Herne affects not to notice the approach of Mrs Maguire, the Deputy Head teacher. The elaboration of Mrs Maguire's hair, a curious arrangement of pins and chemical superstructure, adds five inches to her height and makes her visible in the clear glass panel that divides part of the room from the corridor. Beneath the head height of the average adult the panels are opaque, affording a kind of privacy, but the very tall, and Mrs Maguire, reveal themselves. She's a little island of coiffed artifice bobbing towards the door. As the door opens Miss Herne pretends to be distracted by the scrape of chairs.

The chorus is precise.

'Good morning, Mrs Maguire.'

'Good morning children. Good morning, Miss Herne. It's a pleasure to see manners so well executed.'

'Practice, Mrs Maguire. Practice.'

'Indeed.'

They have a diction and formality, devised for the presence of the children but practiced elsewhere. It's a tacit arrangement that Miss Herne extends to most of the staff room. Mrs Maguire is almost as broad as she is long, in stark contrast with the spare asceticism of

Miss Herne. Mrs Maguire considers she had two advantages over her slimmer colleague that more than compensate for her beam: she is the Deputy Head and she is married. Mrs Maguire thinks Miss Herne denies herself in an attempt to attract a mate. Mrs Maguire thinks this is not a strategy without risk, because everyone knows that thin women age badly. Miss Herne thinks Mrs Maguire is a fat churl.

'I have, Miss Herne, some new members to join your happy assembly.' Through the opaque glass two figures can be seen standing near the door. Miss Herne has been appraising their silhouettes since Mrs Maguire's entrance.

'If only the administration was as sprightly as yourself, Mrs Maguire, I might have arranged a reception. Or some desks.'

It is Mrs Maguire's turn to pretend not to notice as she goes out into the corridor and returns with two children. The silence of the seated children deepens to absolute stillness as they take in these two. They are a girl and boy, evidently brother and sister, but the difference is arresting. The average age in the class is ten, although it has its sprinkling of older children held back. The girl would fit with the average age and height. The boy, however, is hulking, larger than any of the others whose retarded development hasn't allowed them to move on. Regulations over uniform have to be flexible to accommodate the motley attempt some mothers make at cobbling together a uniform. But these two beggar any attempt at classification. The boy wears a man's donkey jacket, with leather reinforced shoulder patches, that hangs on him like a shroud. He has plunged his hands into the jacket pockets in a failed attempt to conceal the redundant length of sleeve. At the other extreme his trousers stop an inch from his ankles. The shoes are a disgrace.

The girl seems to be wearing some kind of kimono that has obviously been cannibalised from some larger garment. A man's belt gathers it at the waist. She at least has a blazer of regulation blue that she carries over her crossed forearms, draped protectively in front of her. Miss Herne conjectures that perhaps the fit is too much of an embarrassment. The boy is scowling in a ferocious attempt to overcome the embarrassment of yet another induction. He appears to be sprouting from his clothes. Taking him in, Miss Herne notices the precocious down on his top lip and chin, and the incipient spots that will form into a crust of acne as his hormones rage. His features are in unfortunate transition. He's markedly unlike the other children in the room. It's as if the miscellaneous features of several ugly men are vying for ascendency.

The girl, on the other hand, is an olive-skinned beauty. She has dark hair drawn back, and beneath the apprehension at her new circumstances Miss Herne can see the tranquillity in those even and symmetrical features. And there is something inchoate in her, a promise of greater beauty to come. Give her a uniform and half a chance and Miss Herne believes she will have the assuredness of only the very beautiful. Miss Herne believes herself to be a connoisseur of art. Like all her accomplishments it's self-taught. She has honed her critical faculty by conscientious visits to municipal galleries and directed reading. She has a particular fascination for devotional painting. It's one of the discriminating factors, like the purity of her faith, or her chosen abstentions, that she believes differentiates her from almost everyone she comes in contact with. The girl, she thinks, is worth the attentions of a Dutch Master. She can even imagine the artist importing a blemish for credibility. The boy, on the other hand, is a crude impasto.

Scanning the space to satisfy herself that there are two vacant desks, Mrs Maguire projects toward the classroom, looking anywhere but at the younger woman.

'Well, Miss Herne, I will leave these fortunate children in your capable hands.'

'I do not believe we have been introduced, Mrs Maguire.'

Mrs Maguire takes a step back while at the same time indicating to the boy that he should move forward to her vacated place. The gesture appears more a theatrical prompt than a command. As the boy shuffles forward she makes her exit, closing the door on his muscular swallowing. His incipient acne is beginning to glow in the heat of the focused attention.

Miss Herne watches the tacky cone of hair bob out of sight before turning round.

'And what's your name?'

'Campbell,' he says, loudly. Miss Herne is performing an instantaneous calculation that has become automatic to her when meeting new people, of assessing the Catholic implications associated with any name, first or surname. New acquaintances, colleagues, names from newspapers and titles from the radio are all indelibly classified according to her private system. She considers the Campbells, as a clan, of having a poor history of Catholic association. Some have practiced an intolerance more public and no less rigorous than her own, with the obvious difference of discriminating in the opposite direction. But the name has become so ubiquitous, 'common' is the word that flashes through Miss Herne's mind, as to be almost religiously neutral. America, she believes, is bursting with Campbells, more concerned with their biscuit box Scottish heritage than religion. However, she has also known several Scottish Campbells as devout Catholics, and is prepared to give the grotesque boy and unblemished girl the benefit of the doubt.

'And what's your first name, Mister Campbell?'

'Campbell.'

There's a ripple of unseemly titters that she suppresses with a glance. Miss Herne isn't averse to employing the class mirth for her purposes, but only when she permits and directs.

'Campbell is your Christian name?'

'Yes.'

'Yes, Miss Herne.' She corrects.

'Yes, Miss Herne.'

She considers. The school register is cluttered with Peters and Andrews and Marks and Johns.

'It escapes me for the moment which of Our Lord's disciples was called Campbell. Yes Daniel?'

'Wasn't he the one with the bagpipes, Miss?'

'For tomorrow morning, Daniel Gildea, you will write out for me the names of the Apostles twenty times. If you don't know who they are I suggest you call at the chapel house on the way home. Father Delaney may be able to oblige.' And turning to the excruciated boy, 'And what is your surname, Campbell?'

'Renton – Miss Herne.'

She doesn't need to calculate any further. His Catholic credentials are dubious.

'And you, young lady?'

'Gig, Miss Herne.'

'Is that an onomatopoeia?' She turns towards the class and projects. 'Onomatopoeia. A word in imitation of the sound of the thing meant. It's derived from Greek. Who can furnish an example? Yes, Lucy?'

'Splash, Miss Herne.'

'Indeed. A good example. Daniel Gildea, I hope this offer is sincere. I'll give you an opportunity to redeem yourself.'

'Plop, Miss Herne.' Another round of titters. Daniel Gildea suffers more from a ready wit than a rebellious nature. He's more often than not the victim of his own spontaneity.

'The names of the Apostles fifty times. You have no prudence, Daniel Gildea. If your parents are curious as to the purpose of the exercise then direct them to me.' She turns back to the girl. Perhaps she is as uncomfortable as her brother. If so, her complexion conceals it. Miss Herne decides that for the girl's sake she will overlook their dubious credentials. Were Campbell alone she might enquire further. Were anyone to question her reasoning Miss Herne would simply remind them that Our Lord, as a fisher of men, did not require testimonials.

'Come, young lady. Your name is not abbreviated to a hiccup. What were you baptised?'

'My name's Georgina, Miss Herne.'

The attempt to gloss over the issue of baptism doesn't escape Miss Herne. A pre-emptive frown suppresses the class and Miss Herne talks to cover the girl's confusion.

'A pretty name, perhaps more suited to the pages of a Jane Austen novel than a Clydeside parish. Nevertheless, it's the contemplation of fine things that elevates us. We now have another pleasant name to adorn our register. Please take a seat, Georgina and Campbell. We will see to the issue of your textbooks and jotters after we have navigated division.'

She turns her attention to the board. The class turns its attention to the twins. Still scowling, the boy pulls a chair for his sister and gestures her towards it in a gentle movement of incongruous courtesy. She sits. They exchange a shy smile. Miss Herne turns round from the blackboard and raps her pointer for attention.

THREE

Prompted by his wife, Stephen Neavie returns promptly from his shift at five o'clock the following evening. He's confronted with a galvanised tin bath on the kitchen floor, half-full of steaming water. The stock pot is at a slow simmer with more water. Deborah pours in another steaming cascade and gestures towards her husband. He undresses in the hall and she accepts each item before he can find a surface to put it on. He lowers himself into the tub, muttering. The blessing of hot water goes some way to relieve his irritation. His compressed spine uncoils in a series of cracks. He has been a riveter in the yards since he was sixteen. He has the hands of Achilles, the palms and fingers callused to reptilian hardness, the knuckles and backs meshed with strata of scars. He has grasped and wielded so long that his hands have pneumatic strength. At rest his fingers curl to a prehensile clutch. He flexes them beneath the water, feels the crepitus of the joints, and looks around. Every visible surface that isn't porous has been cleaned with caustic soda. Placing the dripping sponge on his head he reflects that there's only one thing worse than an unscheduled visit from the priest, and that's a scheduled one.

Deborah comes in, her lips silently moving, as if reciting some internal list.

'Where's the wee man?'

'Cleaned and fed,' she says, returning to her silent monologue. Looking at him sparks another recollection. 'There are stovies in the pot. Clothes are on the bed.'

'I thought we were eating together?'

'I'm not hungry. I'll eat when he goes.'

'For Christ's sake, Debs!'

'Keep your voice down.'

'Is it the neighbours or the wee man you're worried about?'

'He'll only be here for an hour. An hour and a half at most.' She says this to mollify him. He drops his voice.

'It's not the second coming or the Pope. He's from our kind of people.' But it's pointless. She's abstracted again, mentally discarding overcome obstacles. He lies back, luxuriating until the water begins to turn tepid. She must be timing this too as she comes in and hands him a towel. He stands dripping in the tub. The residual heat has turned him tumid and he contemplates the curve of her buttocks. She glances at this and smiles, the conspiratorial curve of the corners of her lips that he loves. He pulls her towards him, jokingly, because they both know this isn't the time. She mimes a shriek and pulls away in mock horror.

And this is what he objects to so strongly, this unaffected intimacy intruded upon. For they both know the purpose of this visit. They were married three years before Michael arrived. This is the exception around here, especially among Catholic families. The birth of a first child is always timed against the date of the wedding. A premature baby is likely to give rise to rumour of forced marriage. Deborah has watched some of the girls she went to school with push out a child a year. There are women in their late twenties exhausted with childbearing, haggard with work, spawning children in a shrinking flat with no room to segregate a growing brood. Deborah wonders where they find space for their intimacies. But they must find it because the families continue to grow. And she's seen these same mothers at the grocer's counter, frantically searching the lining of a worn purse looking for a truant coin, while the queue clicks with impatience. And it's been all she could do not to hand across the money and risk resentful thanks.

She was shocked last year by a back-court exchange. Margo, one of the girls she grew up with, with a flat across the way, seemed to time hanging out her washing to coincide with Deborah's. Margo seems to have spent all the years from her late teens on mostly pregnant. It's taken its toll. Her looks were in her youth. Both have been squeezed out a baby at a time. Standing in the afternoon sun, up-lit from a billowing white sheet, her skin looks granular. Her eyes are sinking as her pelvis and hips spread. Her ankles now flow. Deborah thinks the washing-line exchanges are one of Margo's few escapes. She normally tries to extend them until called in by one of the older children. Last time the meeting wasn't contrived because she was there before Deborah. She'd obviously been crying. It was as if Deborah had interrupted a monologue. Margo turned to her.

'He said all he needs is food, beer money and on-tap cunt.'

Having spoken she looked down, as if evaluating the used breasts, the pelvis, her calves.

'Look at me! Look at me! Look at me and look at you!' The last part was said with some of the vehemence he must have aimed at her. She wiped her eyes on the half-pegged towel and ran indoors. Deborah hung up the rest of Margo's washing. The back-court meetings have never coincided since.

Deborah's never heard a man speak to a woman that way. Not her father. Not her husband. She knows she's fortunate. She knows she has the best in the parish. He isn't her only blessing. They have their own toilet, a conspicuous luxury for a family of three when jakes on the half-landing service many of the larger broods. They have their own kitchen, with an iron range and a deep Belfast sink, not an alcove with a gas ring and a tap above a metal bowl. They have a recessed bed near the range where Michael can sleep in the winter, with the constant heat and the residual smell of perpetual soup. They have a bedroom. They have the 'good' front room, with a bay window overlooking the street, a fireplace kept scrupulous with black lead, and antimacassar, like fringed doilies, adorning the chairs. Although this room occupies almost one third of the flat's floor plan it's seldom used. Life revolves around the kitchen.

There are kids round here who only ever get to spend a dozen consecutive hours around their father at Christmas. There are fathers who have never bathed a child. Stephen isn't like them. Like lots of others they married before they genuinely knew one another. Unlike many the introduction of a baby deepened the acquaintance. They sit and talk. The more they know the more they want to know. Each now has an ingrained sense of the other.

He washes the boy. He pushes the pram. In others this might give rise to rumours of effeminacy. But not Stephen. He has a physique to match his hands. He also has an inherent masculinity that has nothing to do with his size and strength.

Despite her health and his robustness, she took longer to conceive than all the others. Michael was a difficult birth. Stephen stood at the bay window, frowning sightlessly down the hill, while the sound of her animal noises came from the kitchen alcove and the doctor in attendance shouted instructions at the midwife. She came out briefly and handed him the placenta wrapped in newspaper. At a loss, he threw it on the fire and listened to it hiss. By tacit agreement Deborah and Stephen haven't talked about the birth since, and he's unwilling to put her through anything like that again unless she really wants it. There are enough kids round here with something wrong with them. There are even more, without infirmity, competing for love and scant resources. They have a healthy boy. Stephen's content to count his blessings. And here comes this dark smudge of a priest, rounding the corner and climbing the hill, to question their equilibrium.

Stephen wonders if Father Delaney believes the popular suspicion that they've curtailed their family for money. Deborah told Stephen this rumour. He doesn't know how she knows it, and wouldn't begin to ask. He experiences blinding irrational rages at the mental images of the women who accost Deborah, pose oblique questions and exchange looks when she's passed. He's never actually seen this but he's seen her come back from some gathering she'd been looking forward to, subdued and near tears. She's busied herself with the baby to deflect his concern. And he's cracked his knuckles in impotence. He'd drop a tenement on the whole fucking lot if it would do any good. But they would still have just one son.

There's something else that quietly incenses him. He's seen the consequences first hand. He knows men who won't leave their wives alone, who will come home night after night, six pints on, move the baby to the next room to sleep with all the other kids and fuck a still lactating woman. And if asked they'll say they're fulfilling their Christian duties. If this fool of a priest is going to hint about such duties then Stephen will stick his hands into his pockets because he doesn't trust himself not to do anything else. It's never been about the money, or their own toilet, or the aloof privacy he thinks they're accused of. There's the question of Deborah's mother to consider. Myra, half a dozen parallel streets away, widowed in a single room and kitchen. She's managing – just. But when her health starts to fail, as it will, there's nowhere else to go. Deborah won't even have to ask. They'll manage. The flat will absorb her and her possessions. He stands at the window watching the priest's slow progress, as she did yesterday morning from the step below. He can practically feel her smoothing her hair nervously in the next room and it's all he can do not to punch the wall and bawl his love for her through the hole he's made. He mentally rehearses what he'll say afterwards, when the priest has gone and the issue has been ventilated, that he would love another but only on her terms; that her happiness and their family eclipses everything else; that she's better than the whole fucking bunch of them, but he'll leave out the swearing – when he remembers the tin bath.

She'd obviously remembered it because that poor kid with the spots is wrestling with it. Having baled it out down the kitchen sink and dried it with a towel Deborah provided, he's trying to hoist it to stand vertically and fit it into the kitchen press. Stephen takes an end. He doesn't take over. He keeps the pretence of a joint effort while the thing is noisily stored. The boy smiles shyly. Stephen remembers being that size, at that age.

In the street below, Father Delaney continues his progress. Deborah hasn't told anyone he's coming. When people have advance warning of his arrival the priest is preceded by a bow-wave of cosmetic tidying. In lots of his scheduled visits he's presented with an implausible scene of domesticity, like something arranged by a Victorian photographer for the long exposure. Deborah hasn't managed to arrange the effect to her satisfaction before the door goes. Stephen hasn't had his stovies either. Either he's been tardy or Father Delaney's early. In either event it's not likely to put Stephen in a better mood. She's meticulously counting out coins to the boy when the knock sounds. Sensible to the situation, Stephen feels embarrassment on the boy's behalf. He puts his hand on the boy's shoulder and opens the door.

'Come in, Father.' He follows this by a wave in the direction of the good front room. Deborah has bolted to the bedroom to complete some unknown preparation. There's a moment of confusion as the boy, studying the linoleum, tries to leave as the priest enters. Stephen steers him to one side. The boy's presence seems to perplex the priest. He stops on the threshold and his movement stutters, before going in the direction Stephen is still indicating. Stephen follows the boy out on to the landing, hands him another coin, steps back in and closes the door on further embarrassment. He wishes he'd eaten before the priest turned up. And his clothes are constricting and uncomfortable. Can she really believe that the priest thinks they sit about like this? If he does it gives the lie to the Sunday best.

He walks into the front room wondering if the priest is also conscious of its antiseptic cleanliness. The familiar smell has been overlaid. He has to check himself from resenting the man for this halo of artificial sterility he must move around in. It's not his fault. But he must notice it, given he's not so scrupulous himself. From the distance of the pulpit he might pass muster but not at this distance. At this distance there's a weariness to Father Delaney; a morning-after look. At this distance he's a man going through the motions.

They both appear momentarily embarrassed by Stephen's superior size, vitality and cleanliness. It's the biggest room in the flat and their mutual awkwardness somehow makes it seem cramped.

'Please, Father, have a seat. No doubt there will be some tea.'

'There always is.' The priest returns this with a downward smile that elicits a pang of sympathy in the bigger man. The priest sits in the chair. Stephen takes the couch. The unaccustomed furniture groans. It's a mismatched ensemble, what they could manage when first married. The priest's chair is leather, polished to a ceramic gloss this afternoon by Deborah. He feels his arse sliding forward and has to check his motion, like a secretary pushing back the action of a typewriter. Stephen smiles.

'Just passing?'

'I just thought I'd call in and admire the whiteness of your shirt, Stephen.'

He's never been alone with the priest before. The gentleness of the jibe and the six feet that separate them opens him to the other man, his porosity, leaking imperfections. Deborah comes in holding Michael in front of her like a shield. The boy is normally asleep at this time. Stephen doesn't like to think of his son being use as some kind of stage prop.

'Was the boy not asleep?' It's enough to register his disapproval. She slides a look at him before returning her eager smile to the priest. Stephen doesn't like this facsimile either. But it's probably not her fault. Her mother's obsessively devout. It's probably not the priest's fault either that he's treated with even more reverence than the local G.P.

Sliding like yesterday's launch down the slipway, Father Delaney exploits the opportunity to lean forward in a half crouch and bless the child in an automatic gesture. He sits back to a salvo of flatulent noises from the squeaking leather and clears his throat.

'So tell me, Deborah and... and Stephen...' He pauses, trying to form something. Deborah leans forward into the gap. 'Have you had much to do with the people... the people... upstairs?'

She leans back, relaxed, illuminated. Stephen's lost. They're on the ground floor. There are two flats to a landing. There are at least six families upstairs.

'Upstairs?' He looks to her for explanation.

'The Rentons,' she says, flicking her eyes towards the cornices, as if the ceiling's transparent. He's still none the wiser. His stomach makes a churning noise, wanting its stovies.

The priest clears his throat again. 'There's a boy and a girl and a father... I don't know anything about a mother, although presumably...' his voice tails. He waves a hand. Deborah's face clouds at the mention of the absent mother. 'As you may know, we have a hardship fund. You can imagine how often it's called upon in a parish such as this. The children enrolled at school today. I've seen the father who assures me they're confirmed. And confession and communion. He wasn't very good on specifics. I'm not suggesting anything, mind. I think the lack of detail might be to do with the heavy night before. And the boy's shoes were a disgrace...'

Deborah's nodding sadly in time to the cadence of these broken sentences. Apparently this all means something to her. Stephen's still completely bewildered until the mention of shoes recalls the boy on the stairwell he just handed a coin to.

'Is that the kid who emptied the bath I gave a tanner to?'

It's the priest's turn to look bemused. Deborah explains for the benefit of both.

'The boy is called Campbell. I know what you mean, Father, by his shoes and... and hardship. I've had him down a few times to do odds and ends, things I could do myself but I wanted to try and get some money to them. There's a girl too. A beautiful wee creature. I've met the father too. Alan.'

'Alan.' Father Delaney repeats, unconsciously applying Miss Herne's criteria. The significance is still lost on Stephen.

'Yes. Yes, Father. I've only met him in passing. He's usually on his way out. It's normally before Stephen gets home. Sometimes I've heard him coming back. I think I have to agree with you, Father. I mean about the drink. I've heard him bounce off the passage on the way up. I've given the children money a few times. I'm hoping it found its way to where it's needed. As you say though, the poor boy's shoes...'

'The last thing I want to do is pour hardship money down the man's neck. Not, you understand...'

He makes another vague gesture. Deborah gives another comprehending nod. Stephen doesn't understand at all but has decided that he's going to. He's not putting up with tonight's social upheaval and his cold stovies for nothing.

'Have I ever met this man?'

'No, dear.'

'I don't remember a girl either. And tonight's the first I've seen that poor kid. Even if I haven't seen them on the stairs, you'd expect to see them out playing.'

'They're a fairly recent arrival.' Father Delaney explains.

'I'll get some tea,' Deborah says. Grim as the Rentons' situation may be, she's immensely cheered that their hardship, not her fertility, appears to be tonight's topic.

Stephen takes Michael from her. She goes to the kitchen. With one hand round the baby's midriff, Stephen fingers his uncomfortable collar. He's determined still to get to the bottom of this. Availing himself of Deborah's absence, Father Delaney nods towards Michael. To reinforce the point he drops his voice to confessional register.

'He's a lovely boy. I don't suppose there's any... news?'

'Well, there was a big ship launched yesterday not half a mile from this spot, and if you believe the papers, things in Europe have seemed a lot better.'

Father Delaney isn't used to being rebuffed. He leans back with another salvo of creaking. The awkward silence is interrupted by Deborah's return. The marriage crockery and Sunday biscuits belie her attempt to make this look spontaneous. Stephen despises these cups, porcelain equivalents of lace doilies. He feels he could shatter the whole service with a cough. And she puts such store by these trinkets. Biscuits and tea are something to finish a meal with, not a substitute. He accepts the cup as his stomach continues to groan, like the priest's chair. The priest slakes his thirst with two gulps and leans forward for a refill. She obliges and then takes Michael back. Stephen cradles the saucer in one hand and tries to link forefinger and thumb through the fragile handle. And then the unthinkable happens. His hands begin to vibrate. This is something that recurs infrequently, an echo of the thousand concussions his hands experience daily return to visit him, usually in private. The print in front of his eyes will blur and he will fold the newspaper in exasperation until the tremors subside. The cup is now dancing on the saucer, corrugated tea slopping over the lip. Not understanding at first, the priest looks up at the ceiling. It hasn't occurred to him that the source of the vibration is the man opposite. The noise is now too loud for any of them to pretend it's not happening. Worse, the movement has now communicated itself to the chair and adjacent tray. Spoons are tinkling in bevelled saucers. In one fluid movement Deborah puts Michael on the floor, moves the tray away, puts Michael back on her hip, takes the cup from Stephen, disappears into the kitchen and returns immediately with the speed of having been spat out a revolving door. She hands Stephen his large mug that she half fills with a stream of treacle-coloured tea from the elaborate pot. He takes a gulp. The others listen to his swallowing. The trembling subsides.

'Well,' Deborah offers, smiling all round as if they're to be congratulated in surviving a minor earthquake. 'Shortbread, Father.'

'Yes please. Did you make them yourself?'

'It's the work.' Stephen says, having none of this genteel pretence. 'Riveting all day. Sometimes it feels as if the teeth will shake loose from my head. End of the shift and you think you're finished with it and sometimes it comes back, like this.'

'Have you been to see Doctor McFarlane?'

Doctor McFarlane is a practical man of sound common sense who dispenses well-patented drugs when he must, but who mostly prescribes moderation. Most of the ailments he comes across are the result of some excess or another. There are lots of livers in the parish larger than Father Delaney's. He has a credo of vegetables, fresh air and abstinence repeated to the patients with as much effect as Miss Herne, up the hill, intones the catechism to her children. His two main adversaries are poverty and ignorance. Disappointed parents come out of his surgery lacking the placebo they sought, while their children skip in the playground with the three persons in the one God, God the Father, God the Son and God the Holy Ghost, echoing in the whisper of the ropes.

Stephen knows Doctor McFarlane and Doctor McFarlane knows Stephen, and his circumstances. He knows Stephen practices the moderation he advises and that he supports his family the only way he can. He wouldn't dream of telling Stephen to stop work, because the hardship fund's already oversubscribed, and he wouldn't insult his intelligence with a placebo. And Stephen knows all this too.

'No, I haven't seen the doctor. There might be a point if my hands trembled for the same reason as quite a few round here. But if that were true he'd just tell me to lay off the bottle. And as I rarely touch the stuff anyway...' he unclenches a free hand and shrugs a shoulder. With anyone else Father Delaney would suspect this was an allusion to his own habit. But there's something in the other man, his healthily complaining digestion, his white shirt, the power in his still hands that compels him to think otherwise. He's too roughly hewn for innuendo.

'So these people upstairs,' Stephen says, 'nobody seems to know anything about them but that the mother's somehow out of the picture and they're dirt poor. There's not that much about it that's strange around here except the man being left with the kids.'

'She might be dead,' Deborah says.

'She might be. I can think of two widows within half a dozen streets. Both have a clutch of kids and a man that's alive and kicking on the other side of the Clyde. Does this man say he's a widower?'

'We don't know,' Deborah says. 'We don't know anything.'

'We know the children have enrolled at school.' Father Delaney says. 'We know they're called Campbell and Georgina and that the father's name is Alan and the family name is Renton.'

Stephen surmises that this is the nub of it. The priest's looking for

Catholic antecedents and isn't inspired by a roll call of names that don't appear elsewhere in the school register.

'We know more than that, Father. We know the boy has shoes that attract attention even around here, given both of you have an opinion on them already, and if that isn't a qualification for the hardship fund I don't know what is.'

He stands without saying anything further, his silent and large figure suddenly dominating them and the furniture, drawing the visit to a sharp conclusion. Father Delaney puts down his cup, slides forward one last time and uses the momentum to stand. Deborah sits quizzically for a moment, Michael completely asleep on her lap, staring first at one then the other of the standing figures, trying to comprehend what just happened. She too stands. Father Delaney takes a small glass bottle from his pocket.

'May I?'

Stephen nods. The priest sprinkles a small amount and mutters in subdued Latin. Stephen notices the small column of dots strafe the linen cloth she's placed on the side table. She bows her head until the muttered benediction is complete. The priest shakes Stephen's hand. She shows him to the door. Stephen stands at the bay window until he sees the figure appear on the steps. It's turned dark during the brief interview. It's a starless night, the velvety gloom somehow intensified by spangles of lighted windows across the way, and illuminated pools of street light that track the sloping street. There are still children playing, calling to one another in the darkness, the near pool momentarily bisected by the trajectory of a kicked bladder. He follows the priest's descent, swallowed by the gloom only to emerge at the next island in a series of diminishing appearances until a fleck in the pupil and then nothing.

'He hadn't even finished his tea.'

When he turns she has unconsciously adopted yesterday morning's pose with Michael on her outflung hip.

'He's worried about hardship funding going down the neck of him upstairs while everyone from here to Partick Cross knows he's got a habit himself. Don't tell him anything.'

'He hears my confession.' Father Delaney, for all his faults, is her priest. Stephen sees her dilemma.

'Don't tell him anything about the people upstairs.'

Five years from now she'll stand in the same spot as yesterday morning with Michael's sister on her hip, Michael standing in the archway formed by her other hand braced against the sandstone for purchase in the pose of a capital K. The gap between the brother and sister will reduce to contemporaneity if they ever live long enough. Weather permitting she'll stand in this pose when the evening whistle sounds, waiting for him to come up the hill at the shift's end, and he'll seek this architectural arrangement of their placed bodies amid the dispersing throng and think he's been given too much.

knee there wouldn't have been any need to hit him on the back of the head with a heavy object, probably a pipe, wrapped in newspaper, probably *The Daily Express*, from the reverse print smudged on the base of the skull. Perhaps, they conjectured, an honour reprisal. The victim was a notorious womaniser.

Perhaps, Alan thought, a case of mistaken identity. For the man had been emerging from Alan's flat, after feeding Alan's son's cat, when the first blow fell. Alan didn't need to conjecture any further because Campbell and Gig, on the half-landing above, saw the whole thing. It frightened them enough to secure their silence for a day, after which the whole thing poured out like lava, over Alan, who quickly packed their bags. The three of them flitted in the night, like fugitive Bedouins, before the money lender learned of the mistake and sent the hired help back to smash the correct knee.

Despite his appearance, or perhaps because of it, Alan was never short of women: a blowzy woman in Leith of kindred slovenliness; an upright woman in Newcastle who sought to improve him; a devout evangelical in Arbroath who thought she could bring him into the fold. Big, small, fat, thin, mulatto, Hungarian, Irish – none conformed to type. The only thing they had in common was in gravitating towards a man of no obvious redeeming qualities. A single man with children attracts attention, and, usually, sympathy. For some of the women the children were just a nuisance. Some viewed them as evidence of his concealed decency. He was clever enough to know that a little self-effacement went a long way. He never explained that his wife had beaten him to it by deserting first. Her only contribution had been their ridiculous names. He had it in him to run away from them with their mother, but not to leave them on their own. Abandoning his escape was, in his mind, a kind of faithfulness. The simple act of staying exhausted most of the care he was capable of. His parents hadn't even given him this much. He loved his children in his own way, as much as his stunted heart was capable of. This didn't preclude calculation. He kept an unconscious balance sheet, offsetting inconvenience against dividends. He never raised his hand to either, or was ever mercenary enough to put a fuck before their safety.

When he was five, Campbell stumbled into a darkened bedroom in Inverness wanting his dad. He was frightened by something he'd dreamed about. He never got to explain. In the gloom he fetched up against a disembodied mannequin head, complete with wig. He screamed. The lights went on. His father and a parallel mannequin sat bolt upright, spring loaded. The mannequin sprang from the bed, reached past Campbell and snatched the wig to its head. He was too shocked and inexperienced to notice the absence of pubic hair and eyebrows. The woman, large-breasted and terrifyingly fleshy in the sudden glare, automatically adjusted the wig like a helmet while assessing the situation. Her sudden tirade at him was stopped in mid-flow by his father. She, his father pointed out, was in *their* home. This was news to Campbell, whose memories extended through a series of flophouses that smelled of other people's feet. Neither he nor Gig had mentally put down any roots. A continuing series of upheavals constituted their lives. The bald woman pre-empted them that time by stalking off at first light with the mannequin head in a hat box.

Their lifestyle resulted in a sketchy education for the brother and sister. Alan, who seldom thought about religion at all, would, if asked, probably concede there is a God and it's probably a good idea that the kids learned about Him. He wasn't having any truck with these foreign religions. If Christianity was good enough for God it was good enough for him, but he didn't care what form it came in. When he landed this number in the shipyards the nearest school was Roman Catholic. Proximity was all that mattered. He was prepared to give the necessary assurances to anyone, teacher, headmaster, priest, that he had to. He usually found that whenever questions uncomfortably specific, a sad mention of the children's absent mother did the trick.

There's nothing of him in either child to look at. This doesn't make him doubt their parentage because he can't see anything of their mother either. Neither Campbell nor Gig has developed his sense of sponging fatalism. They do have a vague sense of social shame all their own.

The job itself was enough to tempt him without the school, as he said to them both, 'A kick in the arse up the hill.' He's a glorified janitor and spends an inordinate amount of time in his little booth watching people punch in and out. He's good at sitting. He has a token role in security. Within minutes of the whistle sounding to announce the start of another shift the noise is colossal and still rising. He closes the door to scan the racing results, a little insulated pocket of stasis. Winter mornings the shift starts before dawn. Freezing darkness is punctured by welding arcs and the dull glow of braziers that pewter figures congregate around, stamping their feet, breathing through tunnelled fingers, snorting vivid plumes. He has a stove. The extent of his activity can be followed from outside by the glow of his cigarette describing parabola, as he reaches for tea or folds the paper.

There's also a modest return to be made from contraband. There's an astonishing variety of things that go to make up a ship. He'll choose his moment to take the paper to the toilet. His commission is minimal, but it's gratifying to know that even shitting earns him money.

He's never had any plans. He never intends to stay, but he never intends to go either. Their departures have always been occasioned by a growing disaffection, either in him or by the people around him whose tolerance has grown thin and generosity exhausted. Loans are called in. Women want either more of him than he's willing to give or, pointedly, nothing at all. It's usually only a matter of time and he views it as something inevitable, like seasons or tides. It's never occurred to him to alter his behaviour.

Until now. In this place he's better off than he's ever been. The money's modest, even with the back-handers. No female candidate has put herself forward so far as his helpmeet, bit of skirt or conscience. It could be age or encroaching domesticity, but there are appetites that don't demand to be satisfied as they once were. True, it's early days, but he finds he can make do with the occasional foray to Sauchiehall Street. One of the things that pleases him here is the conscience of the district, a kind of unofficial social service that's subtly engaged itself on their behalf.

The appearance of the boy, in particular, seems to have triggered some kind of payment. That Catholic priest, the one with the grog blossom nose who looks as if he'd slept in his clothes, turned up and explained about some kind of fund. He was quite pointed about the fact that it didn't usually contribute to the welfare of the gainfully employed. If nothing else Alan's good at assessing situations. It's an instinctive calculation, practically instantaneous. And he has the added advantage that he doesn't have any pride to wound, although he has found that the appearance of injured self-esteem can work a treat.

'Father...'

'Delaney. It's Father Delaney.'

'Of course. Father Delaney. Although I'm pleased you're here I didn't invite you. And although I'm pleased to hear about this fund I didn't apply to it. If I'm disqualified because I found a job to try and feed my kids then I wonder about you turning up to tell me about it.'

At this point Father Delaney was unashamedly taking in his surroundings. Alan felt that the comparison of what he saw with what he expected could only work in his favour. And he was right. The only disappointment was that it came in kind, not cash. The kids came home with new shoes and a uniform of a kind. Groceries arrived. He rummaged unsuccessfully for cigarettes. An unsolicited canvas bag of root vegetables arrived on the doorstep and he left Gig trying to concoct some kind of basic soup, following the sessions she'd had with that nice woman downstairs, the one with the husband whose hands could be seen a football field away. She was pretty, that woman. Time was he might have tried the sympathy card. But not now. He didn't know Gig was precocious. He had nothing to compare her with. He did know that her growing femininity was causing him some disquiet.

The nice woman downstairs, Deborah, noticed it too. She went some way to adopting the mantle. It was something unspoken between the three of them. He was unashamedly grateful. And there was some kind of understanding between the girl and the woman. Perhaps it was just both of them being women. Nothing in the string of women he'd dispensed with, or who had dispensed with him, prepared him for this. Perhaps it was just her being surfeit with love. You could see it from the same distance you could see her husband's hands, and her having only one kid to lavish it all on.

He'd be appalled at the prospect of anyone treating Gig the way he treated other women. At the same time he doesn't think he's done anything wrong. Campbell's hormones can take care of themselves. Fortunately there's also that teacher. Between her and Deborah they probably have all those feminine issues he's happy not to know anything about covered. The more he thinks about it the more he thinks there's really nothing to worry about.

FIVE

Danny Gildea, class wag, has accosted Gig in the playground. Danny's small for his age, something he feels acutely. He compensates for this by the quickness of his wit and a pre-emptive temper. He gets his retaliation in first. He swears like a docker. The rougher elements of the playground leave him alone. But he's not like them in a number of ways. He's secretly fastidious. His schoolbag and desk are obsessively tidy. When the bell rings and he joins the general four o'clock stampede to the school gates, he'll undo his tie and wear it, Apache style round his forehead in the brief dozen-street walk home. But when he gets there he'll wind it carefully round his hand and place the coil beside his similarly looped snake belt.

There's a mental fastidiousness too and an appreciation of things wild horses couldn't drag an admission of. The farrago of classroom smells giving way to the smell of wet tarmac at home time give him a sense of elation. He's mesmerised by the peripheral trees, whispering to one another. He conceives the heady concoction of smells from the yards as a confection of metal, fire and toil. This amalgam is the same smell as his father's hands after a long shift, the smell of his clothes as he used to pick Danny up at the front door and crush him to his overalls in that nightly embrace. This same smell drifts up the hill with the early winter sunsets and strikes an inner poignancy. Unaccountable tears well in Danny's eyes. It's this last sensibility he's most ashamed of. He's never yet been caught. He's managed to conceal this from his mother as effectively as his playground language. She'd be touched by the tears, furious at the swearing.

And there's something in her, this new girl, that's struck him almost as forcefully as the smell of the yards. He can't place it. It's not unpleasant. It's an amalgam of things, something to do with the symmetry of her face, the fact that she hasn't got a mother, those clothes they first turned up in and that they're manifestly poor among poor people. It's almost an odour. It's not nice in her brother but it's tantalising in her.

She's an enigma to him and Danny's life doesn't admit uncertainties. Uncertainties lead to hesitation and hesitation is weakness. His only solution is to attack problems. His fascination with and liking for her manifests itself in another pre-emptive exchange.

'I like your shoes.'

She looks at him uncertainly, quizzical.

'I'm sure my mum was wearing them last week. Or no... was it... wait...'

He's acting out a mime of forced recollection, staggering now with hands on temples, giddy with effort, collecting an audience. He's done it before. They know what to expect. There's a general air of hilarity centring on him. She still looks bemused, not realising she's the butt. Sensing something from the other side of the playground, Campbell detached himself from the railings and starts to make his way across. His attempt to contrive indifference immediately vanishes with concern for his sister. Danny is still staggering. The laughter instantly stops as Campbell approaches. Tension has spread telepathically. The whole playground is focused on the confrontation. Danny stops, snaps-to like a patient released from hypnotism.

'I remember. It was an old jakey. She woke up and someone had stolen her cider and her shoes.' Campbell's bearing down on him. 'Mind you, more her size than yours. Nice uniform though. There's a pair of curtains,' he throws his arms wide, splays his legs, like a gingerbread man, 'with this shape missing from both. Front and back. Pull yourself together.'

'Campbell, don't!' she says.

But Danny has set it all in motion. He's no idea of the nature of the force he's just provoked. Danny's sense of grievance comes from being slightly smaller than normal and having an over solicitous mother who still licks her handkerchief to clean his face in public. Propelling Campbell is a feral sense of kin, awareness of the indignity of his, her and their father's appearance and the experience of yet another dislocation. He's learned to stamp his authority decisively and early. He's no time for playground escalations of pushing. Whoever he is he's said something to his sister. There's Campbell and Gig and the rest of the world. When confrontations like this arrive everything becomes blissfully simple and he's honed to a single purpose. It doesn't matter that he's smaller. His size won't save him. It wouldn't matter how big he was.

It's over in two seconds. Campbell parts the observers like wheat and punches the boy without breaking stride in a downward motion that focuses a hundred remembered humiliations, flattens the bridge of his nose and sends a delta of bloody spray down his shirt front. Danny's knees fold and he sits down.

Distaining the staff room yet again Miss Herne has watched the whole brief exchange from her classroom, inferring their words and motives. She's thoughtful, not shocked, but is provoked into motion by the sight of Mrs Maguire, acting monitor, rounding the corner. The older woman has sensed something from the absence of a dozen consecutive playground games, but she hasn't seen anything yet. Miss Herne raps the window while the Deputy Head is still out of earshot. The children's eyes turn up. She gestures, unmistakeably, to Gig, Campbell and Danny and summons them with a wave.

Gig helps Danny, suddenly docile, still stunned with the speed and vehemence he only associates with the grown-up world. They walk to their punishment. The playground returns to hopscotch, ropes and football. Mrs Maguire, baffled, has penetrated a dispersed nucleus and stares around accusingly. Miss Herne has glided into the shade before Mrs Maguire sees her.

In the classroom the three children arrange themselves like an identity parade.

'My, Daniel, what a mess you're in.'

He's blinking rapidly and through the shock is still able to discern that her tone is concerned, not reprimanding. She takes his face in her hands and tilts it towards the light. In his confusion he's waiting for further pain, pressure on some sore area, some form of coercion to make him tell. His playground bravado's been shown to be paper thin but he won't tell.

'I fell.'

'So I see. Bruised but not broken. Bloody but unbowed. You are our proper little Trojan. Do you know about Thermopylae?'

'No, Miss Herne.'

'That'll be tomorrow's instruction. They were stoical in the face of pain and they didn't say anything – like you. History doesn't repeat itself but it rhymes. I don't expect you children to understand everything I say as I say it, but perhaps it might sink in and you'll recall it someday when it will be of some use. I see I'm talking to myself. Is your mother at home?'

'Yes, Miss Herne.'

'Then go, explain your fall and your narrow miss. Tell her two feet to the right and the railings might have had more to say about it. Under the circumstances you can forget the lines that I notice you haven't handed in yet, although an acquaintance with the Apostles' names wouldn't do you any harm. You, Campbell, can accompany him. Come back once he's safely delivered.' She claps her hands. 'Go. Now. You, Georgina, can sit with me until we call the class in.'

The two dismissed boys leave, Indian file, Danny in the lead. They cross the playground and exit the school gates in the same formation, both perplexed why she colluded in the lie. Once out of sight, Danny stops. Campbell draws abreast.

Danny undoes his tie and curls this in a careful spiral round his fist. Campbell, misunderstanding, tenses. He's prepared to slap down any retaliation. The tie is spotted with blood. Looking down Danny sees the absent tie has left a clear stripe in his maculate shirt and jumper. The noises and smell of the yards drift up the hill in waves. The combination can make him feel a sense of premature nostalgia for something he hasn't yet lost. The pain in his face and the sense of humiliation wash over him afresh. To sit down like that. In front of all those people.

He's horrified by the sob that bursts from him, spotting the clear stripe the absent tie exposed. Another follows. And another. He's temporarily blind. He can't even see the other boy, never mind gauge his reaction. He tries holding his breath but it doesn't work. He's racked with these sobs, juddering like a marionette in the tenemented street. A huge string of bloody catarrh droops from his nose and when he attempts to wipe it, the loop from sleeve to septum is caught in a curve by the afternoon light. He tries wiping his eyes with the other sleeve and only succeeds in creating another loop.

Campbell shifts his weight anxiously and looks up and down the street. His social vocabulary of blushes, punches and awkward silences isn't equal to the moment. He can sense the boy's humiliation and would be anywhere, rather than here, and add to it.

The sobs begin to subside. Once he can see, Danny wipes his hands and face with his tie.

'You shouldn't have tried to make fun of Gig.'

'I know.'

'I'm sorry.'

'I know.'

Danny's mother, across the street from Michael's, opens the flat door to the boys. Campbell finds this wall of aromas as poignant as Danny does the shipyards'. As she falls on Danny, he's picking his way through the strata, identifying children, soup, bleach and half a dozen things he can't recognize. The interior is so warmly lit he almost feels he would be puncturing some kind of domestic membrane by entering. Having satisfied herself that he's not mortally wounded, Danny is allowed to speak.

'This is Campbell. I fell. He saw me home.'

This unknown species of mother now turns her attention to Campbell. She's even put her arms round him and he stands, paralysed on this tantalising threshold. His sense of dislocation is total. He pines for the awkwardness of the new playground. Her embrace has extended to engulf Danny too. She seems to think them some kind of brothers in adversity. They're ushered into the kitchen and set down at a table with an oilcloth, worn at the four compass points where countless meals have been taken. To Campbell it's the busiest room he's ever seen. There's some kind of simmering pot. Pendant bedding, like a looped shroud, hangs from a pulley in the ceiling. The window drips condensation. A little boy or girl, he doesn't know which, regards him unblinkingly from the recessed bed. The heat from the modest grate seems disproportionate, as does the number of times she touches him, busying herself on some activity that evidently demands his presence. She tousles his hair twice in passing. He hasn't had this much contact in three years. A rising sense of guilt gets worse every time she touches him. She pats his shoulder in the passing and he blurts out words as spontaneous as Danny's sob.

'He didn't fall.'

'We got in a fight.' Danny says quickly. He knows that if the circumstances are teased out, his goading of Gig will come to light. Irene Gildea will put two and two together and find out he was teasing the girl of the new family across the way that hasn't got a mother. And he'll be asked to explain motives that he doesn't understand himself. Better leave her with the impression of a playground scrap that's forgotten. Besides, no one has clarified who was fighting who. They could jointly have gotten into a fight with other boys. He's adept at leaving details unspecific.

'Who were you fighting with?'

'Just some Protestants.'

'I hit him.' Campbell persists.

'I deserved it but before you ask I can't even remember what it was all about and neither can he.'

'So there weren't any Protestants?'

'Did you know Campbell's mother's dead?'

He doesn't know if it's true or not. It's one of these rumours that no one knows where they come from but spread across the playground fast as a punted football. The non-sequitur stuns the other two as it's supposed to. Campbell doesn't know if his mother's dead. Danny knows his mother will pursue her line of enquiry and it will turn out badly for him unless he derails it. Irene looks at Campbell.

'Are you one of the family that's just moved in across the way?'

'Yes.'

'Above Deborah?'

'I don't know who that is.'

'Mrs Neavie?'

'Yes.'

Irene goes to the stove and wordlessly puts a bowl of soup in front of Campbell. The fragrance is so intense it smells about ten feet deep. Tiny dots of fat pool the surface, shining yellowly in the afternoon light among floating pearl barley and chunks of shredded flank mutton. Beneath the surface are large chunks of carrot, potato, turnip and onion. She puts salt, pepper and torn hunks of bread in front of him. He's always on the verge of intense hunger. His embarrassment is temporarily forgotten. Nothing requires any chewing. The whole thing disintegrates into a spectrum of flavours that draws saliva and speaks to his stomach in a way that nothing has before. He eats quickly, as if frightened she'll change her mind.

'Where's mine?'

'After homework.'

Which both of them know to mean he has a mother and isn't a priority. She refills the bowl before Campbell finishes. He slows at the last three spoonfuls, awaiting a reprimand. He's already devoured the bread she gave him and she gives him some more.

'It's for soaking up what's left. Use the crust for the last bit the way you would your spoon.'

He's embarrassed by his ignorance. But a woman who's going to show him how to mop up the residue without drinking it isn't going to shout at him either.

'Well you might have been fighting but you had the good grace to bring him back.'

'The teacher told me to.'

'Have you no more sense than a shite?' Danny asks, despite himself.

She smiles at Campbell for being so remorselessly honest and slaps Danny on the back of the head.

'I won't have language like that in this house. Once more and I'll tell your father. And we'll find out about the fighting after homework.' She knows that's unlikely. Danny's nimble with his evasions. You never get to the bottom of anything. She turns to Campbell.

'Well, now that you've been here and seen his home you won't hit him again, will you?'

'No, Mrs Gildea.'

'You've got a sister, haven't you?'

'Yes, Mrs Gildea.'

'Well she might like the soup as much as you seemed to. Bring her round some time and you can try it again, with her.'

'Yes, Mrs Gildea.'

At her prompting, Danny sees him to the door. The past forty-five minutes have been so beyond expectation or previous experience for Campbell that he feels it requires some kind of acknowledgement, but is at a customary loss.

'Your mum.'

'What about her?'

'I won't tell anyone. About you crying, I mean.'

'I know.'

stretched, gibbeted, but not voiding their bowels. Suffering doesn't seem to detract from piety, but somehow shitting seems to. Certain corpses, we're told, don't corrupt. The odour of sanctity. What do people expect? Is it ever possible to satisfy all their expectations?

You'd have to be a saint. And saints, as far as Father Delaney is concerned, differ from the rest of the world in kind, not degree. No one progresses incrementally to sainthood. It's not like graduation. They're made by God and recognized by the Pope. Supernaturally suited and booted. This thought gives him some comfort, for Father Delaney sees himself as a man of a certain modestly allocated piety. It's an almost feudal view. He has a position in the strata he won't rise above, and hopes not to sink below. There's not a lot of point in straining.

How he wonders, does the Pope recognize a saint? By this time he's buttoned up, washed his hands and is prowling the kitchen looking for something Mrs Quigley might have left him to eat. Spam. There are some tomatoes. He layers the whole thing between two slices of bread and is half way through when his eyes alight on the jellied chicken. Mrs Quigley's talents wouldn't have stretched that far. It must have been one of the parishioners, with an excess of generosity and coupons. He opens a bottle of stout and swigs directly from it. There's no one here to disapprove. Both hands are now occupied. He burps into the silence, grins, beerily, and returns to his speculations. Anyone looking in would see a flabby, drab man munching steadily like a horse and frowning at some invisible blemish on the wall.

What is it the Pope sees that distinguishes the remarkable from the rest? How does he penetrate the sleight of hand, the adulation, the credible hysteria, the crowing gullibility that surrounds the reputation of the candidate? People clamour to be in the presence of grace. It's a narcotic. He's seen it. He doesn't believe it rubs off. Does the Pope see in them something of himself? But that can't be. Popes progress incrementally to become Pope. They're parish priests, like him, with ambition and an allocation of piety less modest. Then they're bishops, then cardinals, and after that his understanding of the hierarchy is as hazy as the smoke that signifies a decision. Or not. That, he thinks, is only a difference in degree. How happy would his Bishop be with his conclusions?

He's finished the sandwich and looks round for a fork. The cutlery drawer is across the room and he can't be bothered. He sticks his unoccupied hand into the jellied chicken and pulls out a thigh. It comes away with sucking noises. He bites, happily. There's a film of grease on his lips shining in the overhead light. He frowns more intently at a memory.

A boy. In Woolworths of all places. He smiled up and handed Father Delaney his dropped evening paper. Said something to the priest. Anyone stopping him in the main isle of a Saturday evening rush would have put him on his guard, prompted him to feel for his watch and wallet, in case he's been a mark for pickpockets. But not this boy. He thanked him, exchanged a few words trying to locate the child's accent, and in that inconsequential dialogue experienced a moment of rare insight. He realised he was talking to someone of immense spiritual superiority. It was doubly disquieting: firstly because unsolicited, he hadn't prayed for any insight; secondly because the child's colour and accent led him to believe that he probably wasn't even Catholic, never mind Christian, never mind Scottish. While it lasted the encounter gave him a sense of spiritual vertigo. He resisted the temptation of praying that there wouldn't be a recurrence. Luckily, he thought, his parishional duties made this unlikely.

He avoided Woolworths for the rest of the year.

When it comes to the parish he sees his role as a continuous rota of administering the sacraments and of baptising, marrying and burying. He hopes he dispenses a comforting sense of continuity. He sees himself as a kind of GP in his own sphere, sanitising as he goes. He knows he's spiritually incurious himself and he doesn't encourage unhealthy speculations in others either. All that musing about popes and saints, the result of a missed dinner, where's that gotten him?

The chicken's now finished and his hand is greasy. He puts down the bottle and reaches for a cloth. Wiping both hands he throws the cloth in the direction of the sink and tuts in disapproval when he notices finger marks ringing the bottle's neck. He picks it up and swigs.

There was an old priest in the seminary who thought slovenliness a sin, not because he thought it indicative of some inner laxity but just because he didn't like untidiness. He gets irritated at the mere memory of the man. There's a difference between etiquette and sin. If it's a sin to drink from a bottle then it's so venial it's not worth bothering about. He knows he's confusing the issue here: the etiquette of drinking from a bottle with the consequence of drinking its contents. He knows that in his case this is indicative of some inner laxity, not because he swigs from one bottle but because he can't stop there.

Why shouldn't they have the money? Having taken an unpleasant turn his thoughts jump the rails. The greatest qualification for the hardship fund is hardship, and one look at them tells him they're extravagantly qualified. What does it matter if he's dubious about their Catholic credentials? Look at the boy's shoes. 'And now there remain faith, hope, and charity, these three: but the greatest of these is charity.' His own faith is as it is. He doesn't hope for much, just a safe berth this side and a niche afterwards. But here's a chance, modest, admittedly, to exercise the greatest virtue.

He'll advocate their cause. He sees himself before the Board, heads nodding in agreement in the wind of his eloquence. Who's he kidding? He is the fund. They've never turned down a case he put forward. At least this will be one needy instance they offered succour to before the Kirk beat them to it.

He opens a second bottle. A family's going to benefit in a manifest way from something he's going to do. He has a more benign image of himself at such moments. He would like to think the congregation shares it. He's not the drab journeyman who fell into this by the weight of family expectations, the young man whose only calling was a desire not to disappoint and now terrestrially administers to a few dozen streets. No, he's something more numinous, a vehicle of grace.

Miss Herne, at her own frugal supper of herring and boiled potatoes, would beg to differ. Father Delaney, in his numerous encounters with

Miss Herne at the school and church, has mentally consigned her to the variety of spinster schoolteacher he's met numerous times. She seems adequate and he has no reason to find fault in the rote learning she instils in the children. He can't vouch for their arithmetic, but they all emerge well-versed in their catechism. He's never suffered a moment of Woolworths' insight in her company. If he were truly to see her he would never hold another preconception. If he were to see the depth of the narrow chasm that separates her not only from him, but from all the congregation on his side of the brink, he would see her isolation as sinfully willed.

She sees him. Sunday after Sunday she sits in the pew intently watching and listening, watching and listening. And from this sustained one-sided collision she perceives a great deal. She doesn't blame him for the obviousness of his homilies. They have to appeal to the least subtly minded of the congregation. Having a calling doesn't always entail having oratorical skills to match. But, as far as she's concerned, he has neither. She can guess at the family coercion. She sees him as a bumbling functionary. In the course of his tedious sermons she has mentally compared their respective chastity: hers, burnished, resplendent, given to God; his as lukewarm as the rest of him, never much of a sacrifice to relinquish, a dull filament that glowed less frequently, a pilot light that blew out when no one noticed and will never be called on again because there's nothing to ignite.

She sits there in the pew, just as she does in any public place, memorising the foibles, noting the shortcomings of those around her.

He's on to his third beer. This thing he will do, this act of largesse is a good thing to do now, furnish the rumour mill with a story of generosity instigated by him. Given the choice he wouldn't have it talked about. But things are as they are, and in a parish this size everyone knows everything – except the news of the new man coming. If he could choose to be remembered for a single act while in sole control, he could do worse. Of course he won't be remembered for that. No one's remembered for a single act, no matter how exemplary. Perhaps martyrs - but who'd want that? 'But the greatest of these is charity.'

SEVEN

'Thermopylae – don't drag your chairs as you sit. We're all Jock Tamson's bairns but you don't have to behave like livestock. Manners are one of the things that elevate us. Thermopylae was more than just a battle. Jean Muir, why are you squirming? Are you infested? Do I have to escort you to the nit nurse again?'

'Can I go to the toilet, Miss Herne?'

'No. You should have thought of that before you came in. If you scratch once more I'll sit you at a hygienic distance. Is that what you want?'

'No, Miss Herne.'

'Then sit still. Listen, all of you. Sadly you'll find that few people in life will say anything memorable to you. Moments like this are the exception. Consider this an opportunity. Be still. Pay heed. And *remember*. If you take only one thing away from these moments, other than bladder control, let it be how to apply what you learn to situations in the rest of your life. I don't expect you all to understand this now. However, if you *remember*, you'll find you have a compass you didn't know you possessed. It might help you find your way. I'm your teacher. I care what you think and I care even more what you will think. No one else does. Yes, Andrew Thomson.'

'What about our parents, Miss Herne?'

'The better of your parents are more concerned about the everyday, about putting food in your bellies and clothes on your backs, to have the luxury of wondering what you'll think when you're their age. And they're the better ones. Look at our new classmate, Campbell Renton, sitting there with his new parish shoes. A committee put them on his feet, not his father. What is it, Andrew Thomson?'

'What about Father Delaney, Miss Herne?'

'What about Father Delaney?'

'Doesn't he care what we think?'

'He *should* care what you think as you're thinking it. That's his job. But, like the better parents, he is preoccupied with the everyday, doling out Hail Marys and the like. Now, for the second time, Thermopylae. As I said, it was more than just a battle. It was a confrontation of perhaps half a million Persians against three hundred Spartans. That's what I said, half a million against three hundred. Imagine Hamden Park filled ten times. Or imagine if the men coming from the shipyards at closing just kept coming for hour after hour. That would be the number of the Persian host.'

'Did the Persians have ships, Miss Herne?'

'Whether they had ships or not is neither here nor there. I mentioned the shipyards only to give your young minds some idea of the number of Persian soldiers. We're talking about a land battle.'

'Were the Persians the bad ones?'

'That's for you to make up your own mind about. The Persians were commanded by a king called Xerxes. He was a man given over to insensate rages. He once had the Hellespont, what your parents would call the seaside, whipped because it wouldn't obey him. You're all staring. People are not above such stupidities. Among his armies was an elite core called 'the Immortals'. The battle was to prove they were far from immortal. That's called irony. What's it called?'

'Irony, Miss Herne.'

'And what is irony? No one? No? I would rather you asked than remain in ignorance. It's Greek for 'dissimulation', but I don't expect you to remember that either. It's the awareness of a discrepancy, a space, a gap, between words and their meaning. They were called the Immortals, which meant they couldn't die, and yet the Spartans killed them.

'The Spartans were commanded by King Leonidas. With him he took three hundred men of the royal bodyguard, the Hippeis. When Xerxes sent a messenger to Leonidas demanding a gift from the Spartans in token of surrender, King Leonidas threw the messenger down a well. Then he set off for war with his trusty three hundred. Even before he left he knew he would never return. He consulted the Oracle at Delphi, the way some superstitious people talk to a fortune teller, and he was told he was going to die.'

'Why didn't he just go to church instead, Miss Herne?'

'Leonidas didn't have the advantage of the Catholic faith that we do. It would be almost five hundred years before Our Lord would come down. I'm not saying fortune tellers tell the truth. They may say correct things by accident, but they're frauds. The importance of the oracle for this story is that Leonidas believed the prophecy to be correct. He believed he was going to die, and that belief didn't stop him from going.'

'Did he die, Miss Herne?'

'Patience. Leonidas had chosen his battlefield well. Half a million Persians on one side and three hundred Spartans on the other. But only a dozen or so could fight side by side. Xerxes told Leonidas and his men to lay down their weapons. Leonidas told Xerxes and his men to come and get them. The battle joined.

'The Persians attacked for three days. Thousands of them were killed but they didn't succeed in routing Leonidas and his men.

'However, a traitor, a man named Ephialtes, a man whose name would come to stand for infamy in the centuries to come, knew of a mountain path that would lead some of Xerxes' men round the

Spartans to attack them from behind. Once they were surrounded there was only going to be one outcome. Xerxes' men rained arrows down on the three hundred Spartans until every last one was dead. There's no need to cry, Andrew Thomson. It all happened a very long time ago. You know the Spartans left the feeble to die at birth. I don't think you, snivelling like that, would have made it to schooling age. I repeat, Thermopylae was just a battle. But what does it tell us?'

'No to get surrounded, Miss Herne.'

'I'm not thinking of military tactics.'

'That arrows are bad for you, Miss Herne.'

'God has granted you scant wits, Jean Muir. He has his reasons that I don't pretend to understand. Take your full bladder to the toilet and don't come back until I tell you to enter. What else, class, does the lesson of Thermopylae teach? It teaches that a small group of free people chose to fight and prevail for three days against an immensely superior army that had been forced to advance under the lash. It teaches us that if people are prepared to die for what they believe in, then they can overcome vastly superior odds driven on by despots, or, as your parents would say, bad men. I say this to you, class. You don't have to die to prove your strength, although willingness to give up your life for your faith is the purest and most beautiful of sacrifices. And we have a faith far more worthy of sacrifice than the Spartans did. You can experience your own Thermopylae every day. I don't mean you'll join in epic battle. There are small resistances against the forces of ignorance that beset us. This is a moral example that shines down through the ages and teaches something worth remembering. Take it from Thermopylae, take it from history, take it from me, you don't have to listen to the prevailing wisdom. The only true authority is the inner one. It's how God speaks to me. You must learn to listen to Him and only Him.

'You may not come in, Jean Muir. You can't have washed your hands properly in such a short time. Go back and do so now. Slovenliness is a sin.'

EIGHT

Times are changing. Deborah Neavie, unaware that her longed for second child will eventually arrive, would willingly freeze things as they are: Michael her perpetual baby, all of them young and healthy, Stephen vigorous and free from accident, the ominous rumblings from that vague entity consigned to the back of her mind as 'Europe' nothing more than distant tremors. But it's not to be. Geography has forced itself onto the front pages. By now everyone's heard of Poland. She sat with Stephen listening to Chamberlain's broadcast and judged the gravity of the situation not by the constrained delivery, but by the slow flexing and clenching of Stephen's hands. There's nothing normally oppressive about his taciturnity. She can normally talk for the two of them. But the gloomy silence that descends when he turns the radio off presses down like a low ceiling and spoils her appetite. She's suddenly exhausted, seeks an early bed and breaks routine by taking Michael in with her.

The nation holds its breath, awaiting the cataclysm. Nothing happens. The nation breathes out in the anticlimax. They go back to what passes for normal. Around here they're more normal still. She doesn't appreciate that it's the riverside cacophony that insulates them; that this proportion of fit men will soon cease to be the norm; that the change from mercantile to warships presages something; that round the clock production will be a race against the predations of the U-boats.

Stephen does. She becomes intolerant of his silences without realising how close to domestic catastrophe their little family is. With some prompting he normally shares his thoughts. But now, to her, he seems to make a virtue of silence. Her intuition has failed her and she's as annoyed at herself as at him, culminating in a slammed soup plate that cracks and dribbles its contents on the kitchen linoleum. She's on the verge of tears for a cracked plate and he stills her hand by covering it with his own.

'Don't worry. I'll stay.'

And she realises the chasm that almost opened and she guesses at his silent calculation: his robustness; the public need; the humiliation of seeing the less able enlisting versus the need for ships, his skill squandered in squarebashing; Michael, herself, her mother, an extended family dependent on his continued vitality. And then she has a sharp mental image of him lying somewhere, anonymous, foreign, his love and vitality haemorrhaged and him broken. It is not an image of war but dredged from a childhood catalogue, probably a catechism martyr. A noise breaks from her neither has heard before. His other hand cups the back of her head. The soup dribbles. She clings and clings to him, denying Europe a chink of admission.

If Alan Renton has subjected himself to the same kind of scrutiny then he disguises it well. He reads the papers looking for standards he can fail until he realises there's no need; he's in a reserved occupation. He could look like that Trojan downstairs, the one with the wife, and he'd still be safe. He sees his war, if it ever comes to that, as a series of gestures sketched out with his glowing cigarette tip for the benefit of whoever's listening.

There are few takers for the programme of evacuation while the

Phony War lasts. Deborah reads and scowls at the sense of dislocation. She imagines Michael transported to someone else's keeping, and she wants to cry for those displaced English children. She wants to cry a lot these days, and Stephen's staying, and the war hasn't really started, and no one she knows has been hurt. How will it be if they are? She resolves to compose herself, for all of them.

Times are changing. The blackout has made a playground of the streets for marauding children. Danny Gildea's perfected a way of slipping out once his brother, Paul, is asleep, dropping on to the bin-shed and returning via an acrobatic downpipe. He and Campbell are now inseparable. He calls for Campbell at any hour and is waved in by Alan. He finds the austerity of these surroundings as fascinating as Campbell does his home. It's not just the lack of stuff that every other home he's ever entered seems to have accumulated to make life possible, it's the complete lack of regulation that goes with it. His forays are surreptitious because his life's hedged with rules. He sees their complete lack of restriction as glamorous.

Not that Gig needs to add to her allure. She seems to attract people with no perceivable effort on her part. She takes it for granted because it's happened to her as long as she can remember. Danny's hopelessly in thrall. He's rescued her from pirates, Indians, Fu Manchu, cowboys with sinister moustaches and all the stock threats of Saturday matinees. Last night's heroic fist fight lasted half an hour until he was shouted at through the wall to GET TO BED. He traded cow-stunning blows with all of her captors, laying out one western desperado after another, culminating with the henchman he punched through the saloon doors into oblivion. He ignored his wounds to console her and pick her up. But here he faltered. Reality intruded and abolished them when he realised she was probably more able to lift him.

He'll haunt their Spartan flat, mostly she's not there, trying to evoke her from the miscellaneous furniture. It might have been deposited by a cyclone. He doesn't understand why but he wants to handle the same things she does. It's proximity – of a kind.

It's convenient that she's Campbell's sister, but their friendship is independent of her. Gig tries to divert some of the attention she gets from other people towards Campbell, to redress the balance. It hasn't worked before and it doesn't now. They've both come to the conclusion that some people are more loveable than other people, and he's drawn the short straw.

Miss Herne perpetuates this discrimination. Her illustrations of municipal charity are only ever focused on Campbell and the other destitutes, never Gig. She's blatantly offered her hand to Gig, in the playground, to lead and summon the class in from the rain.

Deborah Neavie has also tried to redress the balance. She knows the pretexts for giving Campbell jobs and money are growing thin. When he comes in she can feel his prehistoric hunger for the surroundings as much as the food. Just stepping over the threshold involves overcoming chronic shyness, but he'll repeatedly make the attempt and stand, wordless, because the ambience must be worth the effort. And there seems to be some wordless understanding between him and Stephen, because the boy will gravitate towards him as soon as he enters. She sees less of Gig than she would have hoped. Any female company is welcome when her only normal company is male, and the girl's not just anyone. You can see the onset of her puberty alarming her father. His only attempt to deal with it seems to be to foist her on any woman that will pay attention to her. Deborah's beginning to have misgivings about the interest the teacher's taking.

Gig did have a predecessor to Miss Herne's attentions. That girl had a mother to circumvent and a father who paid attention to her. Miss Herne finally released her like an undersized fish to return to the shoal of the playground. Aside from the inconvenience of her parents she had decided that the girl lacked the necessary qualifications. Miss Herne isn't looking for acolytes, and she doesn't always have a potential protégé in tow. She believes her submission to her chosen creed to be absolute. She believes such perfect surrender to be a gift. She believes that when she recognizes these potential and very singular qualities in another it's her duty to foster them. She believes she will never find them in a boy or man because the grossness of their sex interferes.

She believes she has found them in Gig. She believes it doesn't matter whether Gig knows her catechism or not, or has memorised the De profundis, because the combination of very, very rare elements is there awaiting her attention. She believes the girl is a gift, from God to her, and that the lack of social entanglements are His clear indication to her to proceed. And now, more than once, she has invited Gig to share her evening meal. The attention is of a different kind from anything Gig's known until now.

'Is that the marriage china?' It's an expression Gig has heard, that seems to refer to the second set of plates, often displayed, seldom set.

'Do you see a husband?'

'Sorry, Miss Herne, I mean the good china?'

'Child,' her hand covers the girl's 'all the things in here are good. I've no patience with the inferior.'

The table is placed at the kitchen window. The pouring and preparation of the tea is almost oriental in its elaboration. Gig's eyes shine. Campbell can see the pouring arc from the back courts below.

Two more people are shortly introduced to Miss Herne and the class in the course of Father Delaney's next Tuesday. The first is again heralded by the Deputy Head teacher, Mrs Maguire. He's a boy of corn-coloured hair and penetrating blue eyes, mid-way in height between Danny and Campbell, if a shade on the tall side, and with a porcelain complexion that would match Gig's. But there's nothing effeminate about him. His almost Nordic appearance isn't what's most striking to the class. His bottle-green blazer has striped diagonal piping. Those who can muster a uniform here sport the regulation dark blue blazer, often as not inherited, worn to the point of colourlessness, improvised as countless goal posts and shapeless as a sack. But this is an exotic, refulgent green. And it fits. He already carries a mystique around him. Mrs Maguire exchanges a confidential word with the teacher and returns to wherever she dwells, leaving introductions to Miss Herne.

Miss Herne claps her hands needlessly, calling for attention. All eyes are focused on the new boy who seems to exhibit none of the nervousness of Gig or Campbell when first inspected.

'This, boys and girls is Douglas Cunningham.'

'Dougal.'

'I beg your pardon?'

'Dougal. My name's Dougal.'

'And mine is Miss Herne. And that's how you will address me from now on. Always. Is that clear?'

'Yes, Miss Herne.'

'I appear to have been misinformed.' Dougal, nearer the exchange between the two women than the rest of the class, knows she wasn't. 'I stand corrected. Only Our Lord is infallible. Should you feel the need to correct me in future, Dougal Cunningham, you will approach me in private. Is that also clear?'

'Yes, Miss Herne.'

'You will notice Dougal's blazer. Is it not splendid? Is it not incongruous? Do you know what that means? No? It means out of place. And why is it out of place? It's out of place because Dougal Cunningham wore it at his last school. I understand from Mrs Maguire that that was in Perthshire. Is that correct?'

'Yes, Miss Herne.'

'Saint Alphonsus?'

'Yes, Miss Herne.'

'Saint Alphonsus as you may not all know is a *public* school. For those of us who have grown up in less fortunate circumstances the expression 'public school' may not mean anything. There's something ironic here. Yes, children, we are back again to irony. Who can tell me what irony is? Yes, Georgina Renton?'

'It's a gap, Miss Herne, between what a word says and what it means.'

'Excellent. Listen and learn. Here's a young lady recently arrived without a public school blazer who *remembered*. But what is the gap I'm talking about here? Don't be embarrassed – I didn't expect any of you to know. Something that is public is available to anyone. Like books in the public library. But public school education is only available to those who can afford to pay. There are, I believe, token scholarships where the children of ordinary families can get help sending their children there. This is a form of charity, like the hardship fund that put David McClelland's blazer on his back. But on the whole public schools are not public. They're private. That, children, is what is known as a 'misnomer'." She chalks it on the board, separating the syllables with emphatic dashes, dotting the 'i' with a little concussion of chalk dust. 'Repeat the word.'

'Mis – nom – er.'

'A misnomer is a misnaming. It's a mistake. From press reports I understand another example is the 'stand' at football matches. People don't stand in the stand. They sit. Where shall we sit you, Dougal Cunningham? The seating arrangement here indicates the academic standing of my class. Nearest the desk here are my gifted girls – and Malachy. In the diagonally opposite corner are those more challenged by the curriculum. Isn't that correct, Jean Muir?'

'Yes, Miss Herne.'

'Fortunately I'm *not* a slave to the curriculum. Between here,' she gestures open-handedly to the foreground, 'and here,' waving dismissively back-handed without looking where she had tossed their attention, 'is every shade between. Children earn their place. As shall you. Perhaps some of your public school sophistication,' she pauses to write the word on the board in another series of separated syllables, 'will rub off. I'm afraid you may find things around here rather basic. We may not be fortunate enough to see your talents exercised to their full extent if they require your Perthshire facilities. We have blackboards, schoolbooks, a playground, admirable municipal libraries and some of us have our imaginations. It may be a falling-off from Perthshire but we rub along. And if I'm not mistaken, that badge on your lapel indicates some kind of sporting prowess, does it not?'

'Yes, Miss Herne.'

'I doubt if the playground will afford the scope to exercise your talents. We can only wait and see.'

At this point another very singular figure enters. He's a man in his early thirties but whose features and complexion shave ten years off the common estimation of his age. His soutane announces him to be the colleague of Father Delaney, drafted into the parish to quicken the spiritual pulse. He's wearing a beret, something in these provincial circumstances to cause comment in itself, a piece of exotica. He's oblivious of this until the combined focus of the classroom's attention draws it to his notice. He snatches it from his head apologetically, revealing a tousled mop of very dark hair that radiates from his head like static. This, combined with the mobility of his face and eyes that are almost black, give the impression of enormous mental energy that his body can barely contain.

The reason his eyes are gleaming so brightly is that he's intensely angry. He's irritated with himself for being late for his appointment with Mrs Maguire. Prompt time-keeping is one of his numerous standards. Told that she has gone to escort the new boy to his classroom while she awaited his arrival, he went off in pursuit to apologise. And he has spent the past five minutes aimlessly walking various corridors, taking in the sights and sounds and smells. The unconscious conclusion that he has reached, that will uncurl itself as he finally lies down to sleep, is that this place is the poorest he has encountered and poorer than he anticipated. Consciously his mental clock is still calibrating his increasing lateness when he catches sight of a bright green blazer through one of the windows he has just passed. It's so incongruous it can only be the new boy Mrs Maguire delivered. He pauses outside the room and listens to corroborate.

The tone of the teacher he has momentarily glimpsed suggests that there's no other adult present. He looks, again, to make sure. He sees an ageless woman whom he would estimate as being in her late thirties. The calculation is made more difficult by the deliberate severity of her appearance, which probably adds as many years to the common estimation as his appearance shaves from his. Her hair is drawn back in a constricting bun. She wears a matching charcoal skirt and jacket that seems almost clerical, its only concession a fitted waist. There's something about her that immediately tells him she's childless: the narrowness of her waist; breasts that haven't nourished children; the attention to her appearance, austere as it is, that indicates a preoccupation that most mothers around here can't afford; the whiff of money, of a modest salary undiluted. He's listening simply to the cadence of her sentences until their meaning begins to overtake him and he's stunned by this bravura performance in calibrated malice. He thinks this can't be allowed to continue when he suddenly realises that he's standing in the classroom, equidistant to the teacher and green blazer, physically blocking the line of sight between these points. Intense silence has fallen. The children are regarding him with the same awe they would a pantomime magician, levitating from a smoky floor. He realises his mistake but deliberately turns to the boy.

'I knew some ex-pupils from Saint Alphonsus when I went to the seminary.' The focus of the class now immediately pivots from the two newcomers to their teacher. Another grown-up has come into the classroom and addressed his remark to the someone other than her. Even to their young minds it's a blatant slight. She regards the priest very intently for a full five seconds before clearing her throat. It's the preamble that would normally still them if they weren't already deathly quiet. Knowing he's achieved his object and deflected her attention from the boy to himself, he deliberately pre-empts her.

'I'm sorry we haven't been introduced. I was late for my appointment with Mrs Maguire.'

She regards him for another five seconds. All the clergy she has so far met have conformed to type in her mind. But looking at him there, a dark vertical bisecting the diagonals of morning light, beret in hand, the ardency of his eyes tells her she has entirely another quality to deal with here.

Again she needlessly claps. The front row flinches.

'We are fortunate, children, to be among the first to welcome Father Delaney's replacement, Father Paolo Bernacchi - '

'If I may, is it Mrs or Miss?'

'Miss Herne.'

'If I may, Miss Herne, I think it's important the children should know I'm not Father Delaney's replacement. I wouldn't like that mistake to be taken back to their homes.'

'You heard that, children, Father Bernacchi is *not* Father Delaney's replacement.' And turning brightly towards him 'Helpmeet? Colleague?'

'I'm simply here to help with some of the parishional duties.' He takes his cue and turns to the rest of the class, circumventing her. He's also taken an automatic step towards his audience, allowing a clear line of sight between the green blazer and the teacher. She's still looking intently at the priest. 'I'm happy to tell you that I'll be taking over as school chaplain. So I hope to see you and your parents at church and I'm delighted to say I'll see more of you at school. If any of you want to talk to me you don't have to wait until I visit your classrooms, and you don't have to talk to me in front of others. You can come and talk to me on your own.'

'You mean like confession?' Danny asks.

'I will be hearing confessions but I don't mean just that. I mean like a chat.'

Miss Herne inwardly smiles. Word will get around the way word of his arrival did and she predicts one of two things will happen: he'll become prey to every opportunist, spiritual hypochondriac and lunatic in the parish; or they'll remain intimidated by the combination of his office and strangeness, question his sincerity and methods, scorn the informality that attempts to bridge a gap that's there for a reason, and they'll stay eloquently away.

'I've imposed on your good teacher long enough.' And to the boy 'Perhaps you can tell me about Saint Alphonsus. We can compare your version with the stories I heard.'

She knows, as he intends her to, that this is a marker. He's offering to open a dialogue that will keep him apprised of the boy's treatment. He's as aware as Miss Herne is of the reversal in fortune that would transplant a child from Saint Alphonsus here. He's been uprooted himself enough to give him a sense of the boy's dislocation. First days are bad enough without being condescended to by a woman who resents even withdrawn privileges.

As he sees himself out she orchestrates a ragged, 'Good – bye – Fath – er – Ber – nacc – i.' Only when the door closes on him does she notice the intensity of the new boy's scrutiny of her. It reminds her of the sustained one-sided collision of her focus upon the hapless Father Delaney, fumbling for platitudes in the pulpit.

NINE

'So have you been to Perth?'

'I went to school there.'

'She said Perth*shire*.'

'Yes. I've been to Perth.'

'I've never been any higher than Glasgow.'

'I've been to Inverness,' Campbell interrupts. This is so remote from the topic it means nothing to Danny. Perth is a place of green blazers and 'facilities', whatever that might mean. It's imbued with fresh-air glamour. 'Inverness is further than Perth,' Campbell adds. The distance fails to add to its allure. 'And I've been to Perth.'

'What, to his school?'

'No.'

'What school then?'

'I don't remember any school. Dad met a woman there and then we had to leave.'

'*That's* no good,' Danny says. There's a place called Perth and at its nucleus are 'facilities'. To go to Perth and not to be there is just the same as going to everywhere else. In Danny's mind all Campbell's wanderings in tow to an itinerant dad don't count. It's like using the ferry once and saying you know the Clyde. At the first opportunity Danny cornered the new boy in the playground and gestured Campbell to join them.

'Have you been to a zoo?' Danny says.

'Yes.'

'Fuck.'

Dougal retaliates. 'Have you been on a train?'

'Yes. Well... a couple of stops.'

'I've been on a sleeper.' Dougal says.

'What? A train you sleep on?'

'Yes.'

'And then you go home?'

Campbell's Inverness so-phis-tic-at-ion intervenes. 'It travels while you're asleep. When you wake up you're somewhere else.'

'Fuck. Where did you wake up?'

'London.'

'Did you see King George?'

'No.'

'What did you see?'

'A show. Peter Pan.'

'Fuck.' He contemplates his foot, kicks the tarmac, weighs all the new boy's advantages and is at a loss to identify any of his own to counterbalance them. Then the obvious strikes him.

'Is your dad in the war then?'

Dougal's mouthed reply is drowned by the bell. He waits until it's finished and abbreviates it to a syllable.

'No.'

'Dead?'

'Shut up, Danny!' Campbell has the good grace to be angry.

'No, it's all right.' Dougal holds up a hand, volunteering. 'Dead. Yes. My father's dead.'

' 'father'. Who says 'father'?'

'Don't be such a prick, Danny.'

'What's made you all touchy? I know! Campbell's got no mum. You've got no dad. Your mum and his dad could get together.'

Campbell's thinking of hitting Danny again, a warning slap for pushing it too far, not a punch that would involve all the embarrassment of last time. He and Dougal look dubiously at one another, the contrast of Dougal's green and Campbell's motley obvious to both. Campbell has in his mind an image of Dougal's mother, an older, feminine version of Dougal, well-dressed, smelling of perfume, doing sophisticated unimaginable feminine things. Things that involve a future. And he compares this with his dad, pulling on clothes left on the floor, shunting from home to work to pub to wherever, fag end always smouldering in the corner of his mouth, no plans beyond the next drink. His dad and Dougal's mum – they're probably separate species.

'Have you seen a circus?'

'Yes.'

'Fuck.'

The interrogation comes to an abrupt end. In their absorption they haven't registered Mrs Maguire come to supervise the lines. Danny's last word has cut through the descending silence. A disembodied hand appears between the taller boys' shoulders and grasps Danny's shock of hair. He's marched toward the main door and the crowd jubilantly follows, tramping noisily indoors in ragged lines in expectation. This has happened often enough for everyone to know what will follow. Danny will be marched into the presence of Mr Gilchrist, the Headmaster, a perpetually gloomy man who doesn't take kindly to interruption of his unremitting pessimism.

Mr Gilchrist is called upon from time to time to administer punishment for the more severe infractions, not because he's Headmaster but because he's one of the few men on the staff sanctioned to do so. The janitor is sufficiently robust, but he has to confine himself to surreptitious rabbit punches behind the boiler room to those wee cunts who steal his biscuits and try and piss in his kettle.

'And this one, Mrs Maguire?'

'Blasphemy, Headmaster.'

She doesn't know whether 'Fuck' is blasphemy or not, but its pedigree wouldn't stop her. She knows a sin when she hears it. They play out the pantomime of sad consternation, as much for themselves as for the boy because they have become these roles; he sadly shaking his head as he takes the belt from the drawer; she pursing her lips, her flabby cheeks now concave, as if sucking a lemon, stealing herself for what's about to happen.

The Headmaster walks ponderously into the corridor, gesturing Danny to follow. Mrs Maguire brings up the rear. It's her sad duty to witness this. Neither will admit, even to themselves, that this is one of the few enjoyable distractions. The corridor is empty but he always belts them here, to maximise the acoustics. Danny stands arms outstretched, one palm beneath the other, ready to alternate his hands.

The catechism, the chanting of the six times table, the rhythmic recitation of 'Young Lockinvar', the scrutiny of the red-mapped Empire, all give pause as the sound of the strokes echo up the stairwell.

TEN

There are several conversations being conducted simultaneously in the staff room. They don't all stop at Miss Herne's entrance but continue, more subdued, while she stops on the threshold. Several of the women exchange glances. Aside from the one incongruous man they're all women and that, as far as Miss Herne is concerned, is one of the problems. And then there's the man. And he's another problem.

She's thinking where she should place herself. Normally she would gravitate towards the man. This isn't an attempt to redress any balance, it's just that he's preferable to the alternatives. Her choice isn't an endorsement of him, it's an indictment of them. When near him she's conscious of an intense masculinity. Whether it's unique to him or an effect of her sensitivities, only in male company when circumstances require, she can't say. He exudes a spectrum of odours, none of them unpleasant. It's an amalgam of astringent cologne, the fastidiousness of clean cotton and something else, something hormonal she can't identify. And then there's that business with the pipe, its accoutrements and the ceremony of its preparation. There's something almost ecclesiastical in the way he fusses with it. She hates cigarettes and all that go with them. But from a leather pouch he'll draw out tobacco, dark as peat and with a fragrance she can't dislike either. It's the drawing and puffing like a locomotive that irritates, although she doesn't find the smell of pipe smoke objectionable either. But she can't sit next to him today as his name might prove an impediment to the conversation.

'Has anyone other than me had the pleasure of encountering Father Paolo Bernacchi?'

It floats out there like a fragrant cloud from the pipe. Her visits are so infrequent that her comments always command attention. Other conversations stop as the aired issue is now considered.

'I thought his name was Paul,' says Mrs Sharkey. Mrs Sharkey has a certain social cachet. She expressed her disapproval of her son's mixed marriage by timing her departure up the isle to coincide with the Protestant bride's progress in the other direction, dragging the hapless Mr Sharkey in the wake of this public boycott. The extremity of her views lends her a certain gravitas in staff-room politics.

'Perhaps he sought to anglicise it,' Miss Herne says.

'What does that mean?' asks Mrs Adams, brightly blinking. Miss Herne often silently despairs at the level of her colleagues' intelligence, just as she does the spiritual credentials of the uninspiring clergy she's encountered.

'It means he's sought to make it more English, more like one of us.'

'None of us is English,' says Mrs Fitzpatrick. Some of the others nod. Miss Herne sees that Mrs Fitzpatrick has hit upon a correct fact but entirely missed the point.

'I'm not suggesting we are, ladies,' with a deferential nod towards the solitary man.

The reason Miss Herne choose not to sit beside him while airing the issue of the dubious sounding foreign name is because he's called Jacek Tomaszewski. The reason she does choose to keep company with him during her infrequent trips to the staff room is that he's Doctor Jacek Tomaszewski. He's one of the few people Miss Herne tolerates because she suspects he knows almost everything factual that she does, and an unquantifiable quota besides. His shortcoming, in her eyes, is a corrosive scepticism that prevents him seeing what she sees.

'I'm just suggesting that in the light of our current crisis, perhaps Father Bernacchi thought fit to use a name that made him sound less *foreign*, in the nicest possible way.' She nods to the man again. He's standing at the window, half turned away, regarding the playground. He wears sombre horn-rimmed glasses which throw an accidental diamond of light on the opposite wall. It's difficult to gauge how much of his attention, if any, the conversation occupies. Miss Herne's willing to risk offending him and perseveres, 'Because there are certain foreign names that, through no fault of those that bear them, carry certain *associations* in the public mind.'

'What?' says Mrs Adams. 'Do you mean ice cream?'

Miss Herne experiences an urge to cross the room and slap Mrs Adams. It's so intense she can almost hear the report.

'No, Mrs Adams. I am thinking about *Il Duche*.'

'Does he run an ice cream shop?'

'No,' says Miss Fullerton, 'he runs a country.' The appearance of an affinity between the only two unmarried ladies in the staff room is simply that, an appearance. Miss Fullerton is stepping out with a piano tuner from Kilmarnock, and, as far as Miss Herne can see, is starving herself until the man is ensnared. Miss Herne thinks Miss Fullerton has a physique that's naturally bovine, that will relax to its natural shape once the ring is on, but also possesses an intelligence far more lively. She almost admires the younger woman's self-denial in pursuit of her goal. But Miss Herne can't understand how someone can wilfully subordinate their acumen for a man. Rumour has it that Miss Fullerton's intended avoided conscription due to his spine, a curvature pronounced enough to dictate his profession. Rumour has it he was confined to a choice of jobs that involved only looking down: piano-tuner, French-polisher, street-sweeper, stamp-licker or anything that didn't require a horizontal perspective. Rumour has it Miss Fullerton would rather be Mrs humpy-backed piano-tuner than

Miss on-the-shelf desiccated teacher, pretending a vocation to conceal the fact that she never chose, or was chosen.

At the other end of the spectrum, Mrs Adams, the needlework teacher, borders on idiocy. Mrs Sharkey holds opinions so strident that facts to the contrary simply don't exist. And Miss Fullerton has sandwiched herself between these two in preparation for the role she so ardently craves. It's beyond Miss Herne.

Miss Herne has missed the mark with Jacek Tomaszewski in thinking him unobservant. He sees a great deal. He's convinced that, in the main, the world is divided into those who look and see, and those who look and don't; between those who are receptive and those who simply project. And yet this staff room throws up some interesting hybrids. During the first day the whole staff room was treated to his halting explanation, to Mrs Adams, that the title 'Doctor' didn't automatically imply medical knowledge, that there are as many kinds of doctors as there are academic disciplines to confer them.

'Fancy,' Mrs Adams had said.

Miss Herne projects for emphasis, 'Mussolini does, as Miss Fullerton correctly points out, run a country. A fascist country we are currently at war with.'

'I thought we were at war with Germany,' says Mrs Adams, blinking even more brightly as these vistas unfold.

Here, thinks Jacek is an example of a woman who doesn't see because of the restrictions of her intelligence. The Sharkey woman's also interesting. She has the assurance of contrived ignorance and a reservoir of contained anger she's prepared to direct. He's seen examples of her classroom vehemence that leaves him merely sad. He's seen extreme forms of it back home that have proved fatal.

'We're at war with the Axis powers, which means we're at war with fascist Germany and fascist Italy,' says Miss Herne.

'Fancy,' says Mrs Adams.

Miss Herne's conscious of becoming bogged down in detail that's distracting her from her purpose of guilt by association. 'And perhaps Father Paolo Bernacchi thought it prudent to distance himself from his Italian origins.'

Mrs Lesley is one of several members of staff immune to the corrosive female politics of the staffroom. Unfortunately she's the only one of these tolerant ladies present. She leans forward to make her point.

'It would seem a bit strange to change 'Paolo' to 'Paul' and keep the Italian surname. Perhaps he's just one of these people who's called differently at home.'

Few, or none, see that Jacek's bleeding for Poland. His exit was more fortuitous than planned and now he can't get back to his family. He intended them to come here, but the way out, and in, has been closed as irrevocably as a withdrawn ladder. And although he's safe it's he who feels shut out. In less guarded moments, like now, gazing across the damp tarmac, he sees them across a woodland clearing, corralled by wire. Like Deborah Neavie's catechism image of her dead husband, the imagined scene is totally fictitious, but no less poignant for that. Unlike Deborah Neavie's image, his fiction has the possibility of being realised. He's come to the conclusion that his imaginative faculty is a curse.

'Indeed,' says Miss Herne. 'By his Italian family.' This is allowed to float out and perish.

There are many Polish servicemen. Jacek knows half a dozen in the Polish Fighter Squadron inscribing their resistance in the sky. He harboured a quixotic fantasy of joining them, defending his countrymen from the clouds, a knight errant behind a Merlin engine, dispatching fascists. But it wasn't to be. His eyesight alone disqualified him and to drive home the point he began coughing up bloody clots. As communication with his wife dwindled to the occasional fugitive letter, and then dried up completely, he saw his safety as an affront to common decency. And now he revenges himself on his disobedient lungs with a pipe.

He's a pure mathematician and offers his services free of charge outside school hours to anyone who can profit from them. Two nights a week he teaches at a technical college to young men, perhaps destined to become bombardiers or night-time navigators. He's looked at their eager young faces and imagined them shot up over the Channel. And he's tutored the more promising graduates from Glasgow University, hoping that Military Intelligence may avail itself of their talent, having refused his.

And for money he comes here to do this and thinks that perhaps, short of fighting, it's the most worthy contribution he can make. The children are poor, and many of them are bright, and all of them malleable. To have it within his gift to help make better people – it's a responsibility he took on without realising the gravity.

Sometimes he looks at them and envisages their future, as he does the imagined navigators, and experiences a rush of pity. When he mentally wanders, the class misbehaves. Mrs Sharkey has complained to the Headmaster about Mr Tomaszewski's lack of discipline. She refuses to refer to him as Doctor. Doctor Tomaszewski looks at the children and thinks it more important that they're boisterously among the quick than the tidy rows of disciplined dead back home.

'There's an obvious precedent,' persists Miss Herne. She hasn't given up yet.

'Is that a different kind of priest?' says Mrs Adams.

'No,' the urge to slap her is almost irresistible. 'I mean there's an obvious example. The Royal Family changed their name during that last war.'

'Fancy.'

'Saxe-Coburg was felt to be too German.'

'The King's a German?'

'No. There was German ancestry in the family. The old King's grandfather was Prince Albert of Saxe-Coburg and Gotha.'

'Is that what all this is about?'

'I'm not sure I follow, Mrs Adams?'

'You know what families are like.'

No, thinks Miss Herne, I don't, and are you so intensely stupid that you interpret a world war as an escalated family argument? She chooses to ignore this and persevere. 'The old King changed the family name from a German-sounding name to an English-sounding one.'

'Fancy.'

No one else contributes anything. Miss Herne knows it's a busted flush. There's no point in insinuating anything to an audience too dense, otherwise preoccupied or deliberately well intended to pick up the implication. And as a fishing expedition it's a wash out.

When not teaching Jacek haunts the art galleries, the libraries, or he simply walks around the parish. These people – they've no idea. He feels for them in advance, for what's in store, the expanding inferno. When he first arrived he anticipated encountering a sense of urgency and was shocked at the country's unpreparedness. They've been slow to learn their lesson, protected by that sliver of Channel. And this parish is slower than most. They see themselves as insulated, with all these healthy men around in the middle of the day. They imagine things have continued as normal, because their lives haven't changed. They see the shipyards as a refuge. He sees them as a target. Him, her over there, and her, and her, and the stupid one, and the vindictive one, all of them, this school, that church, the sleeping rows of tenements, they're all on the periphery of a pin on a map somewhere in Germany.

He looks at the Anderson shelters and baffle walls and sees them as a bad joke, about to be swept away by forces they pretend to withstand.

And he looks at these people, here, in this room, and their reaction to their task. How can they not see the gravity, the privilege? They use the children as a target for their frustrations. The sewing woman can't be blamed for her stupidity but look at some of the others. The Sharkey woman who ruined a wedding. What would she do if given greater influence? He's heard of devout church goers back home who help hunt down Jews with relish. And the young Fullerton woman who just wants to fit in. That Herne woman, now leaving because her insinuations haven't worked. There's a singleness of purpose there he's only seen on newsreels. The steeliness of her restraint makes the Sharkey woman's outbursts seem harmless.

And this morning, after break, the sound of belting echoing up the stairwell. Beating a child, evidently for saying 'fuck'. Fuck! Fuck!

Fuck! he inwardly bawls in time with the remembered strokes. If they've even the vaguest idea of the aggregate of human suffering being experienced right now, they wouldn't add to it so carelessly, side with the inflictors. Don't they understand we must love one another or die?

ELEVEN

September has eased into a late autumn. Danny savours the piles of smouldering leaves and their earthy rotting. By the age of eleven he's acquired the habit of precocious nostalgia, a genetic melancholy that skipped his pragmatic mother. Gig and Campbell experience their first Christmas spent in any kind of understood context. Six months, with no indication of another upheaval, is longer than either can remember. Their first sense of continuity brings home to both the fact that things are miserably awry. Alan works Christmas Eve and hasn't returned since. By midday they've given up on him and opened the presents they've bought one another. Beyond the imminent radius of the living room fire the flat is ferociously cold. On the pretext of offering their father a Christmas dram, Stephen seizes the initiative and goes upstairs. He's been working until four, and walked back up the hill in an ochre sunset. Reaching the steps where Deborah had stood in the pose of a capital K, he watched the sun disappear like a blood orange, igniting the river and burnishing the cranes before darkness falls and the windows glow. He's still in his working clothes when he knocks on the door and is admitted by the two children. He can see his breath in the hall. Sizing up the situation he hands the bottle to Campbell, the glass to Gig and shepherds both out the storm doors and downstairs. His very size is persuasive. He tells both of them not to worry about their father. He'll come back up if he hears Alan returning. Their misplaced loyalty causes him to slam Alan's door with a force that shakes the close. Watching their bobbing heads descend the stairs in front of him he can sense their excitement and anxiety. If he saw Alan coming in the opposite direction he thinks it's all he could not to choke the little fucker.

The children go in ahead of him. Deborah's confusion is so momentary that neither notice: she sees Stephen's face above theirs and understands. They shuffle on the threshold. Deborah pulls. Stephen pushes. They make a joke of it. The children are agog. The whole flat is warm. It seems profligate. There's a tree in the antimacassared front room and a fire in the grate no one's huddled round. There are threaded wreaths of pine and berries and tinsel above the door lintels. There's a grandmother in the kitchen, tipsy on sweet Christmas sherry, gregarious with the season. There's an iron range, belting heat that flows in dry waves down the hall. There's Michael, engrossed with a pile of discarded Christmas wrapping, a pyramid of ignored presents like a window display. And there's a pervasive smell of food, and not just one thing either. They keep looking at one another, calibrating their reaction in the face of the other.

Irene Gildea calls round later with Danny. She's been friends with Deborah since Gig's age. They've both lived out their lives to date in these dozen streets without a sense of confinement. Danny's heart lifts at the novelty of finding Gig and Campbell here. At the commotion on the stairs Stephen goes out. Alan can't get his keys into his own lock. He's half cut. Invited to join his children he experiences the same sense of novelty at the bright, warm interior as they do, without the least pang of guilt. He accepts a glass and steps into the party mood with the ease of slipping into clean clothes. He takes the food that's offered and eats absently, not with the preoccupation of his children. Campbell ate for a solid fifteen minutes with a protective arm around his plate. Stephen watched. And then he watched his father take everything that was offered with the opportunism of a forager. Perhaps Alan even guesses at Stephen's dislike. Even if he did, it wouldn't dissuade him from sitting there and taking.

When they're all gone and Michael is long since asleep, Deborah finds Stephen gazing into the fire, embers reflected as twin points in his dark eyes as he contemplates the lives of the three children, one in the next room, cosseted, the other two now sleeping twenty feet above his head.

Spring is slow to arrive but the pace in the yards is relentless. There's something in the nature of controlled panic spreading abroad. Alan's occasionally dragged from his booth and is to be seen with his barrow, collecting swarf from the lathes.

As summer approaches, Miss Herne is seen uncharacteristically here, there and everywhere about the school. More than once she has walked peremptorily into the Headmaster's office, turning briefly to stare down the secretary who dared to try and forbid her entry. She pointedly closed the door behind her. No one beside the two in the office knows what was said. The secretary couldn't report of gesticulations seen through the glass window. No voices were raised. But the unmistakeable cadence of Miss Herne's voice prevailed until he fell silent.

It was never any contest. Mr Gilchrist despises change of any kind because it requires effort. He's best in negation, preventing things from happening. His expertise lies in sardonic belittling. One glance at her and they both know he's beaten. She tells him to practice his miserable intimidation on schoolchildren susceptible to it. She tells him what they both know: that if he were to take himself down the street to the yards around *real* men, instead of surrounding himself with clucking women and a Polish intellectual distracted with melancholy, that, like water, he'd find his own level and be an abject menial in three days. She tells him she has more iron in her than all the yards on the Clyde combined and an appetite for a ten-year fight that would leave him like a wrung out dish cloth in ten hours flat. And then she tells him what she wants and that she'll be back at the end of the week to make sure he's arranged it. And then she goes out, closing the door quietly behind her, distaining to look at the secretary.

So powerful is the force of her presence that he continues to stare blankly in front at the space she's just vacated, the corona of a solar eclipse that he blinks slowly away. Eventually he stands, summoning himself to retrieve some of his self-respect by shouting at the secretary for her lack of vigilance. Her sense of being the aggrieved party sends her straight to Mrs Sharkey. At the next play-time conjecture ripples through the staff room. Only Doctor Tomaszewski, gazing pensively at the hopscotch below, remains uncontaminated. Miss Herne, true to type, remains away. Jacek takes a moment from whatever speculations are occupying him to wipe his glasses and listen to the conversation. Why is she politicking so furiously? He returns to his thoughts, saddened. These people. What does it matter if some provincial primary school teacher steals a march on the others? These feuds are so bitter precisely because the stakes are so low. They'll learn their insignificance the hard way.

At the end of the week Miss Herne returns to be preceded by an angry secretary who throws the door open for her and, like a mediaeval herald, needlessly announces her arrival. The fact that she gets what she wants is only made evident by the classroom posting on return after the summer. Of all the teachers only Miss Herne retains the same class. It's such a trivial victory the others let it pass in the general wave of relief. Jacek notes the concession.

It's Miss Herne's intention that Gig should continue her progress up the class rankings to occupy the cherished spot next to her own desk. The method of assessment in determining who should sit where is something of a black art that none of the parents have been successful in having Miss Herne explain. Mr Gilchrist is too frightened to ask. Certainly it has something to do with proficiency in the three Rs. But there are other partisan factors: word perfect recitation of even obscure prayers, familiarity with patron saints, manners, something

Miss Herne calls 'deportment' but makes no attempt to teach or explain.

'Either you have deportment or you don't. Georgina Renton has deportment. Jean Muir doesn't.'

What's more, 'deportment' seems to be something confined exclusively to girls. There's a weighting here that makes it almost impossible for any of the boys to occupy the favourite seating. Almost. Malachy temporarily claimed his spot and in so doing became a token girl in the eyes of his classmates. There's a natural effeminacy there, happier in the company of girls. But this year Malachy is nowhere to be found. Coming to the conclusion that there must be something in the mass evacuation of children elsewhere, Malachy's mother has taken fright and moved him to relatives in Barra. He'll spend an idyllic summer on talcum white beaches before the two-roomed school resumes, his schoolmates laugh at his Glaswegian accent, a Hebridean winter encircles and he wonders if the Germans aren't all that bad.

His spot has been usurped by Dougal, who manages to occupy this with no stigma of effeminacy and no apparent effort on his part. His marks in the more traditional academic subjects are so manifestly better than anyone else's he has to sit where he does to give Miss Herne's system a semblance of rigor. Similarly denied the statistical advantage of deportment, Campbell isn't far behind. Miss Herne recognizes similar abilities in the twins. Campbell progresses despite no encouragement from any quarter. Gig progresses further because of the attention lavished upon her. She's now a tea-time visitor to Miss Herne at least twice a week. Miss Herne not only strains her rations, she'll brave the austerity of a city on a war footing to show the girl what municipal art is still on display and march her round the Victorian edifices, guidebook in hand, pointing out the subtleties of the canvas and the splendour of the surroundings. Danny languishes mid-way between Dougal and Jean Muir, lacking the mental agility to compensate for his lack of deportment.

The additional year they are all thrown together will mark another change, beside the indelible stamp of Miss Herne. Gig has sprouted incipient breasts in a month. The change appears more dramatic in her than any of the others. Campbell's increasing in size and awkwardness. His hands and feet are caricatural. His porous nose now dominates his face. Deborah Neavie nightly ticks off a mental catalogue of those she prays for. Her current entreaty for the boy is that he grows into his features. For Gig the prayers are more subtle. Let her not become prey to the people who congregate round beauty. Let her respect herself and not become common currency because she will be desired.

Campbell's embarrassed by Gig's change. The flat may be neglected but it's big enough to afford privacy. When she's not out with Miss Herne, Campbell gives her space she's not really looking for. When Deborah offers to take Gig out to buy her 'some things', Alan's more than happy to agree. Deborah doesn't mention money. Neither does he.

Campbell's voice drops a precocious octave overnight. Dougal Cunningham's approaching puberty is more gradual and less grotesque. Fuzz appears on his top lip. Only the occasional spot blemishes his complexion and he doesn't seem affected by the mood swings apparent in his classmates. He's as measured as ever, but his capacity to understand is increasing at a rate that outstrips everyone he's sitting beside. It's apparent to him, and Miss Herne, that if it wasn't for the bias of her appraisal there's only one seat he would sit in. If she could she would gladly move him to another class, forego the credit for his progress that they both know she's not responsible for. From her point of view the one saving grace is his déclassée mother, too preoccupied surviving the social plunge to ask why her son isn't top of the class when his marks merit it. The obscure circumstances of Heather Cunningham's arrival in the parish intrigue her.

Dougal now stays late twice a week for advanced maths with Doctor Tomaszewski. Campbell's invited to join them, his marks and aptitude merit it, but without any parental encouragement his attendance is sporadic. Miss Herne, knowing she lacks the abstract abilities of Jacek, redoubles her efforts to champion Gig. And in this atmosphere of surging hormones and seething competitiveness,

Danny Gildea minutely searches his scrotum every morning, with the help of his mother's hand-mirror, in the hope of finding a follicle that might have crept out while he slept. His top lip is as smooth as Gig's. As he's said to Dougal and Campbell, 'Mrs Maguire's a fucking Mexican bandit compared to me'. By Friday afternoon her moustache is visible across the playground before disappearing over the weekend in preparation for Sunday mass. Danny lacks the attention span and the kind of intelligence to move him up the rankings. He just wants to be within touching distance of Gig. Since his main incentive is physical, he's consigned to the academic periphery. And from that arm's-length perspective he notices something alarming.

Last week Dougal said he had to go home from school via the library. Danny volunteered to keep him company. Something about Dougal's lack of usual ease piqued his interest.

'Why are we going there?'

'Why do people go to libraries?'

'Books.'

'Tell that to Miss Herne and she might let you sit nearer the front.'

'Fuck you! It might be heat. Dossers go to the library to sleep.'

'I've got a flat to sleep in.'

'Why are you acting funny?'

'I'm not. You don't have to come if you don't want to.'

'Is it a dirty book?'

'Go home Danny.'

'Is it a medical book with drawings of womens' bits?'

'No.'

'Let's see.'

'No.'

'It fucking well is!'

'It's not even my book.'

'Whose is it then?'

'The library's.'

Danny forms his hands into a megaphone and sings up the length of the terraces.

'Dougal's got a dirty book. Dougal's got a dirty book. Dougal's - '

'It's Gig's!' Dougal interrupts 'She asked me to take it back. I don't even know what it is.'

Neither does Danny. He doesn't have to. Its very existence opens up a vista of intimacies. He feels as if something in the middle of his body has suddenly sagged. He sits in the swing, opposite the library, assessing, while Dougal gets the book stamped and takes back her ticket. Hers.

Danny's dad expects him to obtain his knowledge of the facts of life from toilet graffiti and smutty innuendo, the way he did. He'd sooner face a division of the Waffen-SS than sit his elder son down for a conversation about the birds and the bees. His mother has hinted at 'certain urges'. He might not be academically top drawer, but he has the sense to understand that these urges are heralded by pubic hair, moustaches, erupting acne and the changes he sees around him every day in class and desperately looks for traces of in the mirror.

Irene feels for him. She thinks it a great pity that his obvious sensitivity doesn't manifest itself in his place in the class, or the reports she receives. She knows she has no capacity for introspection. What good would it do, around here, with kids? But she knows he has. She hasn't had an abstract thought in her life, whereas he could day-dream through a typhoon. She thinks it a pity so much of his energies are expended feeling things, and not thinking about them. It leaves him exposed. He's never going to be top of the class, but he will be the one most upset by the world's unfairness. Of all the children she's encountered he's the most delicately calibrated. She thinks she would think this even if he wasn't hers. She's seen other parents try and slap sensitivity out of other children with self-righteous vigour, harden them up, inoculate them against pervasive carelessness by giving them a touch of it at home, as it was given to them. She rages at this perpetuated stupidity. His vulnerability is precious to her. It's one of the things that makes him most different.

'You're a great feeler, even if you're not a great thinker,' she told him. As a consolation it's hopelessly misplaced.

Danny thinks if he can understand things better he might be able to swap places with Dougal. He attacks the problem with his usual subtlety.

'You know how Dougal fancies your sister?'

'Has he said anything?' Campbell's hands begin to clench.

'No - '

'Has he done anything?' His voice jumps an anxious octave.

'No. Calm down.' Danny's been on the receiving end of that fierce loyalty. 'What I'm just wondering about is why. Do you think it's got anything to do with you not having a mum and him not having a dad?'

'What are you on about?'

'Well, you know, that kind of wanting.'

'Wanting what?'

'Well, you and Gig, and a mum.'

'I don't want a mum.'

'Well you could have fooled me.' Campbell changes colour like a cuttlefish. Danny doesn't want this subject diverted by another outburst. 'What I mean is, you think she likes him more cause he hasn't got a dad and that's something she understands?'

'I don't think not having a dad is the same thing as not having a mum. I don't like him any more or less 'cause his dad's dead. How much does she like him? Do they meet up?'

'Yes. They caught a train together to London. They had tea with the King and then the three of them went to see Peter Pan. Calm down! I'm only kidding. When she's not with us she's with Miss Herne so when could they meet? She stays with you so you know better than I do.'

Campbell says: 'At least if it's him it's not someone else.' It's the last thing Danny wants to hear. But he doesn't want just to resign.

'And anyway. I think Dougal likes Jean Muir. Can you make sure you tell Gig that?'

Campbell snorts. Danny decides to leave it alone for now.

The palpable chemistry between Dougal Cunningham and her protégé hasn't escaped Miss Herne either. Like almost everyone else who grew up in poverty, she has an instinctive resentment of privilege. Her own stock of knowledge was hard won. His aptitude irritates her because it can't all be ascribed to six years of private schooling.

The tea ceremony, with Gig, isn't so regular its format is prescribed.

'I don't like crusts,' Miss Herne says, 'but in these austere times we must forgo the delicacy of removing them.' She hands the plate of meagre sandwiches across. 'How, precisely, us eating crusts with our sandwiches will help halt the German advance escapes me.'

'Are you frightened of the Germans, Miss Herne?'

'I believe there are many Catholics among the Germans. I believe they appreciate culture. Some forms of war are indiscriminate. Like bombing. People get killed who aren't supposed to. But I don't believe Our Lord would countenance cultivated Catholics deliberately killing one another.'

Gig later repeats this to Campbell, who repeats it to Stephen Neavie, who doesn't repeat it to anyone and believes Miss Herne is quite mad. He also thinks the staff room probably harbours more zealots and neuroses than the shipyards do.

'Do you imagine,' probes Miss Herne, 'that Dougal Cunningham and his mother are patriotic enough to eat their crusts?'

'I – I don't really know.' Gig's confused by the mention of his name.

'I suppose it depends whether or not this social plunge of theirs is permanent. I understand Heather Cunningham shops at the Co-op in musquash. That doesn't sound like a woman who's reconciled herself to a working class parish in thrall to the shipyards. I find wool sufficiently serviceable. I'm sure the Blessed Virgin, if faced with the rigours of a Glaswegian winter, wouldn't adorn herself in musquash. I'm sure Our Lady would find wool sufficient.'

The wool Miss Herne finds most serviceable is a pearl grey cashmere, and she cuts a distinctive figure in the parish streets for the quality and subdued good taste of her clothes. The girl doesn't know if an answer is expected and mention of Dougal has caused her colour to rise. Nothing's been exchanged but she feels a weight of playground expectation and wonders if he does too. They're blatantly the two best looking people in the jumble of stutters and spots, tics and callipers that constitutes a proportion of the class. Clairvoyantly following her train of thought Miss Herne turns her focus to the son.

'I imagine he's clever in that mechano kind of way that boys are. It may even have practical application. I suppose bridges will always need building. Perhaps he'll design one of these vessels rather than be simply swallowed by the shipyards, like so much fodder. I doubt this is the proper forum for him. What do you think, child?'

Gig shrugs.

'Don't do that, Georgina. We're not given powers of articulation to shrug. A chimpanzee could shrug. I have some Seville orange marmalade I've been keeping. Perhaps a special occasion. Perhaps Heather and Dougal Cunningham's departure. Because, be assured, were their fortunes to be even partially restored, they wouldn't remain. Bear this in mind, Georgina. The selection of our confidantes is no small matter. Our Lord wants us to be constant in our affections.'

If Father Bernacchi or, despite his youth, Dougal Cunningham had been there to hear this, they would have said it's a bit thick. Aside from the guarded promptings of her protégé and incidental disclosures to her small coterie of favoured female pupils, past and present, Miss Herne has no confidantes. Rigorous in her observations of the sacraments, it's believed she distributes her confessions around adjacent parishes. She's never availed herself of Father Delaney's services in this respect and Father Bernacchi doesn't expect to encounter her in the confessional any time soon. The public opinion isn't that she's done anything incriminating that might be judged by the timing of her penance, three cursory Hail Marys and a sprint through the Glory Be, as opposed to the penal servitude of two decades of the Rosary, but that she's so intensely private an individual that she would rather have the burden of her venial sins lifted by strangers. Rumour misses the mark. It's simply that Miss Herne thinks that no priest has the qualification to intercede on her behalf. She sees no contradiction between these sentiments and her Catholic zeal.

Her speculations about Heather Cunningham have no grounding

in any known fact. Miss Herne's even prepared to listen to the kind of public rumour she would normally dismiss, to corroborate her suspicions. She has a mental image of some elegant sophisticate, harassed by the daily rote of tasks now required of her, woefully unprepared for the domestic littleness of this parish's everyday regime.

She meets the lady in question the following Saturday, queuing outside the butcher's. With the exception of Dougal the queue is comprised entirely of women, some optimistically clutching their ration books, the noise and cheer seemingly disproportionate to the attenuated line. Half a dozen conversations are being conducted simultaneously along a line that ripples with hilarity despite the meagre window display: two chains of hanging sausages and a handful of forlorn cutlets. This is in stark contrast to the carnal splendour of his peace-time display, of tiered poultry, of tripes and offal, of marbled rib roasts, rolled briskets, belly pork, of hanging plucked fowls and dangling game. Dougal is at the end of the line and nudges his mother at Miss Herne's approach. They exchange a remark, unnoticed by Miss Herne as she takes her place, still preoccupied. A river breeze has gotten up, collecting grit, funnelled by the tenemented streets. Miss Herne is aware of the figure beside her tightening her headscarf and leaning forward to shout against the wind.

'Dougal tells me you're his teacher.'

First she glances towards the boy the woman has nodded towards with obvious pride, and then she brings her full scrutiny to bear on the mother. She's momentarily irritated at herself. She normally sees people before they see her. But this impulse is fleeting, suppressed by her obvious curiosity. Heather Cunningham isn't adorned in the alleged musquash. In fact, nothing in her appearance is ostentatious or decorative. Miss Herne realises she has been susceptible to another of Mrs Sharkey's small calumnies and is again irritated, not at the lie but her willing gullibility. She mentally catalogues her error, to be unfolded and considered at length when leisure allows, rather than distract her from the spectacle at hand. Mrs Cunningham is barely taller than her son. She appears to be the shape of an ingot, filling her coat with compacted bulk. She has a wide cherubic face that creases naturally into a smile, the cheeks further crimsoned by the cutting river breeze. She wears woollen mittens rather than gloves, and tucks one into the other armpit to free her hand and offer it. Miss Herne removes her leather glove a finger at a time and shakes the other woman's hand, still fascinated. Everything about Mrs Cunningham looks serviceable. She looks like a happy peasant. Miss Herne can easily imagine her cutting peat. Beside her Miss Herne feels stork-like and rarefied. More precise enquiries than Mrs Sharkey's calumnies will later reveal that Mrs Cunningham originated from Grampian farm-labouring stock. The affluent interlude in her life, with Dougal's father, is seen by her as an aberration. His deteriorating health, death and bad investments deposited her back in financial circumstances she took as normal. She's perfectly at home in the make do and mend environment where fate has deposited her. Her only concern is for the children, brought up during that intermission of plenty. The national shortages have helped them acclimatise: it's easier to do without when everyone else is doing the same.

She has two sons, the older with his father's intelligence, the younger already educated beyond her ken. The older boy escorts convoys in the North Atlantic, doing his best to sink U-boats before they sink him. It's never occurred to her to utter a prayer for their financial betterment. She keeps her passion for more important things, whispered entreaties on the boys' behalf: 'Let Colin be safe. Let him not be killed but help him to get our ships through and feed us.' Mrs Sharkey conducts public prayers before her classroom, invoking a God of Old Testament wrath to visit His vengeance on the enemy. She would consider Mrs Cunningham's next entreaty both profane and treasonous: 'Let him not have to kill Germans. But if he does make it quick and not hurt a lot. And have mercy on them because they're probably only doing what they were told and they'll have mothers and sisters. And let it all be over before Dougal gets swallowed up in it. And keep him safe and let him not miss his father. And let him mix and make a home here.'

In the wee small hours Dougal has woken and heard her restlessness in the bedroom through the wall. She's dreaming of her older son, flailing in horizonless black water. Totally alone. Her one blessing is that she's not an imaginative woman, but her restricted faculty is at full stretch when unchecked in sleep. She has a recurring image of strangers, sitting motionless in an unidentified steel cylinder, frowning in concentration. The context is explained by the spray that erupts through a burst weld. They begin to scream as another fissure opens, and another, and another. The dream always concludes with an implosion that finds her sitting upright, gulping for air. Dougal has construed this as throes of grief for his missing father, in concert with his own silent pangs. Every morning, as her feet find her slippers, she buckles on her courage for the day ahead and the benefit of the son left to her. And next door, in his own way, he does likewise. In the winter mornings they eat porridge together and listen to the wireless as the sun struggles up. Miss Herne knows nothing of their silent compact. Nor could she understand if it were explained to her.

'Good morning, Mrs Cunningham.'

'I have been counting this queue, and the sausages and cutlets, and I think there's scarce one per family.'

'My needs are modest.'

'My appetite's not what it used to be either but,' gesturing to Dougal like a magician to a decorative assistant, 'I've others to think of. Goodness knows how those with larger families survive.'

'Indeed,' says Miss Herne, who has never given it a thought. 'One can only hope the ration book ensures to each his own.'

A surly butcher boy with blood on his apron is seen approaching, counting heads with difficulty. He draws an arm down like a level crossing barrier, between Mrs Cunningham and Miss Herne, now third from the end of the growing queue, and makes a dismissive gesture to the final three women, as if denying traffic access. Presented with this fait accompli the two women behind Miss Herne quickly leave. They're too concerned to find another butcher for any protest other than muttered recriminations as they go. Irene Cunningham looks pained on Miss Herne's behalf.

'I'm sure we can share. As long as we both get something...'

'I'm sure Dougal can account for whatever you get on his own.' Miss Herne would sooner cut off her hand than be indebted to this woman. She turns to the retreating boy. 'David Jamieson, how many portions among how many customers?'

He turns, scowls in concentration, counts the fingers in one hand with the forefinger of another, looks hopelessly towards her.

'Start again.' Her tone is peremptory. In his mind her authority hasn't waned in the intervening years. He's back there beneath the chalked numbers, palpitating with obscurity as the clock ticks out his humiliation. It doesn't occur to him he has the whip hand. He gives up with a gusty sigh, marches back up the line and brings down the guillotine again, this time behind Miss Herne, excluding the rest of the non-existent queue.

Dougal exchanges a look with his mother that, this time, Miss Herne doesn't miss.

'Arithmetic was never his strong point. I laboured to find what it was.'

They shuffle forward towards the elemental smell of blood and sawdust. The women already served disperse with their meagre packages. The butcher is a large florid cheerful man with a complexion the colour of the surrounding meat. When dealing with Mrs Cunningham he recognizes a kindred spirit, someone who's been brought up around animals, who sees their rearing and slaughter as part of the seasonal rote she's calibrated the greater part of her life by. She's expert at extracting flavour and nourishment from the humblest cut. He secrets a kidney and a pig's trotter among her allocation and jovially stamps her ration book.

Miss Herne never participates in the ribald banter some of these shopkeepers seem to think a prerequisite. Butchers and sexual innuendo are the worst, slamming down sausages and raising a suggestive eyebrow to the female customers, eliciting a titter along the line. It's something she associates with the grossness of handling meat. She'll walk half a mile to avoid bonhomie. She dislikes talking to tradesmen about anything other than the matter in hand. Even although he doesn't descend to smut, there's a fleshiness to this butcher, accentuated by the hanging joints and bloody sawdust on the floor, that disturbs her. Unlike Mrs Cunningham she doesn't like the look of anything that reminds her of its origins. She takes a single cutlet, handed genially across, and counts out exact payment. She will not suffer bloody change in her purse.

At the doorway the two women nod farewell and go their separate ways, Mrs Cunningham up the hill with her purchases and her boy, mentally browsing a series of remembered recipes to make the best of the butcher's windfall; Miss Herne down the hill to the church, to kneel in silence and draw what she can into her scarcely ventilated heart.

TWELVE

It's a short fifty-yard walk from the church house to the church itself. These winter mornings, his first in the parish, Father Bernacchi has found more difficult acclimatising to than he imagined. It's popularly believed that Father Bernacchi has recently arrived from that exotic region known as 'abroad', a term used synonymously with the equally nebulous 'Europe'. Since 'abroad' is where the fighting is, it's also believed that Father Bernacchi's presence is somehow a harbinger.

It's not a good thing to live with and Father Bernacchi, with a vague idea of this vague prejudice, has done as much as he can to overcome it. Here he has found an unexpected ally in Father Delaney.

'They hate change. I hate change. In their mind you represent change.'

It's not said unkindly. Father Bernacchi thinks that Father Delaney speaks about the will and aspirations of his parishioners in collective terms that gives insufficient scope for their individual souls. He thinks Father Delaney describes them in general terms as he would the habits of migratory birds. But he doesn't say so. He just thanks him for his advice and perseveres in his house calls and chaplaincy duties at the school, trying gradually to insert himself into the life of the parish. He wants them to realise that his recognition of their spiritual sovereignty isn't a change. Or it shouldn't be. He wants them to know that he doesn't perceive them as a herd, mesmerised by Latin responses they don't understand, but as a group of similarly thinking people motivated towards a single purpose by individual piety. The problem is, not many of them seem to want to know it back. They congregate to celebrate Mass but, aside from isolated pockets among the staff and congregation, he's found little evidence of individual piety. He's disturbed by the discovery that the most public evidence of individual piety seems to be that schoolteacher, the one who was so tactically vindictive to that new boy with the green blazer. She can be seen kneeling in the church at all hours, motionless, gazing intently upwards, ignoring her knees and the creeping cold. And there's no question in his mind that she doesn't do this for public approbation. There's something compulsively solitary about her, and a preoccupation that deters.

He elected to come back here, to this working Clydeside parish, to domestic circumstances so different from his own privileged upbringing. It wasn't the poverty that daunted him. He'd seen it almost as bad elsewhere. Of all things it was the cold. Somehow, despite being brought up half a dozen miles away, he'd contrived to forget. Somehow poverty elsewhere seemed more tolerable when it wasn't such a struggle for a large part of the year to keep warm. He doesn't remember the cold being so pervasive. But then his childhood memories of winter are of exhilarating cold outside and a concourse of warm rooms, each with a cheerful fire that other people set, lit and maintained.

Mrs Quigley, the housekeeper he shares with Father Delaney, is older than the older priest and, to him, seems chronically arthritic, making a Calvary of her daily chores. He's seen her, bent like a wind-blown sapling, shuffling through the dim rooms before dawn, listing with the twin weights of coal scuttle and ashes. It's been torture to watch as she lowers herself on cracking knees, this protracted genuflexion as she scrapes out the ashes and re-banks the fire. Thinking she would welcome help he was unprepared for the force of her refusal when he tried to interfere.

'No. Not at all, Father Bernacchi. I won't hear of it. Sit yourself down and I'll make you a nice cup of tea.'

He has noticed that tea is the accepted panacea around here. And now she'll interrupt the tortuous process he's tried to help with, and hoist herself erect, using the mantelpiece for purchase, steady her frail bulk and shuffle off in the direction of the kitchen. Rumours in the parish, that he's a man of private income, happen, accidentally, to be true. He has hinted to Mrs Quigley that he'd be happy to pay for additional help. That provoked protest bordering on vehemence.

'Not at all! Not at all! Sure there's better things you could be spending your money on, and if it's not on yourself then it's the church roof or all those refugees we keep hearing about. Put your chequebook away.' He's empty handed. It's mid-morning. They're standing in the hall. 'I won't hear of it, Father Bernacchi. It would be a sin to spend money on someone like me when there are so many needy ones around. Go and sit down and I'll make you a nice cup of tea.'

There's a chorus of sounds from her old, protesting body that he's unsure whether or not she knows she makes. She grunts at every stoop and wheezes at every elevation. Her knees and spine crack. She farts erratically: reaching for the tea caddy, leaning to wring out the mop, depositing the tea tray. This is ignored by tacit agreement as they maintain the proprieties. Like Father Delaney, she has the deep tartarean smoker's cough, and he has woken in the early hours initially baffled by the acoustics of stereophonic wheezing from either end of the upstairs hall as they cough in concert. He's a light sleeper and is woken each morning by the scrape of a match from her bedroom. He now knows her routine, and lies wide awake, nerves on edge, anticipating the predictable catalogue of sounds. Following the scrape there's the pause of long inhalation, then a series of barks, reminiscent of a performing seal being denied a mackerel, as her lungs protest, a period of silent inhalations as her lungs submit, the grunt as she rolls out of bed and the mattress groans back, and the long shuffle in her housecoat towards her morning toilet. There are two bathrooms and, again by tacit assent, both priests confine themselves to one. He has never seen her bedroom but smelled the years of tobacco as she once exited in his path. They were both temporarily enveloped until she closed the door and the various drafts of the old house dispersed the odour. Despite the fact that she performs a lot of the household tasks with a cigarette clamped between her lips, she doesn't smell of tobacco herself, the way Father Delaney does. She's a collection of smells and the ensemble isn't unpleasant. Although he's never seen her bedroom she has left her bathroom door ajar, and it's festooned with jars and lotions, in glaring contrast to the ceramic starkness of theirs. These unguents and preparations smack of foreign chic. He wonders if she uses them. If this is how she looks when she does, how would she look without? She has various cloths and sponges and some Byzantine regime of hygiene that he doesn't pretend to understand, that seems to involve washing various bits on different days but avoids total immersion. He's never seen her hair wet. That evidently happens elsewhere when she goes for what she calls 'my weekly'. She keeps their bathroom clean by the application of industrial strength bleach, in industrial quantities, that leaves his eyes watering. She has asked him not to make his own bed and keeps his spartan room spotless.

Father Delaney seems immune to it all, the shuffling, groaning, coughing, farting and surprisingly, the food. Her cooking is catastrophic. Father Bernacci had hoped that, like many round here brought up on necessity, she'd be able to make the most from what's to hand. The first time she presented him with a mound of lumpy mashed potato, sprouting sausages like cactus spines, he looked askance at Father Delaney who didn't turn a hair. And she insists in presenting him with a morning fry up that leaves him with a film on his lips and a greasy ballast. He'd like to repeat the house calls to Mrs Gildea and Mrs Neavie, more for the aroma than any spiritual necessity on their part. In every sense these two seem among the least needy of his parishioners.

Aside from the other rumours that surround Father Bernacchi like so much smoke; that he's a man of independent means; that his origins are unimpeachably 'posh'; that he's a spiritual fifth-columnist, sent to oust Father Delaney; is an additional rumour. Father Bernacchi is labelled an 'intellectual'. Unlike the other indistinct labels applied to him of coming from 'Europe' and having lived 'abroad', this isn't a definition that can be clarified with reference to a map. And if asked to explain what 'intellectual' means, those who have bandied the term about would be at a loss to explain. It's freighted with both respect and suspicion. No one has ever accused Father Delaney of being an intellectual, despite his rote Latin. It's popularly believed Father Delaney understands these chants and responses no better than the congregation does. They could all be reciting a Roman train time-table, circulated as a Papal joke, were the Curia not so humourless.

Nor is Doctor McFarlane considered to be an intellectual, despite his prescriptions and understanding of life at a cellular level. Doctor McFarlane's pragmatism denies him this label. In better times, when Chepstow and Aintree and Ayr provided the venues, he was a betting man, frequently seen between house calls to stop off at the bookies and put a line on the 2.30. He followed form and dispensed tips with as much efficacy as his placebos. His very approachability, and the fact that he deals in tangible commodities, disqualifies him from a category he'd feel insulted to be lumped in with anyway.

There are two other people in the parish, aside from Father Bernacchi, who deserve this label. No one knows the extent of Miss Herne's self-taught efforts. Even if they did she's considered too self-appointedly aloof, and social standing, in the parish mentality, has nothing to do with brains. Then there's Doctor Tomaszewski. If anyone has the right to the label it must be Jacek, but he's *too* remote, *too* abstract.

If Father Bernacchi's background and path to the faith were made public knowledge, it would reinforce, not dispel the rumour. Unlike Dougal, his public-school education wasn't aborted. Considered something of a prodigy he matriculated at Edinburgh University's Law Faculty when just turned sixteen, looking young even for his years. From the outset he was marked out, not just for his abilities but for a certain precocious sobriety. His parents and advisor were worried he might be intimidated by the antics of his older classmates. They needn't have been concerned. While these freshmen, for they were all men, got tipsy on freedom and unaccustomed alcohol and genially rioted in the Grassmarket, he read, and walked, and thought. And after two years and a stellar display that justified his acceleration and with no prior hint, he announced that he was abandoning law for the priesthood.

His tutor was disappointed. His parents were horrified. They practiced a lenient form of Catholicism that didn't include the Pope's strictures on contraception. Unlike Father Delaney, the weight of public expectation for him was in quite the other direction. With his gifts they merely expected him to excel, but in something more tangible than the faith. It had been a mistake to parachute him in among people he failed to socialise with. The unaccustomed solitude had affected him. Hopefully it was only temporary. Bring him back, rehabilitate him to company and he'll see.

He indulgently agreed to a year out and returned home to humour his parents. His mother contrived a hectic social schedule. And in the midst of protracted visits to and from friends he was genuinely fond of, his parents came to realise his solitude had nothing to do with unpopularity, absence of loved ones or lack of social opportunities. He simply abstracted himself. They pointed out that this was too young an age to relinquish things he couldn't possibly yet know the value of: a partner, children. He patiently pointed out that he hadn't made any decision and wouldn't have to for a number of years. And in the face of these level responses they experienced a glimpse of vertigo felt by Father Delaney in a Glasgow Woolworths, and were similarly silenced.

He visited a Jesuit friend of his father's, who tried gentle dissuasion. After three conversations the Jesuit visited his parents and delivered an opinion. Paolo studied in Scotland, and in Salamanca. He was ordained in Rome. His inward life blossomed. As previously, his talents singled him out. He could have attained the kind of preferment his parents wanted for him, supplanting the ecclesiastical for the legal hierarchy. But that wasn't what he wanted. It was what he consciously sought to avoid. He explained his motives to his superiors. If his humility was assumed, it would soon be tested. He was assigned to a number of parishes in Liverpool. There wasn't any time for abstraction. Faced with other people's ordinary problems his reserve fell away. They sent him to Belfast. And now he's washed up on the Clydeside, entrusted with his poorest and coldest parish to date.

'Father Delaney is a man who has been in the parish a long time. And he's a man of his time.'

The Bishop is a man of Father Delaney's time. Paolo is unsure what's meant by this and merely nods.

'His path wasn't the same as yours. There weren't the same options to be considered in his case. There were clergy in the family. Do you follow?'

'That there were certain expectations?'

'Indeed. And meeting those expectations doesn't make a man a bad priest. The reverse can be true. I've known people strain what talent they have in order not to disappoint. And it's been the making of them. I'm not saying that's true in Father Delaney's case.'

'Presumably it depends on how realistic the expectations are.'

'Precisely. I knew you were right for this. As I said, Father Delaney has been in the parish a long time and there were certain laxities... I'll not say they were common but I'll say they were generally more overlooked when Father Delaney began his career than they are now.'

'Which particular laxity are we talking about?'

'Something... venial. Don't worry, I'm not asking you to take the strain caused by anything too serious. You'll see it in him when you meet.'

'Forgive me, but doesn't the veniality of it depend on what he does or doesn't do? Does he drink to excess?'

'That depends on what you consider excessive. You're not going to have to hide the communion wine.'

'Does it affect his parishional duties?'

'Why do you think I asked you here, Father Bernacchi?'

'What do you want me to do?'

'I want you to help stop certain things being repeatedly brought to my attention, and that of others.'

'Have there been complaints?'

'There's been a general sense of disquiet. It's spread abroad and members of his congregation are visiting neighbouring parishes rather than receive sacraments from him. I'm told you're clever. I'm sure you're capable of discretion. Father Delaney has tried, he really has, with what faith he has. I don't think it would be such a bad thing if we could all say as much for ourselves. The best of him has never come out in the pulpit. It's a funny thing to say of a priest but I think he's shy of crowds. It's not an ideal qualification for someone whose job is congregational. His virtues, such as they are, are best teased out in private. He's old. I don't want him to become ridiculous. And I don't want the office compromised.'

And on a windy spring morning Father Bernacchi finds himself staring down the hill at rows of russet-coloured tenements, regular as wheat, flowing towards the sheet-metal river, their momentum checked by the shipyards. Even at this distance the clamour can be heard, carried on the wind in waves, with the odour of worked metal. And in that brief hinterland, after the tenements stop and in the lee of one of the yards, he can see the stunted urban spire of the church, at this vantage an excrescence, stained by the fumes, permeated by the smells, illuminated by the flashes, fabricated by its elemental neighbour.

And behind and above him, the school.

THIRTEEN

Three weeks into the job and Father Bernacci's been left with a key to Jacek's flat. It's the kind of gesture that's dispelled what small reserve the priest had left. He's no less private in his opinions, just more publicly forthcoming in his dealings with the parishioners. Random kindnesses always make him give pause, but it was the unsolicited generosity, rare, he would guess, in the environment of the staff room, that took him aback. He'd been introduced by the Headmaster and didn't know if the obvious tension was the result of Mr Gilchrist's presence, his own, or the combination of both. He's become almost accustomed to the artificiality of the few house calls he's made, though familiarity with the awkwardness doesn't help. His few attempts to dispel the formality have been met with fixed grins of resistance and a barrage of tea cakes or placed biscuits. He gets the impression that even if Father Delaney hasn't fostered this tension, he somehow thinks it his due. Father Bernacci's first introduction to the assembled staff room is no less tense.

Two things he notices in quick succession: that the woman who had been so appalling vindictive to the boy with the green blazer isn't here, and that the tension visibly slackens when Mr Gilchrist, having made introductions, leaves. He wonders if her absence is somehow tactical. But he doesn't have time to wonder long. The Headmaster's introduction has been brief to the point of rudeness, little more than a calling of the register with a brief inclination of the head in the direction of the named individual. He tries to make amends, capitalise on the thaw, by going round and introducing himself to them one at a time. That woman he was late for the first day, the Deputy Head whose name he's immediately forgotten, stands at his elbow like some irritating sentinel. It's as if she somehow feels herself responsible for his initiative, sucking up imagined credit. There's a hard-looking woman, who asks him in a challenging tone what he thinks of ecumenicalism, a woman with a vacant smile and a stare of indeterminate focal length, he believes she has something to do with sewing, and between them a younger woman with hollow cheeks and abundant hips. It isn't an inspiring assembly but perhaps typical. What, he thinks, do I know? It sometimes happens to him that an anonymous congregation is easier to imagine as a collection of individual souls, than is a gathering of discrete people he's supposed to be able to supply separate identities to. Despite the fact that he's just introduced himself and half-memorised their names, he sees them as a clump of mediocre attributes and reprimands himself for the thought. The one who seems separate, literally, is the studious-looking man with the imposing glasses, sucking a pipe. As he crosses towards him the Deputy Head woman falls away. Perhaps she thinks this introduction isn't worth supervising. Perhaps she doesn't want to trespass on some imagined masculine exchange. He doesn't know and doesn't care. He's just glad she's no longer at his elbow.

Later on, on the many occasions when he thinks back to this first exchange, he can't remember what they first said. But he can remember the vividness of the first impression, of a discernable intelligence and of melancholy coming off him in waves as dense as the perfumed smoke. They spoke briefly about some book or other he hadn't managed to take with him on his travels, books, you know, being heavy and sometimes continually being in transit... Jacek had nodded and simply said, 'Borrow mine.' Being so flatly put it was difficult to refuse. And when, for form's sake, he tried to turn the offer down, Jacek looked quizzically at him in a way that made him faintly ashamed, practicing half-felt etiquette in the face of a larger courtesy.

'If you're sure. I could come round tomorrow evening.'

Jacek handed him the keys.

'I'm not sure I understand.'

'I give lessons tomorrow evening. In case I'm not back.'

'If I'm not there how will you get in?'

'The neighbours all have keys.'

'Why don't I use them then?'

'You don't know the address.'

'You could tell me it.'

Jacek points to a smudged luggage label attached to the key ring with the address, disingenuously scribbled in slanting cursive script.

'If I lost them, if you lost them, someone could steal everything.'

'I don't have the kind of things people would want to steal.'

He knocks, tentatively, three times, and stands on the twilight landing. What if he's hard of hearing? He didn't seem to be. What if he's preoccupied? That seems feasible. So he knocks more forcefully, and waits a sufficient amount of time that would allow Jacek to return from the toilet. Then he notices the shared toilet on the half-landing he'd passed moments before. He contemplates the grubby luggage ticket and superfluously knocks one more time.

The door at his back opens. An elderly Jewish-looking gentleman detaches a key on a string from a nail on his doorjamb.

'You must be the priest.' He brushes past Paolo, unlocks the door, gestures him towards the glimpsed interior and returns quickly to his own flat. Paolo exhales a thanks towards the closing door and registers the brass nameplate: Morris Levy. He turns back in the direction he was first facing and goes in.

He's seen so many tenement interiors in his house visits he can memorise their identical ground plan. Most have been festooned with drying washing and the stuff of cramped family life. There's an odour to this kind of living and this place doesn't have it. It's got a desiccated odour, overlaid by the smell of old paper he's only ever encountered in archives. Standing in the hall, the kitchen, with what he knows to be the recessed bed, is to his left. The 'good room' is to his right, admitting a cascade of light from its bay window. He's only ever been to the good room, although by inclination he'd always gravitate towards the kitchen where the living and birthing and dying takes place. He can turn to his right and take in the whole sweep of the flat. Unlike the others he's seen, the good room doesn't look good. It doesn't look like a mausoleum of Edwardian gentility. It looks every bit as used as the other rooms.

He goes into the kitchen. Doctor Tomaszewski has fastened makeshift bookshelves haphazardly, with no thought for utility or the volumes they're supposed to contain. Large volumes slant diagonally or rest horizontally on top of others, too tall for the allotted space. The facing spines are irregular in depth because, on closer, inspection, they're double stacked. There are two libraries in here, one on top of the other. In one corner stands what looks like a double-ringed camping stove, surrounded by tins and packets of tea, one open, tipped, spilling a charcoal fan. Clean dishes are stacked in the draining board and in the sink sits a bowl, half-filled with water and a standing milk bottle inside, shrouded with a damp cloth to prevent it from turning. A small deal table is covered in papers and more books, a ragged crescent framing the spot where he must eat his makeshift meals. As expected, the bed recess is there, with its tangle of abandoned bedclothes. How, Paolo wonders, does he remain so obviously fastidious? He must use public baths. He must send his linen out. The impression of this room is not of a kitchen with books but of a haphazard private library with a sink and a gas ring.

He walks through to the front room. The same studious disorder prevails. A folded step-ladder stands against one wall for access to the books that are ranged in shelves reaching almost to the corniced ceiling. The most spacious room in the house is reduced almost to a niche. There's a cheap wardrobe, a slanting parallelogram beneath the weight of books piled on top of it. Inset among other bookshelves it gives the impression of being slowly absorbed. Against the wall, opposite the fireplace, is a large ottoman, the fabric worn smooth in patches and sprouting burst horsehair like algae. It's incongruous here. He can imagine it seeing better days in a Viennese consulting room. There's another tangle of bedclothes here too, which doesn't give the impression of another tenant but of Jacek settling where convenient when too tired to read. Paolo can imagine him, breathing slowed, the disregarded volume tented on his chest beneath the frowning spines of the others, looming in tiers to the tobacco-stained ceiling.

There are a few photographs on the mantelpiece that he stops short of going across and handling. He may as well for the way he leans and peers. There's a formal framed photograph of a family grouping that might be anywhere in Europe since the technology has existed to capture it. Tiers of people radiate out from the central patriarch. Several children sit, cross-legged at the front, with what he imagines to be a childish Jacek, minus the glasses, solemn in his sailor suit. Next to this curls an unframed photograph, decoratively scalloped at its edges, of a laughing Jacek, perhaps in his early twenties. It's a frieze of captured hilarity. In front of him, perched on a picnic table is an infant. On the other side of the table sits a woman, Jacek's age, smiling at them both. Jacek's electrical hair is caught in a penumbra of light, the baby's a soft downy corona. It's difficult to tell the direction of the light because the table is perched on a riverbank. The water's surface scintillates with daubs of light in the sepia landscape. It's worth the indiscretion: he picks up the photograph, flattens and examines it and turns it over. In the same hand as the smudged luggage label he reads: 'Konstantyna. Pawel. Poznań. maj 1936.'

He prizes a book at random. It's in a language he doesn't understand. Polish, he presumes. The next three are in English, the last comprised mostly of mathematical formulae. There's an identifiable leather bound edition of Britannica and another of the Waverly novels.

He guesses Jacek has been buying them by the yard from departing university students. He recognizes this for what it is, this bibliomania. It's an obsession he would have fallen prey to if he hadn't disciplined himself. It's easier to buy books than to read them. He's known people who do as much to establish credentials they don't have. He doesn't think Jacek feels the need to impress anyone. He picks up another that's on a side table beside the ottoman, Jacek's current reading. He flicks through. It's covered in annotations in Jacek's handwriting he can't understand.

The front door opens. Jacek comes up to him and looks at the book in his hand. It's an edition of Vasari.

'I get the impression a fair number of them wouldn't be nearly as famous as they are if their reputations hadn't been tended by him.' Jacek says.

'Surely their work would speak for itself?'

'Walk around this city. Look up at all that architecture. A few big names come to mind of those who have taken the trouble to find them out. And they account for a fraction of the buildings. Most people don't know the name of anyone responsible for any of it.'

Without asking he walks off to make tea. Half-way through the brewing Paolo hears a coughing fit so violent he feels compelled to go through. Jacek's doubled across the sink. As the fit subsides he sluices water round and flushes something away. He straightens and pours out two cups. While Paolo is drinking, Jacek finds the book they had been discussing at school. He hands it across.

'Keep it.'

'I couldn't possibly.' He didn't amass this eclectic library by giving books away.

'Keep it. I won't read it again.'

Paolo looks around. There's a lifetime's rereading here. Perhaps Jacek has reached a selective phase in his life when there's more to read and revisit than hours left to do it in.

'You don't know that.'

'Yes I do. Keep it.'

FOURTEEN

Danny's volunteered for an early night without the usual complaints. He's perched at the bedroom window and raises the sash the instant he hears his mother sit down in the next room. His dad's on night shift. The novelty of the blackout hasn't faded and he can find his way infallibly in the dark. He positions himself outside Miss Herne's close entrance. He's convinced himself that his sense of smell is as acute as his sense of direction, that her unclassifiable odour will announce Gig. As it is he's looking for distractions from boredom, haltingly skipping as he peers at chalk marks in the gloom, when she emerges suddenly and bangs into him. He's standing on one leg and is bumped off the pavement.

'For God's sake, Gig! Watch where you're going.'

She's bigger, and probably stronger, and this display is embarrassment enough. He's been caught playing hopscotch, a girl's game. That compounds things. Ever since she arrived his life seems to have become a series of gestures of punctured bravado.

'What're you doing?'

He has a reputation to keep up. He wanted her to find him composed in the darkness, reassure her, talk to her, tell her.

'Out for a walk.'

What he wants to tell her he's not quite sure. He wants it to be something that will close the gulf that's opening between him and the gang enjoying collective puberty, her and Campbell and Dougal, but especially her.

'At this time? In the dark? On your own?"

He wants to put things on a more equal footing.

'I usually take a stroll about now.'

'Or play hopscotch.'

'Like fuck.'

'You were standing on one leg.'

'Like fuck.'

'I *saw* you.'

'I saw *you*.'

'What does that mean? It doesn't mean anything. Were you waiting for me?'

'Like – I mean no.'

'It's all right if you were.'

'Why would I wait for you? And anyway, what do you do up there all the time? Pray?'

'I don't mind if you were waiting for me.'

'Maybe it's revision. Private lessons and stuff like that. Does she tell you all the answers? No wonder you get such good marks.'

'Would you like to walk back together?'

'It's all one to me.'

But she's already steered him by the shoulder. At the slightest touch he can feel something flooding him. He doesn't trust his hands and thrusts them into his pockets. It's what he wants, to be with her, but not like this. Something's gone badly wrong already and he can't yet place what it is. She's *managing* him. They're not out together, she's seeing him home, probably because she feels indebted to his mum for all that fucking soup. The moon suddenly clears and casts their shadows forwards and he's struck by the incongruity. Elongated as his shadow is, hers is much longer, and he's old enough to recognize the shape of a small boy against the shadow of someone who's not just a small girl. Her attenuated shadow shows the beginning of the flare of a woman's pelvis. He's a stretched matchstick figure. As they pass the tram stop he catches their reflections, his forehead level with her shoulder. He looks up and round to her profile, the light catching her cheek and a glimmer of mobile lip as he senses her smile.

'At least I've got a fucking mum!' he shouts, running away.

He sprints. He doesn't hear anything behind him. He doesn't want to be humoured but he wants the option of refusal. Perhaps she thinks he's not even worth arguing with. He runs until his lungs hurt, the singular figure of a small boy sprinting through the gloom. And when he's forced to slow he bends double, hand on knees, and as his breathing slows, assesses his chances. For him, all their meetings are fraught. Things she would not even consider meetings, his awareness of her in the class, touch him. The way she pushes her lower lip forward and blows air up at her truant fringe touch him. She dismantles him and doesn't even know. And he has a reputation to keep up. Probably the only meetings with him that she can remember ended up with him shouting insults and either being hit or running away. Did she notice their shadows and reflections? What did she think? He's further away from her than he was this time yesterday. It's going to take some kind of grand gesture, something that completely upstages getting on a train and seeing Peter Pan, kid's stuff. He's now so morose, hands again plunged in pockets, that he climbs the stairs and raps the front door without thinking about it. Irene Gildea answers. Her momentary horror flames in three seconds into intense anger. He takes it with a kind of mature fatalism. Just like the fucking thing.

She takes hold of his hair.

FIFTEEN

On his first Sunday in the parish Father Bernacchi says the early mass. Miss Herne sits in the front pew. Father Delaney retains the privilege of saying twelve o'clock mass, the best attended of the week, now with Father Bernacchi in attendance. Miss Herne sits in the front pew. Shes has subjected both to the same scrutiny and it's instantly obvious to Miss Herne that in Father Bernacchi she has an entirely different commodity to deal with.

Father Bernacchi wonders if she knew how penetrating those casual remarks aimed at him in their first classroom encounter were. Replacement? Helpmeet? Colleague? Was she that astute or was it just a vindictive salvo that just happened to hit the mark? He hadn't properly answered because he didn't properly know what to say.

He started with the early weekday masses, short services that conclude before the eight o'clock shift starts, to accommodate the yard workers so inclined. He loves them, this sparse assembly, not instinctively congregating together as the women do but standing individually, peppered among the pews in the half light, stifling yawns, muttering responses in the gloom, like him, giving up an hour of bed to participate in the mystery, taking communion on an empty stomach. And then being summoned by the whistle into the maw of the yards.

They normally all wait until the priest leaves the altar before dispersing. Father Delaney would have taken a dim view of anything else. But with these early services, and the imminence of the morning shift, he's told them they don't have to. He's had to wave them out to overcome protocol. 'Go. Go to work. Go.' Often he'll stay behind a few minutes, sit in the front pew and collect his thoughts for the day ahead. Three weeks into this routine finds him standing absently in front of the Stations of the Cross. The service is over. He's not considering what he's looking at, he's thinking of the day's commitments. He's roused by the awareness of a figure at his side. It's one of the congregation, not yet left; a man, perhaps in his late thirties. He's obviously a shipyard worker. Paolo's noticed that adds on years. He's got the distinctive outdoor complexion. He wears the standard jacket with reinforced patches on shoulder and elbow. His cap is in his hand. He's not looking at Paolo, he's looking at what Paolo was looking at without noticing. Their suspended breaths merge in the cold interior. The man speaks.

'And he was about to go through all that, and they just didn't care.'

Paolo can't think what to say. It strikes him that perhaps this man has more feeling for all this than he has.

'Goodbye, Father.'

Goodbye.'

Three hours later an apprentice comes at a screaming run into the church house. Paolo runs back to the yards with him, Father Delaney barely at the front door before the younger priest is out of sight, clutching his bag. A boiler has exploded. The prone man is barely recognizable, scorched to a charcoal semblance. He knows he only has time for the abbreviated rite. The ambulance crew, in his wake, put down their stretcher. They all know there's only going to be one outcome. As he touches the forehead with the unction the eyes swivel towards him with a look of entreaty. There's a moment of comprehension in the stare from the blackened face. Paolo recognizes him from their exchange in front of the Stations of the Cross.

'Through this holy unction may the Lord pardon thee whatever sins or faults thou has committed.'

There's a spasm. Paolo watches him pass. The circle of doffed caps breaks to allow Paolo passage. He walks back. He seeks sanctuary in the deserted confessional and weeps violently and in silence. He realises this is the luxury of catharsis that that man's family almost certainly can't afford. He gathers himself, returns to the yard for the address and starts back up the hill to see the family. He's wretched and apprehensive and more than ever convinced he has made the right decision. If there is anything to be learned, it's this. If life is anywhere, it's here.

'Bloody shame,' says Father Delaney. He is sitting in front of an early evening fire, staring contemplatively at the embers and smoking. 'Did they pull the wee ones out of school?'

'Yes.'

'Were they all there?'

'Yes.'

'How many wee ones?'

'Five.'

He'd been completely unprepared for the crush of human grief in the small rooms.

'You know there's a hardship fund?'

'Yes. Have there been many accidents in your time here?'

'It depends on what you mean by many. Several. One's too many. At the rate they're working here because of the war I'm only surprised there aren't more.'

'Does it get easier?'

'No.'

Paolo goes upstairs to wash. Father Delaney throws his cigarette end into the embers.

Father Delaney presides over the funeral with Father Bernacchi in attendance. It's not the first spectacle of public grief Father Bernacchi has witnessed, and it won't be the last, but it's the most concentrated to date. The church is packed to capacity. The five children are washed and dressed and arranged in descending order of size in the front pew, the smallest balanced on her mother's hip. Paolo thinks about the logistics of this, and wonders if other mothers have taken these children to wash and dress them, sponging a neighbour's child at their own kitchen sink, getting them to look their best to bury their father. From the older three, who must range in age from five to nine, there's an aura of dreary bewilderment. The mother wears an expression of ferocious concentration. At her side, an older version of herself, clearly her mother, stands with a hand round her daughter's waist in an aspect of human scaffolding. The older lady's other arm is extended round the waist of a woman on her other side, the same age as herself, evidently the dead man's mother. Although the wife's face is fixed her eyes are swimming and the hand at her side mechanically dabs her face with her handkerchief. A few men wear suits. The vast majority are in work clothes, clocked out by special dispensation. The coffin is cheap. It looks porous as cardboard, incongruous beside two ornate floral tributes. In his service Father Delaney does his best to evoke the man. A conscientious father, a good tradesman, a diligent worker, a good man. Neither he nor Father Bernacchi know if it's true. The best testament to the dead man's credentials is the manifest grief stamped on the faces.

Afterwards he's committed to the ground. Suited mourners help lower the coffin. And after that a thankless reception in the borough hall. The complexion of the gathering has markedly changed with the return to the yard of the workers. Aside from the priests there are only a dozen men, all suited, all accepting the offered dram and murmuring in low tones. Father Delaney accepts a whisky and deposits the empty glass on the departing tray, picking up another before it's out of arm's range.

'No one wants silence and no one wants to speak up.'

Paolo wonders if he's just saying this to contribute to the deferential murmur, but he's wrong anyway. The women are talking in as natural a fashion as is possible in the circumstances, until the mood is sharply broken. There's a sound, almost like two abrupt barks in quick succession. People are staring in the sudden silence. The noise is repeated and becomes comprehensible in the context. The dead man's wife is standing with her back to the dismal buffet. Divested of her children she stands in a pocket of isolation her noise has made. Her face is a furious mask.

'It's not right! It's not! It's not right! It's not right!'

Each exclamation is a unit of sound. She is staring. All her vehemence is directed at Paolo. Her ardour deserts her and she leans against the table, suddenly bewildered, confused at her outburst. She hides her face in her hands. Her mother is first there and suddenly she's encircled by other women. The men all look embarrassed. Paolo is transfixed and refuses the dram Father Delaney offers him.

The school was always going to be Paolo's responsibility, the general feeling being that the children, and most of the staff, would be more likely to respond to a priest nearer their age. Having been glad to relinquish the early weekday mass Father Delaney starts divesting himself of other commitments: the later masses, the house calls, Stations of the Cross. He has gout, and it's worsening. He doesn't submit himself to Doctor McFarlane's diagnosis because he knows in advance he's not going to change anything. With Father Bernacchi here the gout's a reason to restrict his movements. His inactivity piles on the weight which is even more reason not to venture out. He knows acedia is a sin, but this intelligence doesn't prompt him further. He retains twelve o'clock mass on a Sunday. The congregation comment on his stoutness, as he limps from tabernacle to altar, raises the chalice with an arthritic grunt and seeks solitude as soon as he's decently able. With his early masses Father Bernacchi has escaped Mrs Quigley's breakfasts. He finds he's growing thinner as the older priest spreads. As Father Delaney becomes more sedentary his aches multiply and he withdraws, spending more time in solitary thought in front of the living room fire than ever before. He now never complains. The querulous edge, that trivial twinges previously brought out, has left his voice now that the protests of his body have become more clamorous. These are deeper, more enduring pains, indicative of something. Father Delaney feels that the various aches that have taken up residence are the late accumulation of a debt soon to be cancelled. Risking presumption Father Bernacchi has offered to hear his confession, or find another priest if Father Delaney prefers. 'Not yet,' has been the only response to date.

It's nine o'clock in the evening. Father Delaney is sitting in front of the fire. He throws yet another spent cigarette on the embers, the only decisive gesture his repertoire seems to have retained. Father Bernacchi comes in from the latest house call to the dead man's family. He sits in an adjacent chair and massages the bridge of his nose with forefinger and thumb. He looks weary and his figure gradually relaxes in the ambient glow. Father Delaney's bandaged foot is raised and seems to the older man somehow unreal, some stage prop signifying inactivity. In this light he could almost believe it to be something discreet from himself until he flexes his ankle and feels the pain. It's almost reassuring, a recall to mortality from this room. He never spent much time really thinking about anything, and now he can't seem to do anything else. It's not just the inactivity. This directing of attention inward is a compulsion he can't understand or control.

'How was she?'

'Much the same.'

'And the wee ones?'

'God help me but I forget their names every time, and when they're introduced they all seem interchangeable.'

'Refer to them collectively. That's all I've ever done.'

There's a companionable silence. Father Delaney can sense the younger man's tiredness. It's more agreeable to sit like this when someone's doing it with you. Paolo feels it too.

'She asked for you.'

'When you mentioned the fund?'

'No. She just asked for you anyway.'

'But you did mention the fund?'

'Yes.'

'And she asked for me anyway?'

'Yes. About your foot. You're their priest. I hope if I stay around as long they'll feel the same way about me.'

They both know Paolo is drawing a complimentary parallel. They both know he's made inroads already that Father Delaney hadn't made after a decade.

'If you live here this long I think we both know they'll feel very different towards you. I can see it already.' Paolo smiles tiredly across. 'And I can't see you with gout either.'

'You never know.'

'Oh, I think you do.' He gestures towards his foot, the bandages crimson in the firelight. They both regard this and the implications of the word and gesture. The embers slide. They're both absorbed by the ascending sparks. They sit some minutes in total silence.

'You love them, don't you?' Father Delaney asks.

'I try to.'

'I think you're too modest. I think you default to love. I think it would only be in extraordinary instances that you wouldn't love, and I can't begin to think what an instance of that would look like.'

Paolo attempts to interrupt but the older priest raises his hand. There's a time and place for candour and Paolo thinks this might be the nearest thing to the suggested confession he's likely to hear.

'I used to try, to love them I mean. But I found it too hard, really hard. There were individual instances of course, people you can't but feel your heart go out to. But even that was temporary. They die, or their circumstances improve and that love, or sympathy, or whatever it was just drains away. And then one day I just stopped trying. It doesn't make you a bad person but I'd no right to...' he gestures to encompass the room, the parish. 'I just had nowhere else to go. To walk out of here was to walk into meaninglessness. Do you understand?'

'I think so. Thank God I've never felt that way myself, but I think so.'

'I'm not apologising, although I might even do that yet. I'm explaining.'

'I understand.'

'Did it occur to you to ask why that woman at the wake shouted at you and not at me?'

'Yes. But I don't think she was in a fit state to answer, then or now.'

'You want them to think. I only ever wanted them to obey. That's the main difference. They'll come to you with questions now. I only hope you've got some answers.'

'So do I.'

SIXTEEN

Doctor Tomaszewski's visits to the staffroom have become less frequent of late. His pipes, in their rack, adorn the top of the staffroom mantelpiece and appear lonely to the few who wonder. Mrs Lesley risks rumour by visiting him in his empty classroom and asking if he'll oblige them with his company. They miss the smell of his tobacco, she explains. He smiles, shyly, follows her back and obliges them all by cleaning the pipes, knocking residue into the grate and, with due ceremony, puffing out a fragrant cloud. The effect is spoiled by his fit of coughing, violent enough to derail Mrs Sharkey's anecdote. She pauses in irritation to glance across. The next day he chooses to remain away and Mrs Lesley chooses to let him. Lunch times have found him beyond the school gates, in almost all weather, walking and thinking. Some have guessed at a family. It's known he carries photographs because he once dropped them in the playground. His accustomed calm momentarily deserted him. He got down on his knees. The girls who helped him reported images to their teacher: a woman and a baby in funny looking foreign clothes, and Doctor Tomaszewski holding the photographs to his chest with his mouth twisted in a way they hadn't seen before.

Mrs Lesley, guessing at his desolation, has arranged a voluntary rota with a number of colleagues to relieve Doctor Tomaszewski of certain responsibilities. He no longer supervises gym or takes in playground lines. He's sufficiently removed not to seem to notice the favour. Not only does he stop coming to the staff room, he stops coming to the school entirely. He has had a series of consultations with Doctor McFarlane and the good doctor was even seen leaving the Headmaster's office looking very serious. Jacek has done some kind of calculation, dividing the outgoings of all his all too foreseeable future against what resources he has, and has evidently decided that a salary is surplus to requirements. His wanderings are another sacrifice. Like Father Delaney, his ambit is shrinking, but in his case it's a forced contraction. Since most people in the parish were only ever aware of him when he hove into sight, or looked conspicuous as the only male teacher on the occasional parents' night, he has disappeared with the minimum of notice. The local shopkeepers miss him. He shopped erratically, without thought for economy, always frowning at something beyond the visible horizon. He wasn't sombre, just preoccupied, and they knew that if they grasped his attention he was delightful. In return he was the subject of numerous kindnesses that to most went unnoticed: the day-old papers passed on without charge; the cutlet in its bloody paper, slipped underhand like a card dealt from the bottom of the deck; the rattling potatoes, bagged before the scales settled to show the generous error. They never asked for thanks. He never gave it, directly. He always handed across too much money and never counted the change. No one ever dreamt of swindling him. And now they ask tentatively of that new young priest how the Polish gentleman's keeping, the one they haven't seen for days, because of all the parish he was one of the nicest.

During one of Miss Herne's rare forays to the staffroom the relationship of Father Bernacchi and Doctor Tomaszewski is discussed. Someone mentions they're a bizarre pair of surnames to be mentioned in a conversation in a Clydeside primary school. No one can remember who raised it, but it's strangely coincidental that topics that preoccupy Miss Herne more frequently get an airing when she's around. Miss Herne praises Father Bernacchi's Christian charity, yet somehow succeeds in leaving her listeners with the impression that he's only doing this to establish his reputation.

'Well he's spent lots of time with that poor family of the man who died. I hear he even managed to get something for them from the hardship fund.' Mrs Lesley makes a point of projecting this to the whole group, leaving no doubt in their mind where her loyalties lie. 'And now he's spending most of his time with Jacek.'

'Is he even a Catholic?' asks Mrs Sharkey. The same righteous anger that prompted her to interrupt Mendelssohn and nonplus a bride is prepared to be roused if the new priest is squandering compassion on Protestants.

'The priest?' asks Mrs Adams.

'The teacher,' hisses Mrs Sharkey. 'The one who's no longer here. Try and keep up.'

'He taught at a Catholic school,' says Mrs Lesley.

'That's no guarantee of anything,' says Mrs Sharkey, looking around. 'Did anyone ever ask him?'

'Does it matter?' says Mrs Lesley.

'Of course it matters,' says Mrs Sharkey.

'He's Polish,' says Miss Fullerton.

'What does that mean?' says Mrs Adams.

'It means he's from Poland,' says Miss Fullerton.

'And most Poles are Catholic,' concedes Miss Herne.

'Fancy,' says Mrs Adams.

Miss Herne mentally notes that this is a reminder to herself, if one were needed, of why she comes here so rarely.

Jacek wouldn't be surprised or saddened by their gossip because he saw and listened far more than any of them appreciated. They were quite unguarded in his presence, as they wouldn't have been had another man been there. With the exception of Mrs Lesley and a few others, and Mrs Adams who didn't think of anything at all, they thought of him as some kind of idiot savant, as assured of his silence as they would have been of a mannequin's.

As his horizons have contracted to his ottoman and his book-lined rooms, he spends more time running through past events. His clarity of recall is formidable. He could disarm the staff room with a verbatim recital of past conversations, with him taking all the parts. But there's no one to listen and he's never had any inclination to impress anyone. And he's found that the paper padding of these walls not only insulates sounds, it distorts time. He'll discover himself perched on the ottoman, or sitting at the kitchen table, perhaps cold or with a crossed leg having gone to sleep, with no recollection of having gone there or how long the interrupted reverie lasted. And he thinks perhaps he deserves the staffroom reputation he acquired for strangeness because only yesterday, or was it the day before, an undergraduate friend of his who was drowned in their second year at Gdańsk walked in, at the age he last set eyes on him, and asked for a cup of tea. It took a lurch of his heart and a series of rapid blinks to dispatch his friend. He's never come back. Jacek would like to blame this on the side effects of the medication Doctor McFarlane prescribed, but he can't. The Doctor didn't prescribe anything because he knows Jacek wouldn't take it. Jacek thinks this is solitude taking its toll, the isolated mind inventing companions. He now momentarily vets everyone who comes to see him. It's a little existential test to verify to himself what realm they've arrived from. He's dreading the arrival of his mother.

He keeps a covered bowl beside him that he hawks or coughs bloody mucus into. Since it's his respiratory system that's failing he fails to see why his brain is joining in. His material wants are dwindling to the point of disappearance. He's reconciled himself to the acceptance of hot meals because he thinks it ruder to refuse than accept. Movement is becoming more painful and he's also reconciled himself to the use of the bedpan, which he's scrupulous in emptying into the landing toilet. Yesterday, on his way down the short flight, he was caught unawares, expectorated bloody spray over the hall tiles and dropped the bedpan. He had to sit and watch his waste drip down the stairs. The pan rolled to the half-landing in a series of concussions before coming to rest, like a spinning coin, in a crescendo of rattling. Morris was at his side in a minute, allaying the worried calls coming down from the floors above. He helped Jacek back into his room, wheezing into a dappled handkerchief. Ten minutes later the rinsed bedpan is discreetly replaced under the ottoman. Jacek hoists himself to his feet and makes the front door, leaning heavily on the jam, to inspect the mess and offer apologies. There's no one there. All that remains is a sheen of dampness and a tang of bleach. He's reduced to allowing those who bring his food to dispose of his waste. Sometimes he'll drag himself to the front door and stand with it ajar, listening to the muffled sound of human occupancy integral to tenement existence. It is a form of communion. 'It's come to this,' he has said to himself, without rancour. It wasn't so long ago he was young, and healthy, and companioned. And now he is here, watching the scales of his independence tip, with a failing body in a foreign country, being dependent on the compassion of comparative strangers. Who would have anticipated such a conclusion?

He has continued teaching his Glasgow University students. They now descend the hill in twos and threes for impromptu tutorials in his cramped kitchen. Dougal Cunningham, his especial protégé, comes to see him. And Dougal has told his mother, who has told Deborah Neavie, who has told Stephen Neavie, of Campbell's squandered mathematical talents. And Stephen has trudged upstairs to talk to the boy and found him unsupervised, Gig with Miss Herne and his father in the limbo indicated by a shrug of the shoulders. And Stephen has sat opposite Campbell and talked to him with an earnestness underlined by a passing bout of tremors. And the boy has been enthralled, that someone cared enough to talk to *him*, that it matters enough to Stephen that he's allowed *him* to glimpse a grown man's vulnerability. He's so overwhelmed that he barely understands a thing, just something about the opportunity too good to pass up that he's agreed to accompany Stephen to the sick Polish teacher's house for some lessons.

The university students' attendance dwindles, and within two months of his confinement the number of people Jacek has contact with can almost be counted on the fingers of two hands: Dougal and Campbell; Heather Cunningham, who's prepared to lavish on Jacek the attention forfeited by her absent son; Deborah Neavie, who feels Alan Renton's debt for the free lessons given his son, even if he doesn't; Paolo; occasional visits from Mrs Lesley who tries to revive his spirits with staffroom innuendo; neighbours, who manifest themselves from the scufflings beneath the floor or above the ceiling and deliver small portions of what they've been cooking. Sometimes there are disembodied deliveries, votive offerings. He has answered a shy knock to find the caller gone and a herring staring from its oatmeal crust, framed on the hearthrug plate.

And there's Stephen Neavie.

A curious bond has established itself between these two that perplexes the others. It seems to have little to do with conversation. On first delivering Campbell, Stephen loitered. Jacek talked to the boys. Stephen inspected his books. Two days later, on the return from his shift, he called in for fifteen minutes on the way home. An hour later, Deborah, delivering stew, is surprised by the tableaux of her grimy husband sitting next to a reclining Jacek, in the attitude of Viennese doctor and patient.

'I'd no idea where you were.'

'I'm here.'

'I've got Campbell out looking for you.'

'No need. I'm here.'

'I can see that *now*.'

Jacek is entertained by this glimpse of domestic friction. He wonders if they realise the privilege of everyday grief. When she leaves, Stephen goes with her. On the way home she's determined to maintain an angry silence. He angers her further by pretending not to notice. His own silence is more articulate. Eventually her curiosity gets the better of her.

'What did you talk about?'

'Nothing much.'

'Well you can go and find Campbell!'

'That's reasonable.'

'And your dinner's cold.'

'I should have stayed and shared Jacek's. He says he's never been so well fed.'

Stephen's taken to calling in with a bottle of stout, after dinner, when his whereabouts have been accounted for. They're a curious couple with nothing obvious in common. The physical incongruity is marked. Rather than feel jealous, Jacek seems to take some kind of consolation from Stephen's vigour. In his declining presence Stephen feels his full strength, and would lend him some of his vitality if he could. They talk of trivialities, the shipyards, the war, in general terms, always skirting the personal. There's no topic Stephen has raised that Jacek isn't interested in. Even with his health failing he's still insatiably curious.

Within a month Stephen thinks he knows Jacek as much as Jacek will ever allow himself to be known, in this country at least, and he likes everything he knows. Paolo has arrived to find them sitting at the kitchen table, drinking stout, and has joined them. For two hours they make a happy trio and Jacek, his glasses flashing back the light, looks from one to the other in a kind of rapture, as if having discovered, or revived, something dear.

Paolo is pleased that Jacek has some other adult male company, beside himself. He's first to leave. Stephen has suspended his judgement on Paolo. He's prepared to wait until he can frame him in his mind in isolation, not tarnished by association. For all his seeming vagueness, Jacek misses nothing.

'Do you know what I like about your young priest?'

'I'm sure you're going to tell me.'

'He never tries to talk to me about God.'

'I thought that's what he *was* supposed to do.'

'You should like him more.'

'I didn't say I didn't like him.'

'I didn't say you didn't like him either. You're waiting for a reason. Don't. Don't ever, ever, waste time.'

Stephen walks home mulling over the advice, conspicuous because he didn't ask for it and it being the only specific topic in a series of conversations that avoided everything private.

Eventually the lessons with the two boys stop. Jacek wishes it. Although Dougal no longer comes for instruction, his mother still calls with regular meals. Stephen no longer knocks. By mutual agreement he now reaches through Jacek's letter box to retrieve the key on a piece of string, long enough to allow him to open the door and let himself in. Eventually the others do the same. Stephen calls in every night and watches Jacek incrementally sink. He's seen the mantelpiece photographs and guessed, concocted a scenario of exile and forced estrangement. He's tried to imagine himself in the other man's position, across a strange sea, in a different country, denied access to Deborah and Michael by the marshalled forces of Europe. It's an act of imagination worthy of Danny Gildea and he gives up the attempt when he envisages his wife and child, sinisterly encircled. He and Jacek now seem to speak less and communicate more.

Paolo notices this, and it piques him slightly that for all his concern and diplomacy, he knows his communication with Jacek isn't on the same level. He thinks perhaps all the books they have both read separate them. Two men who ought to have more in common don't, and he somehow thinks it's his fault.

Father Delaney's health is failing and the younger priest is run ragged. He arrives one evening at Jacek's and takes the chair near the ottoman. Jacek returns from the kitchen with two cups of tea to find the younger man asleep in the chair. Paolo wakes when he realises he is being watched. He takes the cup gratefully.

'I came here to do that for you.'

'There are still some things I can do. I know it may sound ungrateful but it's tiring always being on the receiving end.'

'I can think of some people who'd have no difficulty always taking.'

It sounds like a petty, irritable thing to say, and Paolo immediately wishes he hadn't said it. They both know it comes from tiredness. He's here. He really wants to see Jacek. But circumstances have loaded all the parishional duties on him. As Jacek talks to him he's conducting a mental inventory of all the things he intended to do today, and reprimanding himself for all the tasks left unaccomplished. And he's saying early mass tomorrow. He has to force himself not to look at his watch. He's carrying forward the mental catalogue of tasks deferred, and doing a quick calculation of the number of hours sleep he'll get if he manages to get home at a decent time. His head tips forward.

Jacek relieves him of the suspended cup and drapes the throw from the ottoman round his shoulders. Paolo is awakened by the pressure on his upright back almost two hours later. He goes through to the kitchen to find Jacek, sitting crouched beside the wireless, a battered mahogany affair with Bakelite dials. He's so engrossed, one ear pressed almost against the wireless itself, that he doesn't immediately notice Paolo. All the priest can hear is some distant, fugitive voice, asserting itself in a language he can't understand through waves of static. Looking up, Jacek starts. He looks as if he's been caught eavesdropping. He considers, and places Paolo among the living.

'I forgot you were here.'

'I didn't mean to intrude. Please, don't turn it off because of me. I don't understand it anyway.'

'It's a voice. Trying to come out of Europe. I don't think you need to speak the language to understand.'

Jacek makes another cup of tea. All his movements are laborious. This time they sit at the table. The crescent of books has gone. It's a thing Paolo has recently noticed: gaps in the bookshelves. The older man is about to say something when he's suddenly overtaken by a fit of coughing that hunches him forward. He finally straightens and wheezes out the deferred question.

'How is Father Delaney?'

Paolo hesitates, then remembers the gift of the book. The very least he owes Jacek is candour.

'I don't know really. Reconciled, I'd like to think. But the fact that I'm unsure somehow makes me feel it's my fault. I'd hate him to die in a state of indecision.'

'If there's a final reckoning then I don't think it's something you should be worried about.'

They drink the tea. The volumes surrounding them, leaning into new gaps, seem suddenly tragic to Paolo.

'Jacek. There's something I have to say. If there's anything I can do for you then, for God's sake, please don't be frightened to ask... I'm sorry, frightened is the wrong word... But, I need you to know...'

For the first time in memory he's caught flat footed. Even visits to the dead man's family didn't find him this inarticulate. He's never stooped to cliché but he would now if he thought it would work, and the power of speech hadn't suddenly deserted him. Jacek smiles, sadly, and reaches across to pat his hand in an almost paternal gesture. The tide of concern has reversed. This is wrong. He's young, vigorous, devout. He has a philosophy of continuance and yet it's he who's being comforted by a dying man of no discernable beliefs. He feels suddenly wrung, and Jacek keeps his hand on his until the silent spasm passes.

Paolo leans back, withdrawing his hand, transfixed with embarrassment. He doesn't understand what just happened.

'I really must be going.'

'You haven't finished your tea.'

He drinks in thirsty gulps, suddenly parched, and stands. Jacek says, 'Don't go. Like this. Embarrassed. What you feel and how you want to help does you credit. You're a good man and you'll become a better one. It's a rarer quality than you think.'

'I have to disagree, on both counts. I don't feel that good and I don't think people like me are that thin on the ground.' This time it's him who's smiling, sadly. There's something final in the cadence of Jacek's voice, dismissive without being off hand. Paolo feels he's being permitted to leave a moral tutorial that has exhausted his powers of debate. As he reaches the front door he turns. Jacek takes both the priest's hands in his, as you would steady a child learning to walk.

They look at one another for several seconds and Paolo, suddenly, triumphantly, feels that this is the silence that Stephen enjoyed with this man that he only felt he intruded on. It's heady. How Stephen perseveres he doesn't know. Jacek lets his hand go and speaks before closing the door.

'Some in the staff room are stupid and at least one is bigoted. But Miss Herne in her way is neither. She's not biased towards any one person or group. Her discrimination is almost total. And she's far more dangerous than any of them.'

He totters down the stairs, light headed with this piece of intelligence, and makes his way to the church house. Mrs Quigley opens the door to him before his key can turn in the lock.

'I've had people out looking for you. The doctor's with him now.'

Doctor McFarlane is simply sitting in a chair at the bedside, looking at the old priest. There is no stethoscope, pills or any of his professional paraphernalia visible. His closed and battered bag stands at the foot of the bed. Father Delaney's face is distorted. One side appears crushed with the eye on the compressed side forced closed. The other eye is glassily fixed on the ceiling. On the same side of the fixed eye the corner of the mouth slants askew and is puckered open, like a caricature of an old sea dog minus his pipe. Paolo is suddenly reminded of Popeye, awaiting his spinach. It's an incongruous, irreverent image, but he can't help it. Through this gap comes alternate sucking and gurgling noises as Father Delaney breathes.

Doctor McFarlane stands, offers Paolo his chair. There's very little to be said. Father Delaney obviously isn't going anywhere. Better to die here, among the familiar, and as soon as possible. Paolo declines the offer and goes to fetch his own bag, brushing past Mrs Quigley who stands irresolute at the foot of the bed, silenced by the imminence of death. He has time on this occasion to perform the full rite.

There's no sign of acquiescence or understanding from Father Delaney. Behind him Paolo can sense Mrs Quigley's growing agitation. Every so often she moves forward to wipe sputum from the corner of Father Delaney's mouth before retreating back behind Paolo. Perhaps she expects billowing curtains, a Jacob's ladder of celestial light, music of the spheres, something proportionate to what she perceives as his spiritual status having doggedly put in the hours, year after year, accumulating piety. The Doctor and Paolo have seen these endings often enough to know they're far more mundane.

Doctor McFarlane excuses himself. From the waft of scented soap up the hall Paolo knows he's used Mrs Quigley's bathroom by mistake. As the Doctor goes, Father Delaney's mobile hand begins to pick at the counterpane. The breathing accelerates to a series of whistling puffs. Mrs Quigley rushes out and Paolo can hear her knock in panic on the bathroom door, summoning back the Doctor who wouldn't revive him even if he could. In the silence, punctured by laboured breathing, the hand becomes more agitated still, like an instrument recording some seismic eruption miles away. Much as he and Mrs Quigley might want it, there's no discernable gesture, no benediction, just a tremor that becomes more violent. Paolo leans forward, but it seems that whatever powers of articulation the old priest had, have now contracted to the spasmodic twitching of a single hand. He wonders if this is merely electrical, the random misfiring of nerves, or an attempt at contrition? The puffs accelerate, culminate in gurgling froth. Then nothing. The eye is still fixed. He can hear them come in and wipes the corners of the puckered mouth before Mrs Quigley sees it.

The funeral is conducted with Episcopal pomp that would have gratified him. The Bishop, who directed Paolo to the parish, presides. Clergy from neighbouring parishes are also there. Paolo wonders which of these informed the Bishop of the disaffected members of Father Delaney's flock. He wonders if his efforts are causing the haemorrhaging to stop. Two Monsignors he has never seen before are also in attendance. Most of the parish have turned out and the service is punctuated by the occasional wail of various infants who couldn't be foisted on relatives. Half the workforce appears to be crowded into the small church, which grows stale with the exhalations and candles. The air is perfumed with incense. Those who couldn't get in crowd on the steps outside. All through the services Paolo feels the weight of focused expectation on him, now that the mantle has all but formally passed. It won't mean more work because he's been doing it all for the past months anyway. The elaboration of the ceremony gives him a sense of unreality. Through it all, the hymns and responses, he is rehearsing, over and over, Jacek's last words and pondering their meaning. He can't leave it like this. He'll go back as soon as he can.

He's dazed as they emerge into the daylight. With the Bishop in the lead they follow the coffin on foot. The cortege unfurls the length of the hill, those who waited on the church steps joining last. The vanguard crests the hill, sweating in their ecclesiastical finery in the spring heat, before those waiting on the church steps have even begun to move. Deborah Neavie, carrying Michael, passes her own close in the midst of the cortege and shields her eyes to scan the window for sight of Stephen. There's no movement there, but directly above, Campbell and Gig are framed, watching the procession with pagan curiosity.

As the last of the cortege disappears over the brow Stephen Neavie retrieves the key on the string and lets himself in. He knows, immediately, in the premonitory stillness. Jacek is lying on the ottoman, glasses still on, clutching the mantelpiece photographs.

SEVENTEEN

'Will Father Delaney go to heaven, Miss Herne?'

'Father Delaney will go as far as his pieties and belief will carry him.'

EIGHTEEN

Jacek's funeral is as modest as his domestic requirements. Those who knew him and loved him as much as he would allow, constitute a dense confraternal knot on the right-hand side of the aisle. There's Deborah and Stephen Neavie, Irene Gildea, Dougal and Heather Cunningham, Campbell and Mrs Lesley. Several pews behind are various staff members, volunteering or volunteered as representatives of the school. Across the aisle the mourners are more dispersed. Shopkeepers mix with neighbours. Half a dozen young men in sombre jackets have come down from the university in belated thanks for their free tuition. The service is barely started when four unexpected Polish airmen, resplendent in their uniforms, arrive and file into the vacant front pew on the left. A different, curious, equilibrium is established.

Paolo delivers the eulogy, emphasises Jacek's privacy, intelligence and popularity, this last attribute seemingly given the lie by the scarcity of mourners. He elaborates: Jacek was popular among those he chose to pay attention to; he was a fundamentally private man but his compassion extended beyond his social circle. He glosses over how little they all knew of his circumstances, but makes reference to the sense of dislocation Jacek must have felt, separated from family. He's tempted to look askance at the airmen. Can they provide details, fill in the gaps? A thought strikes: what if they did know and informed all the mourners. Would it make him or any of Jacek's friends any happier? It would satisfy curiosity, but if he had the name of a wife and child to allocate to this body in a box, like a luggage tag, wouldn't it somehow render this obscure, abbreviated life a little more desolate?

Are they alive? Contactable? If they had been, Jacek would have contacted them, and something about the purity of his solitude tells Paolo this didn't happen. If they are alive then God knows what they've had to endure, and if he could contact them and add to the aggregate of their misery, he wouldn't.

As soon as he finishes the service and leaves the altar, one of the airmen genuflects in the aisle and approaches him. Paolo nods in agreement and passes the request to the undertaker, who nods in his turn. The four airmen take position at each corner of yet another cheap coffin, one placing a belated wreath on the top. They hoist him onto their shoulders, he weighs nothing, interlink supporting arms and march out slowly in perfect co-ordination.

It's not raining at the graveside but the spring air is saturated with suspended moisture. The grass looks unnaturally vivid. He's seen embarrassing attrition rates before, but everyone who was in the church also appears to be here. He's never seen that, not even at Father Delaney's graveside. And there's something else: the atmosphere that prevailed in the church seems to have transplanted itself intact. He's experienced grief dissipate in the fresh air. Not this time. After a few formal words he repeats what he said at the conclusion of the church service; there will be a reception in the church house for anyone who cares to come. He crumbles some of the friable earth between his fingers, letting it fall on the coffin, and watches the airmen do likewise. The whole silent congregation await their turn.

The nucleus of mourners is persistent. All of them, minus the students and dragooned staff members, turn up at the church house and descend on Mrs Quigley's morbid sandwiches. He's obliged to send out for a tray of pies. Either they're ravenous, and he's seen grief do this, or they're eating to cover their consternation of having nothing in common except the man they left in a box, in a hole, at the top of a hill. There's sweet sherry, for the ladies, and whisky and stout for the men. He's obliged to send out for more of that too. Two of the airmen produce vodka in unmarked bottles and hand that round. The air is still subdued, as if they're frightened to disband and disperse what's left of Jacek, abandon him to the fickle preservation of public memory.

He has to send out for more pies, a contact in the yard canteen who fills something that impersonates pastry cups with mystery meat to remain this side of the restrictions, and yet more stout. Michael is delivered by a neighbour, as are three other children. Either the parents have exhausted the good will of the babysitters or another shift has started and they have to be handed back. Michael takes up his usual perch on his mother's hip. The other three boys are slightly older and weave their way through the adults, chasing one another. Their presence suddenly lightens the atmosphere. It's as if someone took the roof off. One of the airmen gets on his knees and pretends to box two of the boys.

Mrs Quigley is pointedly and ineffectually trying to tidy up. She's largely ignored. She's never been small minded and Paolo wonders at her as he watches, until he realises what's piqued her: for all the formality of his send-off, Father Delaney never engendered this. At that wake the Bishop's departure started a rout. And these people are here, now, their tongues loosening, the volume of crossed conversations rising, their smiles intruding because they've had some drink and because they want to be here. They're not seeking ecclesiastical preferment. They're not insinuating their way into photographs. There's no *advantage* in staying but they're doing it anyway. And what's this Pole done that would create an atmosphere like this, whose sympathy you could bottle, when all Father Delaney got stuck with, once the Bishop had put on his coat and all those high up ones flitted like Bedouins now there was no one to be seen with, was half a dozen hangers on? How does explaining difficult sums deserve this when all there was to show for the years and years of sacraments, and novenas, and Stations of the Cross were the usual handful of parasites, who tried to trouser the remaining half bottles when told to leave?

He goes across and murmurs to her that it's going well but she refuses to be mollified. It's so unlike her usual generosity that he finds it all quite funny and tries, unsuccessfully, to conceal a smile. She notices and moves off, offended on Father Delaney's behalf. It occurs to him that Jacek would have loved this. He would have found her injured theology delicious. He would have loved the light and the glasses and the rising hubbub. He recalls that conversation over the bottles of stout in Jacek's kitchen, with Stephen, when Jacek's glasses flashed and he looked briefly ecstatic at their little accidental gathering.

The airmen have been circulating, offering condolences. Stephen stands in their midst, talking with more animation than Paolo has seen. At least two of the women are unashamedly trying to pump Jacek's countrymen for information. Either they know as little as the rest or they're not saying. They make their goodbyes, thanking Paolo and shaking his hand last. Three days later a crate of bottles will arrive on his doorstep. Each contains clear liquid with a hand-written label: 'Polish Free-Spirit'. The smell alone clears his sinuses.

By the time they leave there's nothing sad about the gathering. He feels an irrational impulse to sing. They filter out into the spring night in ones and twos. He stands at the door shaking hands and thanking them. Michael's asleep, now draped across his father's shoulder, flaccid as a pelt. Deborah calls him 'Father'. Stephen calls him 'Paolo' and shakes his hand. He looks down his forearm to the sight of his hand completely engulfed. There's something almost frightening in the latent strength, like resting your hand in dormant gearing. It's strange, but at the funeral of a man he obviously cared for, Stephen looked happier than Paolo's ever seen him. He decides to use the moment.

'Jacek said something to me, the last time I saw him. You knew him better than I did.'

'I knew him as much as he wanted me to.'

'Which is more than he wanted me to.'

Stephen acknowledges this with an inclination of his head. 'He said something to me too.'

'What was that?'

'You first.'

'I don't think this is the occasion. Would you object if I came round?'

'Any time.' He claps Paolo on the shoulder. Deborah calls him from the darkness outside. He doesn't notice the slight buckling of the priest's knees. 'Tomorrow. Come tomorrow. Tomorrow night.'

'Tomorrow night,' Paolo repeats. With the hand removed from his shoulder he feels suddenly buoyant, like a fairground balloon. He feels more complimented by Stephen's attention than the Bishop's. He watches them walk away. Mrs Quigley farts good riddance from the recesses of the room behind. He turns to help her with the clearing up.

NINETEEN

The following night Europe comes calling. There's an air raid. Sirens wail. Searchlights probe the sky. Some claim to hear the distant droning of Henkel engines, or simply residual noise from the yards that, these days never stop. Families duly filter to the shelters. The nearest underground station immediately fills, wardens patrolling the length of the platform to ensure no one spills onto the tracks.

In Miss Herne's flat Gig suddenly stands in confusion at the first wail. Miss Herne glances over the spine of the book she's been reading aloud from.

'Sit down, Georgina. If Our Lord wants us He will find us. If He has decided to call us to Him it wouldn't matter if we were a mile underground.'

Paolo takes shelter with Mrs Quigley who sucks her teeth throughout. He decides to postpone the night's visit.

The following evening is the first Friday of the month and he calls in after the seven o'clock service. Michael is getting washed in the kitchen sink. Stephen is sitting at the table, braces trailing, surrounded

by the aftermath of his meal, reading the paper. Deborah answers the
door and looks shocked to find him standing there. She dishevels her
hair in agitation, gestures him towards the front room. Realising she
can't leave Michael standing naked in the sink she changes her mind
and indicates the kitchen, blushing.

Stephen is making bubbles and bursting them. The little tableaux
makes Paolo suddenly very happy.

'Hello, Stephen.'

'Hello, Paolo.'

'Hello, Michael.'

Stephen takes one of Michael's hands and waves it at the priest,
then pours a saucepan of tepid water over the child's head. Michael
laughs. Deborah takes a towel that's been heating next to the range,
nudges Stephen aside with her hip and wraps the boy like a parcel. Still
holding him she fills the kettle in another continuous movement and
puts it on the range.

'If only you'd let us know you were coming, Father, I could have
had something ready.'

'Please. The last thing I want to do is put you out. I came to
apologise for not appearing last night.'

'Last night?' Her voice carries an unmistakable edge. She shoots
a glance at Stephen who shrugs, affably. The situation is immediately
apparent to all three. He deliberately didn't mention it because he
didn't want the fiasco of usual preparations. Paolo knows Stephen
would never have allowed Father Delaney a glimpse like this. He
doesn't know whether Father Delaney would have wanted it.

Stephen says 'I'll make the tea.'

'When did you ever make the tea in this house.' It's not a question.
Although she's smiling at Paolo she can't keep the asperity out of her
voice.

'I've come to talk to you about something rather... difficult...'
Stephen gestures him to a chair. He sits and Stephen sits opposite,
braces still trailing. If she could change only one thing right now it
would be that, even more than her own hair. Her sense of awkwardness

is receding as her curiosity increases.

'If we can help...' Stephen says, and adds, 'It won't go outside this flat.' He reinforces this by looking intently at Deborah who is now doubly irritated.

'Of course. That's why I came. To be frank, although I've been here a while I don't know that many people that well. And since what I wanted to talk about concerns Jacek, and you knew him better than I did, I thought I would talk to you.' He stops, looks around for inspiration. Perhaps he should have thought about what he intended to say before he came, but so much depends on the circumstances when you come to speak it can't always be rehearsed. His eye catches something on the mantelpiece.

'Are those Jacek's glasses?'

'Yes.'

'I could have given you any number of books.'

'I didn't want his knowledge. I'm not qualified. I just wanted something of him.'

His books are dispersed. His clothes are gone to the poor of the parish. His miscellaneous furniture, mismatched crockery, haphazard cutlery and other accoutrements of his exile have gone up and downstairs to the other inhabitants of the close. In a corner of Paolo's room rests the Viennese ottoman with its throw. Beneath is a shoebox of latent tragedy containing all the photographs that Paolo hasn't yet had the courage to examine. He'll have to choose his moment.

The perched glasses impart an air of supervision.

'I think Jacek had certain reservations about the school. Or more to the point, about certain members of staff. One in particular.'

He pauses. They stare. She speaks.

'Michael's not yet at the school – as you know. All we know about the school is hearsay.' She's managed to trap some errant strands beneath a hairclip. Her entire awkwardness has disappeared.

'I appreciate that. He said something to me the last time I saw him. It was the last thing I ever heard him say. The significance of it was lost on me at the time because I was too busy with Father Delaney's arrangements. But when I thought about it afterwards, I think perhaps he knew he wouldn't see me again and it was important to him to say it to me. And I can't help thinking about it. He timed his words.'

'Did he warn you about Miss Herne?' Stephen interrupts.

'Yes.'

'Did he say why?'

'Yes. No. I can't remember. It seems stupid now but the thing I remember most is feeling complemented that he thought me worth confiding in.'

'Did he say she was a fanatic?'

'No. I'd have remembered that. That wouldn't have alarmed me. I've come across any number of fanatics of different stripes. I remember now: he said she was dangerous.'

Stephen leans back and nudges the trailing braces with his foot. Deborah has been following the exchange like a tennis umpire, screaming with curiosity at her husband's prescience. She no longer notices the braces.

'Excuse me, Father...' She turns to Stephen, 'How did you know?'

'It's there for all to see.'

'What's there...?' There's almost a note of pleading in her voice.

'Her face. The way she holds herself. She's there at morning service, before the shift.'

'So was I, before Michael.'

'It's different. It's the intensity. You think you're part of something. She thinks we just interrupt. I don't think I've ever been in the church when she's not there – except Jacek's funeral.' He nods towards the presiding specks. I can't be certain she wasn't there but I'd put odds on it.

'Why didn't you *say*?'

'I'm saying now. Paolo asked. What would have been the point of saying before?'

She's nonplussed, susceptible to conflicting impulses. She's angry at him for his silence and admires him for his perception. What would have been the point? It's a part of him that drew her in, this refusal to have truck with any rumour. What else does he know? What other insights has he brought to bear on these two dozen streets she trundles Michael round. And all these times, when she's come back with small pieces of intelligence and the groceries, was he just tolerating her when she unwrapped the latest piece of news?

He might have shown greater prescience over the issue of Miss Herne but he seems oblivious to his wife's rising confusion. She feels she's about to mist up when Stephen covers her hand with his. He's still looking at Paolo, who's polite enough to pretend not to notice what's happened.

'The reason I came to you, aside from what I already said, is because I'm worried about the children upstairs. I've tried to see their father and he's never in. This has to do with Miss Herne too. The first time I ever saw her she was being vindictive to a new pupil.'

'Dougal Cunningham.' Deborah supplies. There's a tinge of triumph at this contribution.

'I'm not concerned for Dougal. He looks as if he'll succeed anywhere. And he's got Heather. I'm concerned for the boy upstairs because he's abroad at all hours of the night and the father does nothing. But I'm more concerned for the girl because she's never with her brother.'

'She's with the teacher.' Stephen says.

'Yes.'

'And Jacek knew.'

'Sorry, are you asking me or telling me?'

'It's a guess but I think I'm right.'

'I think you are too. He would probably notice until his health confined him, then he wouldn't know anyone's movements.'

'I think he was right to tell you. I think the girl's better bearing the Luftwaffe, if they ever get here, than spending time with that woman.'

They talk on. He loses track of time. Michael sleeps in his towel. Deborah expresses her misgivings more openly to Paolo than she ever has to anyone other than her husband and her mother. She's so preoccupied that she forgets the obligatory cup of tea. Paolo finally

TWENTY

Autumn arrives again. Paolo's second in the parish. Danny and the others' second year of Miss Herne's tutelage. There's a noticeable change. The sirens are more frequent; the drills more rigorous; the wardens more vigilant. For the first time infractions are penalised, accidental lights extinguished at first challenge. Half a dozen times in two months, residents are roused by the sirens.

There are mists on the industrial river, jamming its early-morning commerce. Danny's now taken to wandering down the hill before school, risking a late bell and punishment to satisfy the compulsion of being there. There's something in the morning fog, the dunting of berthed shapes in their obscurity, the horns, forlorn on the opaque air, the blotched masses resolving themselves as they nose along the river that draws him again and again. He's as giddy with these sights and sounds as he is with the scent of the yards. Campbell and Dougal have taken to joining him, risking the same penalties, not because they're seduced by all this but because his silent enthusiasm is contagious. They stand and stare as he does but barely see the half of it. A dirty river with inconvenienced traffic. And after two minutes the only interesting thing to look at is Danny, mesmerised. But that soon palls, and they drag him back, and up the hill.

Paolo finds himself curiously unprepared for winter. It's not the cold, he's come to terms with that, it's the absence of Father Delaney. He misses the older man far more than he would have anticipated. Now that he's no longer surreptitiously in charge, the view from the top can be daunting. At night Mrs Quigley does whatever Mrs Quigley does. When he returns, tired, he stares at the solitary fire, prods the embers to raise a spark, create the illusion of some kind of motion. From his brief exposure to solitary control he now thinks he understands Father Delaney better than before. He imagines these same environs, year after year, a slowly haemorrhaging faith and the sense that things stood still and turned sinister. He kicks the fire, sends up a shower of sparks and thinks that the old priest deserved the Episcopal pomp of his send off.

The cold creeps back.

Although he's preoccupied by all the duties, the thought of the Renton girl continually recurs. He tries twice more at the flat and is answered on the second occasion by Campbell. No – his dad isn't in. No – he doesn't know where he is. No – he doesn't know when he'll be back. No – Gig isn't in either and he doesn't know where she is. At the suggestion that she might be with her father he blurts out a laugh.

Having exhausted the alternatives he goes seeking Alan Renton in the shipyard. The morning shift is well underway. He's waved through the gatehouse and past the clocking-in station. Like his predecessor approaching his house calls, there's a local dampening of sound at his approach that resumes in his wake. The only other time he has been here is to attend to the dying man.

He finds Alan's booth following shouted instructions and pointing. Everyone seems to shout here to overcome background noise, even when it's not there. Alan isn't in. Paolo opens the door on an interrupted game of solitaire played with pornographic cards. Alan arrives at his shoulder, takes in the scene and shrugs. He collapses the game and puts the cards in a drawer.

'I've called round at your house a few times.'

'Ah, well, there's your mistake, Father. I'm not often there.'

'I left a note.'

'There's a war on,' he says, ignoring the last comment, 'with all these shifts and production and what not...' Paolo looks at the desktop vacated by the cards. Alan doesn't follow his line of sight or reasoning. 'Tea?' he asks, cheerfully.

'I did find Campbell there, last night. He didn't mention it?'

'I haven't seen him. You go into houses. You must know how it is.'

'No. I don't know. Perhaps you can explain it to me.'

Alan frowns. He doesn't like seriousness that can't be dispelled by his breezy affability.

'I'm a single man. You must know how that is. But I've got children, the way you've got responsibilities. I've got to work. And what with the shifts... You can't see to everything.'

Paolo's quietly angered by the implied comparison but keeps it from his voice.

'If I'm late there's a bored congregation. There aren't two children left alone.'

'You should try being a single father – no pun intended.'

'I'm not here in some official capacity. I'm not here to remonstrate with you.'

'Yes, but...' he pauses to fish a nipped cigarette end from his pocket; it leaks dust until he lights it, winces at the first inhalation, turns towards the window as he exhales leaving a spiral of smoke in the mid-morning light and nods towards the workforce outside '... they don't know that. Do they?'

'I'm sorry if I've embarrassed you. If there had been any other way I wouldn't have come, but I've run out of alternatives. As I said, I'm not here to remonstrate. I'm here to help if I can. God knows it must be difficult enough with two children on your own.'

Alan takes from this that he has somehow prevailed and that the nasty bit is over. 'Tea?' he asks again, again cheerful, brandishing his tin mug. Paolo nods. Alan busies himself finding another mug and, whistling, walks to the communal urn. Paolo can see him from where he sits. There's a short queue. Alan says something that allows him to go first. As he fills the mugs he nods towards the booth and says something that has several of the men in the queue laughing. They're still laughing when Stephen Neavie joins them. Paolo sees a brief exchange between Stephen and the man at the back of the queue, who also nods in the direction of Alan's booth and apparently repeats what Alan said. The hilarity breaks out once more. Stephen turns and waves towards Paolo and also says something. The laughter immediately stops. Alan, suddenly thrown into confusion seems to be making a lot out of two mugs of hot water. He's at pains to excuse himself from the group, or at least Stephen, and returns with a mug in each hand. He opens the door with his elbow. The minute cigarette end has smouldered to a glowing callus on his lower lip. He spits it on the floor and stands on it while simultaneously handing the mug across.

'What d'you think, Father – seen the end of the Germans? Given up for Christmas?'

Paolo thinks it an odd remark given they've never seen a German. He thinks it odder that Alan seems to assume their previous conversation is over.

'I was wondering what help I... the parish... might be able to offer. With the children I mean.'

Alan has a small stove to heat the booth that he now busies himself with, crouching down and blowing with irritated puffs to revive the embers. His back remains resolutely towards Paolo until something occurs to him and he turns.

'The last one. The older one. Your colleague, Father... Father...' He snaps his fingers in remembrance. 'Father Delaney! He got us some money from some fund.'

'The hardship fund.'

'What are the chances of getting some more?'

'It's oversubscribed, I'm afraid. It's always going to be oversubscribed in a parish like this. And you've already had support.'

'Just a thought.' He turns towards the fire, losing interest already.

'Also, when you received the contribution I think you'd just started work, whereas now you've got a history of continuous employment.' The only response to this is an irritated twitch of the shoulder blades. Paolo momentarily closes his eyes and reminds himself whose benefit he has come for. 'However, having had help doesn't automatically disqualify you from receiving more.'

'No?'

'No. There are some more rules than last time. We arrange follow up visits to ensure the contributions have been put to good use.' He has turned the fund from an instrument of Father Delaney's modest patronage to an accountable donation. Personality, at least of those who dispense it, has been done away with. At the mention of these balances Alan shrugs. Any effort dissuades him.

'Anyway – they never gave me money last time. Just some clothes and groceries and stuff.' The stove can no longer offer a pretext to divert his attention. Paolo waits in pointed silence until he turns round. Alan has as little appetite for confrontation as for work.

'As I said, it must be hard, with two children not far from their teens. We'd like to offer help.'

'What help?' The question is feral in its instantaneousness. Paolo wonders if he has any control over his opportunism.

'Well – extracurricular activities for one thing.'

Alan's patting his pockets until he delves for another remnant cigarette. He finds one, tears a taper from the newspaper and lights it.

'That Polish man helped Campbell with his sums but I hear he's dead now.'

'Yes. He's dead. There are other things, activities he could do, and I was thinking also of enlisting your daughter, Georgina isn't it?'

'No need.'

'I'm sorry?'

'She's taken care of.'

'I don't understand.'

'That teacher of hers. Miss Herne. Gem of a woman. Museums,

galleries. Tea a couple of times a week. Nothing's too much trouble. And she's made her top of the class. Or so I hear. Gem of a woman.'

'Well that's to be applauded. But don't you think it would be... advisable to spend time with other people too?'

For the first time Alan genuinely grins. For the first time Paolo sees the whole dental array. What looked like dull milk teeth he now realises are carious pegs.

'What? You mean, spend time with *you*?'

'No. Not me. Or certainly not only me.'

'Could you, or whoever, keep her top of the class?'

'How could I guarantee that? How could anyone? I'm not a teacher. It's precisely to give her a break from teachers and the school environment that I'm suggesting she broaden her horizons.'

'And yet you didn't object when the dead Pole, who was a teacher, took Campbell and the other boy for lessons afterwards.'

'No. I didn't object.' Half a dozen refutations spring to mind: it was an influence that wasn't pervasive; it wasn't focused on one individual; he was never alone with any of them; it was an extension of the curriculum; it never blurred any distinction. But he doesn't say any of these things. It would be tantamount to defending Jacek to Alan. There's a distinction in kind and not degree if ever there was one. He's trying to correct himself for so manifestly disliking this man, partly because he knows this sense of revulsion is something Father Delaney wouldn't have resisted and might even have cultivated. He's reminding himself that we're all children of God and that Alan may be the only means of access to children who need him more. And there's something else: for Alan Renton to admit Miss Herne might be harmful to his daughter will require more than passive acceptance, it will create a gap that will need to be filled. That's two different efforts and they both know that's two too much. The cost of this man's apathy threatens to blur Paolo's vision with anger. He puts down the cup.

'What? Aren't you going to finish your tea?'

He doesn't trust himself to say anything further. He leaves. Alan retrieves the cards.

TWENTY
ONE

Miss Herne's patronage is select if not extensive. She can do more than intimidate a butcher's boy to count the queue again. Gig has predecessors, perhaps not cultivated with the same degree of intensity but nevertheless there, dotted around the parish and beyond. Her less successful protégés are, Miss Herne fears, destined for marriage and the thraldom of washing and children and husbands, fates they would have achieved without her interference. She finds it sad they appear to have reconciled themselves to such a cramped domestic destiny. It doesn't occur to her it might be a conscious choice.

There are what she would consider to be her successes from the earliest cohorts who first passed through her hands when she was barely ten years older than them: a junior librarian, an ambitious trainee planner in the Town Clerk's office, the first apprentice female pilot of the Renfrew Ferry. And there are others. They took from her the same ferocity of independence without saddling themselves with her theology.

Unlike Miss Herne they aren't chaste, but they've taken on some of her prejudice. They view men as implements and disposable. The pilot is destined to come to the attention of the Luftwaffe, not plying her trade, vulnerable in the middle of the Clyde, but fucking a dock worker in a darkened shop alcove. They're both vaporised as the chance encounter lollops to its spectacular conclusion. The protégés who do survive will progress to modest pinnacles of childless success and cast around for someone to share it with.

The boys who passed through her hands may not have come out so consciously fashioned, but few escaped immune. The butcher's boy isn't a solitary case. Past pupils, apprenticed a few years after she sent them to high school, are now young tradesmen, and lift their hats to her on their way to and from work. They're civil and still faintly intimidated. She got them at the right age.

The idealistic young priest still comes to school and delivers simplified versions of his Sunday sermons at assembly hall services. Talk in the staff room and elsewhere is of his superior oratorical skills. She would grudgingly agree, if she voiced her opinion aloud. It's not just that he's a better speaker than his predecessor, or that there's a coherence and easily-followed progression, it's that he's blatantly sincere. Father Delaney gave off an air of time-served scepticism from day one.

She's been told by Gig that the young priest left a note at the flat for her father. It's just a passing remark, and obvious to Miss Herne that Gig doesn't attach to this the importance that she does. The priest, she knows, has had at least one lengthy interview with the Headmaster. She thinks she has little to fear there. Whether she was the purpose of the visit, or even the topic of conversation, she knows she's bigger than Mr Gilchrist and she knows that he knows it too.

She thinks it a testament of how neglected Gig is that news of her father's dinner invitation had to come from Miss Herne and not him.

'You invited him to dinner?'

'Tonight, in fact.'

There's something quietly seismic in Gig's reaction. Her mind's in fragments. Miss Herne registers her discomposure. She watches for a moment with an almost forensic curiosity and then, turning diplomatic, pretends not to notice.

'Perhaps you can set the table.'

Gig obeys, mechanically at first. The act of following the routine they've established helps her draw the threads together, as Miss Herne intended. By seven o'clock the table is set for three places, the blackout blinds are drawn to conceal the celebratory candle from the Luftwaffe, and a combination of smells is coming from the cooker that can almost make Gig forget.

Almost.

At the first tap on the door she gives a start and Miss Herne, standing behind, slowly places her hands on Gig's shoulders to pacify her.

'Be calm. I'm here.'

Alan Renton only has two social tactics: gregarious familiarity that assumes a level of intimacy, even with those he's just met, and, when that doesn't work, retreat. But starting on a crescendo has its disadvantages: the pantomime is so absorbing he can't take the temperature while in character.

Although she's seen it often enough, Gig can't explain. Her worst fears are realised when he breezes in with the smouldering fag end. He carries a clinking bag of bottles of stout, and in the other hand brandishes an unwrapped bunch of blooms of various stem lengths that have been blatantly plucked from gardens on the way. From the brightness of his eyes they can both see he's already had a few.

'Hello, princess.'

The next part of the charade includes a display of fatherly affection so manifestly false that Gig squirms out of it. She wants to die.

'A bit embarrassed in front of your teacher? What? Not even for your old dad?'

His arms are cruciform, waiting for the theatrical hug. Hell will freeze over before she'll oblige. The weight of the bottles tilts him. 'Refreshments,' he says, handing the clinking bag over, 'and flowers.'

'How very serviceable. Georgina, can you put these precious

blooms in a vase. I don't drink...' looking into the bag, 'stout myself, but perhaps you'd like one.'

'I never drink until...' he makes a pretence of consulting his watch that's been languishing in the pawn shop since his arrival in the parish, 'half an hour ago, but since you force me.'

Gig, now second guessing Miss Herne's fastidiousness, has taken a pair of scissors and cut the stems to uniform lengths. She puts them in a vase and runs water. She's now looking at her father with an expression of repellent dread, and picks up a saucer to improvise an ashtray. Miss Herne is drinking it all in. Gig hands her the vase. She hands Gig a bottle and nods towards the pantry. Gig returns with the opened bottle, balanced on a saucer, and a glass. He takes the bottle from her and turns towards the cooker. As she extends her arm with the glass Miss Herne gestures her to return it to the pantry.

Alan goes to the cooker, lifts the pot lid and for the first time takes the fag end from his mouth. He inhales theatrically, rhapsodises for a moment and concludes with: 'Like I told that priest, she's landed on her feet in finding you.'

'Please,' implores Gig. Miss Herne, still unseen by Alan, gestures to her again, this time to be quiet. It's precisely for this intelligence that she's allowing this nauseating man to pollute the flat. That and the salutary lesson that Gig receives in the process.

'Indeed. Perhaps you can tell us more over dinner.'

He takes a seat, uninvited, and continues with the bonhomie. The cigarette is such a permanent fixture it's as if he fails to notice. Irregular puffs escape in tandem with the plosives as he speaks. Random ash dots the slope of his waistcoat as he leans back. Gig slides the saucer towards him. Grasping its use he stubs the tiny remnant half out. She takes the saucer to the sink and douses it. She'd do anything rather than return to the table and watches the butt bloat and disintegrate in the cold water.

'Georgina. I think our guest is ready for the soup.'

She has hoarded the scant ration of bread and margarine and this is set out with the steaming soup. It's a concoction of root vegetables and, if he's not mistaken, a piece of flank mutton. The main course is a small piece of basted pork loin with boiled potatoes and actual broccoli. There's even a pudding. She's even found rhubarb from somewhere and has fashioned it into some kind of dessert he can't name. Either she's got black market connections, or she's pulled out all the stops, or both. He'll ponder the significance of this later but not now, with dinner on the table. Charm can wait. He always eats what's put in front of him, is unabashed about asking for seconds, and thirds, and keeps going until the hospitality stops. He pays cursory attention to Miss Herne's running commentary, through the first two courses, of Gig's progress, nodding when he thinks something's required of him. When the dessert is put in front of him he pauses long enough to ask.

'What's this?'

'Eton Mess. I couldn't get strawberries. You'll have to make do with rhubarb I'm afraid.'

'And this stuff?'

'Meringue.'

'Do you get stuff like this all the time?' he asks Gig.

'No. Georgina and I make do with simpler fare. This is for guests.'

'As I said to the Father, you're a gem.'

'I'm fortunate enough to have a vocation and I only do the best I can with what I have for those who come under my care.'

'Do you see any of the other teachers putting on a spread like this for any of the other parents, never mind the kids?'

'I'm as in the dark about my colleagues' activities as I am for the reason you and Father Bernacchi were discussing me, Mr Renton.'

'Alan.'

She doesn't want to use his name. It's playing into his hands and she doesn't want him getting the idea there will be any reciprocal familiarity. But she doesn't want discord at this stage, until she gets what he doesn't know he came for.

'As you like.'

'I don't know about your colleagues' activities either but I'm fairly sure no one's feeding Campbell.'

'Isn't that what you're supposed to do, *Dad*?'

There's a look of resentment on Gig's face overlying her embarrassment and a restrained anger close to tears. Studying her for a moment Miss Herne thinks she's even quite ugly, in a temporary way. She puts her forefinger to her lips. It's the first of the gestured instructions Alan actually sees.

'You tell her, Miss Herne. My God, if I'd spoken up at that age...' he cuffs an imaginary child sitting between them. Miss Herne reflects that violence against children is probably the only indictment she can't bring against him in the whole deplorable catalogue of neglect.

'You're not interested in helping Campbell too, are you? Room for one more at the inn?'

'In class time – of course. Other than that my resources are limited. I can't offer all the help to everyone. Perhaps Father Bernacchi can offer assistance.' He's studying the now empty bottle. Having engineered the conversation round she doesn't want it deflected. She nods in the direction of the pantry and Gig returns with another opened bottle. He takes this from her mechanically, without acknowledgement.

'He says not. Well that isn't quite true. There's help although I can't say I understood. He talked about activities and I don't know what. Getting them away from the school environment. Other influences or something of the kind. Broaden their horizons and what not.'

'Them?'

'What?'

'You said getting them away. Was that your plural or Father Bernacchi's?'

'His.'

'Who was he speaking of, other than Campbell?'

He points the bottle towards Gig. The liquid slaps in the neck.

'Was he specific about existing influences?'

'I can't mind. I don't think so. Don't think your efforts have gone unappreciated. I said you were a gem of a woman. That's the exact words I used. I said, 'That Miss Herne's a gem of a woman.''

She nods her appreciation. Having eaten he's starting to sweat. He's on to his second bottle here, on top of several before, and he's starting to repeat himself.

'Are there any actual, tangible plans?'

He snorts, derisively. 'Don't ask me. Nobody tells me anything. After all, I'm just their dad'.

She didn't think it was possible to dislike him anymore. She was wrong.

He can see that there isn't going to be any more Eton Mess on offer and he's sizing up the situation. He's never received an invitation from a woman before, single or married, that didn't lead to one thing. Is that why he's invited here? This woman's difficult to read. It hasn't escaped him that she hasn't offered her first name back. It's hard to say what age she is but she hasn't let herself go, he'll give her that. She's thin, but it's not just rationing thin or drink thin. She's scrawny in that kind of holy, self-denying way. He probably wouldn't have looked at her ten years ago but ten years ago things were different. He just hasn't got the energy to put himself about any more. Something domestic, on the doorstep, wouldn't be bad. When she leans towards the candle a band of scalloped shade appears, cast by the swell of her breasts, and it's mesmerising him. She's actually got quite good tits, he tells himself, calculating the pros and cons. He can imagine himself in here, putting his hands on her. But it's difficult to see how all this can be achieved with Gig around. He needs a clearer steer. What he won't do is jeopardise the convenience of her taking on Gig by trying his hand too early. Better to take it slowly. She's not going anywhere and he's sure she's too buttoned up to put it about. He's comfortable he hasn't got any rivals.

In their separate ways they both realise they're not going to get anything more out of this night. He sees there's no more food and only one last stout. He's happy to wait to try his hand with the teacher and he's fairly sure that's what she's got in mind too. Why else the candle? But he knows they'll have to spirit Gig away somewhere. She can go home and he can come here. He'll give Miss Herne the nod at the first opportunity. Who cares if they're on first name terms or not, as long as she eventually puts out.

She now knows that Father Bernacchi has tried to undermine her position with this man. She knows she's not going to get any more information. He's too stupid to realise the implications of anything he relays and she knows he's unreliable as a reporter.

For the first time in his life he's encountered the pleasure of gratification deferred. He's content to sit here, for a bit, continue with a bit of chat, drink the remaining stout and imagine what she'll look like with a bit of handling. As he searches his pockets for another cigarette there's a sudden mystifying acceleration of events. Something about a school night and papers to mark and an early start. The candle's out, the overhead lights on, a clinical glare has instantly replaced the cosy ambience. He finds himself on the doorstep with the bag he arrived with, clinking with the two empty and one full bottle of stout, staring at her immaculate brass nameplate. He wonders if he should knock the door again and have Gig come home with him. Having set the tone, he's in the mood for company and having her return with him might help his reputation with Miss Herne. But Gig might have homework and she might ask him to help. There's always a first time. If she's got homework then where better to do it than with the person who set it and there's still time for a half before closing.

He finds the cigarette and makes the street, shielding the sulphurous burst of the match in case it attracts the warden's shout. Above him the windows are flung wide, lights extinguished, curtains drifting in the exorcising breeze. Miss Herne stands in the dark kitchen, holding Gig's hand as the smoke disperses, contemplating the forces arrayed against her. She'll choose her Thermopylae. But history won't repeat itself.

TWENTY
TWO

Christmas approaches, Gig and Campbell's second in the flat. Continuity has given them a sense of semi-permanence they've never known before. Stephen doesn't want them running the risk of a repetition of last year and has even stopped that little fucker on the stairs to invite them all round for Christmas dinner. It's a ludicrously long notice period but he doesn't want any mistake, and those two freezing upstairs. He's asked Deborah to invite the children separately, in case Alan doesn't make it known for any reason. He's finding it increasingly difficult to be civil, especially after finding him sniggering at the priest in the yard. The old priest wouldn't have put himself out like that. The more he likes Paolo the less he likes Alan. There's an equilibrium of affection here. He's amused by that little parasite practically shitting his pants on the stairs when he hailed him, mumbled some thanks and ran upstairs.

For the first time someone's paying attention to Campbell. And it's more than just the sympathy of Deborah and Irene. Miss Herne has called him out in front of the class and publicly praised the 'consistent improvement' of his work. She brandished his essay aloft. He's been moved up the ranking and weekly vies with Dougal for top spot behind the untouchables. Miss Herne had stopped short at a tea invitation, but Gig has returned to the flat with a pie and some shortbread, wrapped in a tea towel. 'You're to give the tea towel back when you're finished and I'm to tell you it's no more than you deserve.'

Miss Herne took delivery of the returned cloth in the classroom and publicly commended its prompt return. 'I'm pleased you enjoyed the food. More importantly, you *earned* it.'

He's puzzled because he can't think of anything he did, or didn't do, in the past two months that he did or didn't do before. Gig's equally baffled.

'Perhaps she just...' she shrugs her shoulders and gestures towards him, palms up '*sees*'. He knows she means sees *him* and not just the awkwardness. He's so happy he's prepared to believe it.

Danny isn't. 'That old cow's never done anything for nothing.'

Campbell knows Danny's angry at his enforced separation, halfway down the class. If anything the distance is increasing. The more frustrated he becomes the more the quality of his work deteriorates. Miss Herne announces the new placements each Friday afternoon. There follows much scraping of chairs and changing of desks. Danny's the first ever to question these pronouncements.

'How do you work all this out, Miss Herne?'

They're in the midst of upheaval. The question arrests progress. There's a collective intake of breath.

'With the help of Our Lord.'

He knows he's beaten. She's upped the ante with this infallible terminus. He's thinking of asking *how* the Lord tells her: a chart? a list? a register? Gig shoots him a warning glance. Anyone else and he'd have considered it an additional challenge. He changes places with the boy behind, another increment away from her.

Dougal says nothing. Campbell sympathises, but not so much that it interferes with the pleasure of the attention being paid to him.

The last day of term has usually been, for Gig and Campbell, less a cause of celebration than it has been for the others. Heat and school dinners aren't to be sniffed at. They've been immune to the Christmas spirit before, but spending a second Christmas in the same place changes things. And they've been invited to dinner. They've caught the bubbling optimism in the class as the holiday draws near. Despite Miss Herne's repeated emphasis on the *true* meaning of the season, the final morning of term is conducted in an atmosphere of suppressed hilarity. They're to be let go at lunch time. The playground is already seething with the snowball fights of two prematurely dismissed classes when they're told to go. Her last admonitions, walk don't run, go straight home and don't loiter, are drowned in the stampede. Danny's first out with Dougal and Gig not far behind. Campbell's following when Miss Herne hales him.

'A moment, Campbell.'

He wants to join them but this might be some end of year accolade. He colours, embarrassed and excited, and contemplates his shoes. He outgrew the hardship fund's largesse within months and his appearance bears more resemblance to his first-day than it has since. The shoes are his father's cast-offs, with two pairs of socks and heel grips to stop his feet from sliding. It's the first time he's ever been alone with Miss Herne.

'I wanted to congratulate you and thank you for all your efforts this term.'

'All I did...' He stops, abashed. His voice has dropped an octave after the first syllable.

'You did well. It's just a pity that Doctor Tomaszewski isn't still with us to instruct you in the higher mathematics. I never had the capacity for mathematical abstraction. I believe you either have it or you don't. It's a gift. You're fortunate. I've been fortunate with other gifts. I'll ask the Headmaster if anything can be done for you.'

He studies his hands, not knowing what's expected of him. From his bowed head she can see incipient acne on the back of his neck climb into the hairline.

'And how did those extracurricular lessons with Doctor

Tomaszewski come about?'

'Dunno really...'

'Enunciate, Campbell. You're not a stupid boy.'

'I'm sorry. I – I don't know really. Dougal was already there and Stephen Neavie downstairs took me...'

'Strange. I thought the lessons had been arranged by Father Bernacchi.'

'Well he was there... sometimes. I think?'

'Don't you think that was kind of him?'

'If he arranged it then, yes, I suppose it was. But he's a priest and I thought they were supposed to be kind. I think it was even kinder of Doctor Tomaszewski to give them.'

'Perhaps. How was it that Father Bernacchi selected you?'

'I can't remember really.' Selection to him suggests something formal rather than the loose arrangement that seemed somehow just to come about. 'Perhaps Father Bernacchi said something to Stephen Neavie.'

'It's strange, given that I'm your teacher, that he never consulted me.'

'Dougal was there too.'

'I'm not saying you're not the most appropriate candidates, I'm just wondering how he came to know that you were.'

'I don't know. Doctor Tomaszewski must have had something to do with that.'

'Indeed.' She knows it's pointless to pursue this line of questioning and she can sense his restlessness to join them outside. 'I hear Father Bernacchi visited your house.'

'Well he left a note. Dad wasn't in.'

'Yes. I know, but I understand he visited your father at his place of work.' From his sudden alertness she knows she's just told him something he doesn't know. 'He's very generous with his time, Father Bernacchi, very persistent in a good cause. It was nice of him to pick you for extra lessons. With all these good causes requiring his attention. I wonder how he picks the ones to adopt.'

'I... I don't know. Father Delaney got us uniforms and stuff...' He's blushing at the memory. She doesn't want that. She doesn't want a sense of humiliation to deflect him from following her thread.

'Indeed. But to come to your house and then visit your father at his place of work, that really shows extraordinary care. You know he's even suggested that there are other extra-curricular activities you and Georgina can get involved in. Yes. I can see that that's news to you. My only concern regarding that is that if they're elsewhere they might be segregated. Don't look alarmed. For obvious reasons they keep the boys and the girls separate. With most children that doesn't matter so much. But, forgive me Campbell, without a mother and with a father who has to work demanding hours to compensate, I know any separation for you and Georgina would be hard. Georgina spends time with me, but I'm a matter of streets away. You've always been welcome to join us.' This is news to him. He's watched her incrementally close the door between Gig and the rest of the world over the past months. If the prospect of being separated from Gig hadn't thrown him into confusion he might even have questioned her.

'No one's said anything to me.'

'I don't think any formal arrangements have been made. Perhaps it's just another example of Father Bernacchi's friendly interest. Perhaps he's waiting for something more concrete before mentioning it. He already made arrangements for you to study with Doctor Tomaszewski. It's not his fault they're now over. I imagine he wants to do something similar for Georgina.'

'Has he spoken to her?' His voice fluctuates even more widely.

'It's not for me to say, Campbell.'

'Is he going to take her away? Where? Who else is going?' It comes out in a rush.

'I don't know. Has Father Bernacchi paid this much attention to Georgina in the past?'

If he wasn't panicking he'd realise that no one has had the opportunity to spend time with Gig since Miss Herne monopolised her.

TWENTY
THREE

New Year is ushered in with a public sermon from Father Bernacchi exhorting the congregation to pray for a speedy and bloodless conclusion to the war, for the repose of the souls of *all* dead and for the comfort of their loved ones. Mrs Sharkey blows her nose loudly. Many of the congregation are not quite so catholic in their sympathies, and, like Mrs Sharkey, feel there's something unpatriotic in trying to evoke blanket compassion that includes the Gerries. Does Father Bernacchi honestly believe that they, on the other side, are praying for them? Whether Father Bernacchi believes it or not there's a spiritual arms race going on, just like the rush to build ships. We've got to pray longer and harder than they can pray back just to beat them.

But the beginning of the year doesn't augur well. Casualties mount, and for the first time the parish starts to feel the immediacy of more than the occasional death. Five of the congregation who waived the option of a safe haven in the yards die in three weeks in Africa. Telegrams are dreaded. Masses are offered up for the repose of the souls of *our* boys. Father Bernacchi conducts what are, in effect, a series of separate funeral services to a full church without a coffin, and parents denied the final compensation of putting their loved ones in the ground. Stephen Neavie stands at the back at each service, taking it personally, feeling somehow obliquely culpable, his absence contributing to every defeat. There's a slowly dawning realisation by the third service that the parish's isolation is conclusively punctured.

Alan buttonholes Miss Herne in the street. It's a blustery and cold Saturday afternoon. She has shopped late and, as a consequence, most of the provisions are gone. She has coupons to no corresponding merchandise. The meal she had planned will be more frugal still. She's annoyed with herself for her lack of foresight, her heels click on the pavement to an inward chant of fool-ish, fool-ish, fool-ish. She's so preoccupied he sees her first, another cause for reprimand. He stands directly in her path, swaying from heel to toe, back and forth, smiling leeringly, hands in pockets, the only man in the street without a coat. When she's eight feet away he snatches off his cap and describes an arc as he bows with cavalier gallantry. She detests this public flamboyance, his obvious consciousness of how he's perceived, and veers slightly to pass without slowing down. He pretends to dance with an invisible partner and executes a quick step to block her path.

'Sure, you weren't going to pass without saying hello now, were you?'

He now stands holding his cap in front of him with both hands, wearing a look of mock contrition. It's difficult to tell whether or not he's been drinking. He's so accustomed to it that his speech and co-ordination aren't affected unless he's drunk.

'I'm sorry, Mr Renton, but I'm in rather a hurry.'

The sky reinforces this with a sudden scattering of hail, finished as soon as it begins.

'And here's me thinkin' we'd gotten over this Mr Renton Miss Herne stuff.' The accent is a contrived Irish brogue. She wonders if he imagines he's charming. How did someone this loathsome produce Georgina? She steps sideways. So does he.

'Really, Mr Renton. I'm damp. I'm tired and I'm trying to find some groceries before the shops close.'

'Let it not be said that I stood between a woman and her victuals.' The brogue has been dropped for some non-descript sea faring dialect. He stands aside with another flourish. When she's abreast of him he says, 'Poor fare tonight?'

'It's whatever I can concoct. Good afternoon.'

'I'm not fussy.'

'I'm sure of that.'

He watches her go as she clicks her way out of earshot. No one is watching to observe the transformation. The cap is replaced on his head, the arms allowed to fall loosely to his sides. The debonair air sloughs off. As he continues to focus on the point of her disappearance round the corner, the lips are gradually drawn back over the moist brown teeth and the nostrils dilate. He scents the air. Now that he's not trying to manufacture the atmosphere he can take its temperature.

Four hours later he appears on her doorstep. This time there's no doubt if he's been drinking or not. He's generally a genial drunk – except when he's not. He generally generates good humour, usually towards someone, usually in repayment because they've subsidised his habit that night. But he's spent the intervening hours since his last encounter with Miss Herne drinking alone.

' 's Alan. 's Alan,' he repeats, knocking in time with the syllables. All the flats have storm doors and an inner door. Usually the outer door is only closed-over last thing at night. He is standing in the small tiled interval between. The inner door has an ornate panel of frosted glass, shaking perilously as he bangs the adjacent wood. His co-ordination is haphazard. The inner door opens wide enough to allow Miss Herne to slip out, closing it behind her. He finds he has been somehow guided in the wrong direction and is now on the landing, facing her, framed in the light coming through the opaque glass. He doffs his cap, attempts another theatrical bow and staggers slightly.

'Would you care for a... ?' He pats his pocket. The liquid slaps in the bottle.

'No, Mr Renton.'

'Perhaps we could talk inside.'

'Perhaps you could tell me what you want?' She hears the guarded creak on the landing above that escapes him and projects over his shoulder, 'Good evening, Mrs Timmons.' His eyebrows float upwards. She listens until she hears the click of the replaced latch and returns her attention to him.

'I'm not used to having unaccustomed guests and this isn't a suitable time.'

'Time? It's Saturday. What's time got to do with it? Let's talk inside.' Outwith working hours he has no appointments.

'Time is what regulated people, and that's most people, regulate their lives by. I wonder what business you think you can possibly have with me, arriving uninvited at this time of night.'

'Unfinished business.' He nods, meaningfully.

'We never had any business to finish.'

The theatricality sloughs off, exactly as it had four hours earlier when she turned the corner out of sight. He has reached that point that has occurred in many of his conversations and all of his relationships: the tipping point when the novelty of whatever charm he deployed is exhausted or refused. When there's nothing to be had from the other person he invariably reveals himself and becomes what he is.

' 's like that, is it? Well pardon me all over the fucking place.'

'If you raise your voice again I shall call the constable.'

'Constable? Fuck me! Constable? One night it's dinner and Eton Mess and whatever and weeks later it's the fucking constable? You can keep your fastened down tits. You know your problem – ' He has stepped back to deliver pronouncement. The storm doors close in vertical halves. She closes one. He wedges his foot to prevent her from shutting the second. 'Your problem is that you put out the wrong signals.'

'Here's a signal even you can understand. Never come here again. Never. Never speak to me in the street because I will not acknowledge you. There's no need to warn you not to speak to me elsewhere because you've never exercised a parent's prerogative.'

'Y' can keep your holier-than-thou attitude an' your precious fuckin' chastity. Y' can die with your cunt like a prune and take your bit of learning with you. But you can do it on your own 'cause you're not taking my daughter with you.'

'You're vile. And negligent. I will have her removed from your care.'

'There's a fuckin' war on! The Germans might come ridin' over the hill any day now. You think people don't have more to worry about than two kids without a mother?'

'The mother's absence isn't the issue. Your negligence is.'

'You want her? You want both of them? Because they come as a pair. You don't, do you? You're a fuckin' ghoul, feedin' off her – '

He has tottered back in his vehemence. She slams the other storm door. He shouts, incoherently, until the effort wearies him, stumbles downstairs and slams the close door with a force that rattles the letterbox on the first floor. Sandwiched between the storm doors and the inner door, Miss Herne executes a turn on the spot and lets herself quietly into the flat. Gig is standing in the hallway shaking.

'You see, Georgina? You see what they're like? It's as I told you. He isn't alone. Calm yourself, child. We'll finish our meal.'

TWENTY
FOUR

After his conversation with Miss Herne on the last day of term, Campbell walked out to find the snowball fights in full swing. They're all drunk with freedom. The playground is one huge pulsing mêlée. Presenting the novelty of a new target, he's pelted the length of the playground as he makes his way to the gates, ignoring Danny's shouts. He trudges home, heavy with the intelligence of Father Bernacchi's intention to separate him from Gig.

He spends an anxious holiday. There's the reprieve of Christmas Day with Gig and the Neavies. Alan arrives late, for once morose, introducing a discordant note that Deborah strives to ignore and Stephen dispels by pouring a cargo of drink down Alan's neck. Aside from that, Campbell's days have been tense and interminable. Without the imposed discipline of school, the structure of his day collapses. He haunts the library for books and heat, going over in his mind what he knows about Paolo, imagining destitute scenarios, trying to remember exactly what Miss Herne did say. He spends time with Danny and Dougal. Their respective mothers have him round for meals as often as they reasonably can. It's some comfort, assuages the loneliness for the length of the visit, keeps at bay his prehistoric hunger. But all consolations are temporary. Danny and Dougal find him at the library, angst-ridden by eleven o'clock in the morning. He has thought himself into a state of panic, staring sightlessly at the periodicals. With some urging they tempt him out into the fresh air and go to their usual spot on the river. The water is grey, lustreless, chopped with traffic. He confides. Dougal asks the obvious question Danny wished he'd thought to ask first: 'Why don't you just ask Gig?'

'It's not that easy – now. The more time she spends with her the less she talks to anyone. To me.'

Dougal says, 'So the only person you've heard say anything about this is Miss Herne and you can't remember what she said.'

'Yes.'

'Fucking old bitch,' Danny says.

'Yes. But that's not the point. Miss Herne can get across a lot by not saying something. Do you see what I mean?'

'No.' Danny says.

'You can't accuse her of saying something she didn't say.'

Campbell's too anxious to pay attention. Danny's scowling at the water. He still doesn't understand. Dougal starts to recite, slowly, all the things Paolo's done for them. The list penetrates Campbell's thoughts. He stands up and nods. The cold is getting to him. He's going back to the library. Dougal doesn't know how much of what he has said sank in.

The following Thursday evening Paolo's hearing confession. The hour is almost over and he has to resist the temptation to glance at the pews to find out how many are left. The catalogue he hears is always predictable. It's usually the same people he hears all the time, mostly women, all devout with the same litany of venial infractions. The people who confess regularly are the people who don't need to. No one ever comes here to admit to being bigoted, or vicious. The sins they admit to are usually minor omissions: forgetting such-and-such an observance, being habitually late for mass. He wonders if this is all they recognize as being wrong with themselves. He looks at himself and sees gaping shortcomings. Do they lack all capacity for self-scrutiny or is this all there is to their lives: a series of observances, doggedly followed, mentally ticked off that, in their minds, add up to rectitude? He'd prefer them to measure themselves by the good they do and not the temptations they congratulate themselves in avoiding. No one's ever sat opposite and admitted to the worst omission, of simply not caring enough. And meanwhile those in genuine need of absolution keep their distance.

'Bless me, Father, for I have sinned.'

He's surprised at the age of the voice. Most children's confessions are heard at school. Occasionally he'll hear a child in the evening, usually accompanied by a mother. He's no difficulty recognizing Dougal.

'How long has it been?'

'Eight weeks...' there's a pause, 'Father' he adds, as an afterthought.

'Eight weeks. Are you sure?'

'I've told lies.'

'Is the eight weeks a lie?'

'Actually, I haven't told lies. Or none that I can remember. Or none that matter.'

Paolo thinks the boy's even precocious in his own dispensations.

'All lies matter to God.'

'But if I can't remember them either I didn't lie in the first place or they couldn't have been that important. But anyway, I'll take your word for it... Father. It wasn't so much telling lies as listening to them I was thinking about just then when I said that.'

Paolo doubts that. Dougal's not prey to confusion.

'Hearing bad things isn't necessarily a bad thing in itself. We can hear bad things without meaning to. It's how you act on what you hear. The worst thing to do with a lie is to perpetuate it, to pass it on.'

'So you think I should keep it to myself?'

'Yes. Is there something else you want to tell me?'

'Even if by keeping it to myself someone else might get hurt by it?'

On the other side of the grill he's forced to smile. The catalogue of children's confessions is usually even more boring than their parents'. What's interesting is the domestic indiscretions they sometimes give away. He can't remember being asked questions like this by a child.

'If a greater sin comes out of keeping it secret then the lie has to be exposed for what it is.'

'I've got a friend and he's got a sister.'

'Is this the lie?'

'No – that bit's coming. The sister's got a teacher. The teacher's told the brother... something. I don't know the exact words. Whatever she said, the brother thinks there's a man interested in his sister.' He stops. Paolo's listening intently. 'That's the lie, and I think it's important that the man know what the teacher said about him even although I don't know exactly what it was.'

There's a long pause. Dougal can hear the controlled breathing.

'Is that all?'

'Yes.'

'Thank you.'

'Have I got any prayers to say or anything?'

'No.'

TWENTY
FIVE

Danny's now in a state of contained panic since their conversation on the quayside. He didn't understand it all. What he took from it was that there are other forces at play circling Gig. Larger forces. Adult forces. Forces whose motivation and reach he can't guess. His growing awareness hasn't refined his social tactics. Most of his interactions with her haven't changed much from their first meeting in the playground, or when he waylaid her outside Miss Herne's. He knows his usual tactic of attaching problems won't work, that something more subtle is required. He thinks it's not her fault she makes him feel the way he does. He thinks she's the victim of her own allure. In his mind he's got a new role. He's the Clydebank Zorro.

He's calculating how he'll make his approach. Door-stepping her didn't work last time. He's thinking of getting her to his flat by the simple expedient of inveigling his mother to invite both brother and sister, and then simply forgetting to tell Campbell. But then there'll be his mother, and definitely his brother, and maybe even his dad there too. And what to say in a place like the flat? The problem resolves itself. He's kicking a stone into the January wind, on his way home from school when he turns the corner and she's just there. Barred shade from the railings stripe her in the afternoon light. The saplings behind her are rattling in the sere wind that also catches the untucked hairs beneath her beret. Everything about her clothes now speaks of a supervised quality so absent from Campbell. She wears a blood-red scarf of arresting poignancy with fringes that ripple in time with her drifting hair. No one's ever seen anyone so beautiful. Ever.

He stands in her path, leaning at a ludicrous angle against the railings, and times his opening gambit at her approach.

'I've... I've been saving up.'

'Marbles?'

She's touched a nerve without knowing it. For a moment he sees himself as she must: a little boy whose stick physique and hairless armpits the communal gym classes have cruelly revealed, now half lying across her path. He straightens up and looks sheepish.

'Do you ever think it might not be safe around here?'

'Not really.'

'People can be in trouble and not really know it.'

'Are you going home?'

'Yes.'

'I'll chum you.'

She turns and they both follow the kicked stone. He's trying to regain his assumed nonchalance. This is it. If he doesn't convince her by the time they reach his close then he's lost everything. The rest of his life will be an anticlimax if he fails to persuade her.

'Do you ever think of going away?'

'There's a war on, stupid. For people who are in it *this* is away.'

'Well there are other things that can hurt you 'sides bullets and stuff.'

'Yes. Boredom. Sitting in a flat with no heat and no radio and no food and no parents. Try that some time.'

'Parents aren't all they're cracked up to be...' He tails off, remembering their last discussion on the topic and his Parthian shot that at least he had a fucking mum. If she remembers, she's diplomatic enough to let it go. He nudges the stone to her foot. She doesn't even see the courtesy. She steps over it. He kicks it on. 'We've got relatives. Up north. In the countryside.'

'Dad says the countryside's for shit-shovellers.'

'Well what the fuck does he know? He's either drunk at work or drunk in the pub...' She stops and stares down at him, '... so I hear. I'm sorry. I don't mean to hurt your feelings.'

She walks on and this time she kicks the stone. He construes this as forgiveness and trots to catch up. She's biting her lip. He aches to take her hand.

'What would you think of up North?'

'How would I know?'

'Campbell says you've been there before. Inverness or something.'

'It was always just flats. Dad and women and then leaving. It could have been anywhere.'

'It doesn't have to be up North. England can't all be on fire.' His envisioned geography is a train that departs Glasgow Central and deposits you at a theatre playing Peter Pan. The rest spreads concentrically with London in the foreground sprouting London Bridge, St Clement's, Shoreditch and other nursery rhyme landmarks, the Tower of London, Buckingham Palace, recognizable post-card staples, and beyond that periphery the nebulous haze of England.

'That's not what the radio says.'

'I thought you didn't have a radio?'

'Miss Herne's got a radio.'

They've turned into his street. He's dreading his mother at the top step, or one of the sprawling, perpetual games of street football they try and conscript him into.

'Don't you ever fancy a holiday, the kind of one you don't have to come back from if you're having a better time there than here?'

'I don't know. I've never been on holiday. There's your mum at the window.'

She's standing at the bay, holding Paul's wrist, waving his tiny hand in their direction. They can both see she's speaking to the child, probably urging him to shout to them, their exchange silent at this distance. There, framed in the window, is a tableau of everything she craves. It's transfixed her and he stands at her side, confused, as the longing flows from her.

'I... I've saved up. We could go away. You wouldn't have to bother about any of them. I can help.' She isn't listening. Perhaps it would help if he proved his sincerity, provided credentials.

From her vantage point, to the sound of the radio in the background, Irene Gildea sees Danny delve into his bag and come out with some white bundle. It looks like a hanky at this distance, wrapping a smaller bundle. He opens it carefully, like a magician, raising it in both hands for the Renton girl's inspection. Irene's intrigued. The girl hasn't paid attention. She's too busy looking back at them. Gig waves towards her and the baby, inadvertently tipping the bundle Danny's holding up. Bright coins tumble to the pavement. Irene bangs the window.

'If that's your Christmas money you had no right taking it out the house!'

She's saying it as much to herself because she knows he can't hear. Danny's scrambling to retrieve the rolling scattered coins. Gig, distracted from her reverie, stoops to help. She hands the last one back.

'My savings...'

'Good for you.'

'Where are you going?'

Where she always goes now. She needs to suppress that insistent longing. The sight of Irene and Paul has hollowed her. The only place she's got.

'Miss Herne's.'

He watches her walk up the hill. He ignores the insistent rapping from the window, now within earshot, bundles the wrapped coins into his blazer pocket and turns in the direction of the river.

TWENTY
SIX

Miss Herne was wrong in thinking that Paolo had already talked to the Headmaster about her. He had been in Mr Gilchrist's study, but not to discuss her. After what Dougal told him he feels outmanoeuvred. He's at the disadvantage of not knowing what she said, and to whom, and has only a second-hand schoolboy's interpretation of what she implied. He can't say she lied. And he can't tease out whatever she hinted at without drawing attention to himself. If he did he can imagine the closed-door pronouncements. He can imagine Mrs Sharkey, strident, no smoke without fire, staring down contradiction.

He feels he must do something. Alan Renton was worse than no help. Under the circumstances any direct approach to the girl would be open to misinterpretation.

At his next scheduled meeting with the Headmaster he dispenses with the preliminaries and gets straight down to business.

'Is it normal to teach the same class two consecutive years given all the other teachers don't appear to?'

'Well, Father, it depends what you mean by 'normal'.'

'It's not an obscure word, Mr Gilchrist. You teach English here don't you? Should we send for a dictionary?'

The Headmaster lapses into a baleful silence. He's considering the age of the younger man. He guesses he probably belted scores of the priest's contemporaries. If he hadn't gone to a posh school he'd probably have belted the priest too. And now he's sitting, being cross-examined. The Headmaster's dislike is like a directed light. So is his weakness.

'It's not difficult to imagine the influence a teacher can have, keeping a class twice as long as her colleagues.'

The Headmaster flinches at 'her'. The last thing he wants is for the priest to name names and force him into a repeatable opinion. He pretends to look for something in his desk, ratcheting up the level of awkwardness. Paolo isn't deterred.

'Perhaps I should be clearer, Mr Gilchrist. I'm asking you if you can imagine it?'

'Yes.'

'Who determines the rota?'

'It's not that formal. If someone applies and no one objects...'

'And you sanction it.'

'As I say, it's not that formal.'

'Either you sanction the allocation of duties or you don't. If you don't then I must be missing something. You're the Headmaster. If you don't determine who does what then what are you head of?'

Mr Gilchrist is finding a point in the ceiling fascinating. He's staring at it while his colour deepens. He flicks his gaze down twice to the priest who's staring directly at him. From these fleeting glimpses he recognizes in the younger man something of the determination of Miss Herne.

'Was anyone else given the opportunity to teach that class?'

He's noticed a blemish in the plaster.

'Were they even consulted?'

He'd almost volunteer to be buried under the rubble if only it would collapse in on them now and end this conversation.

'If I don't get an answer I'll go to the Board. Am I going to have to?'

'They'll be at the High School after summer and rid of her!' The Headmaster has leaned forward in his chair and roared. It's not resolve, it's the last defiance of a trapped animal. And it's taken whatever determination he had with him.

Paolo looks at him intently. This sieve of a man was in charge of Doctor Jacek Tomaszewski. She's got something on the Headmaster, either by implication, genuine evidence or who knows what. He's not going to get anything else out of him.

He feels there's something almost understandable in the purity of Miss Herne's ruthlessness, a vocation gone awry. She's got the Headmaster like a crucified butterfly in a display case. She's not going to get him.

TWENTY
SEVEN

The temperature drops still further as February approaches. Early mass, before shift begins, is concluded while it's still dark. The sunsets are spectacular and brief, drawing down by five o'clock. Visits to the sick, and others, are almost all now conducted after dark. It seems a long time since Christmas, celebrating the mystery on the bestial floor. And the reprieve of Easter's resurrection, that culmination that annually galvanises his faith, seems even further to him during these dark mornings. He thinks back to his days abroad, with the sun on his back. Is that what it was like for Father Delaney, a gradual whittling away, a nucleus of faith that eventually became less than the sum of its scattered parts?

And then he sees her, turning a corner, the way Danny saw Gig and haemorrhaged. The surprise isn't that it's happened. The surprise is that it hasn't happened before. He's seen her, in church, in the school, in crowds, at a distance on her own, but this is the first solitary pavement confrontation. He doesn't know how he appears to her, on the spur of the moment, but any surprise on her part is concealed. They're separated by perhaps fifteen feet. Both have stopped. She's stiffly erect but bows her head slightly in a movement that puzzles him. Mock deference? But it's simply the resumption of her forward momentum, a graceful motion, like the lowering of a gazelle's head to initiate that flow of movement. Everything about her is elegant. She waits until she's nearly abreast of him, says, 'Father Bernacchi,' in acknowledgement and swivels her head to bring her full attention to bear on him. There's no hint of triumphalism, her ageless face isn't wasting, but he can see the skull beneath the skin, the total composure and her complete absence of doubt. Beside her he feels suddenly porous. He realises that his sense of fallibility puts him at a terrible disadvantage in the face of this stark assuredness that will never entertain the possibility of being wrong. It's chilling. She doesn't break her stride and the sustained glance lasts only a moment. But he's dumb for as long as it's directed at him and mutters a hasty, 'Miss Herne,' when she's already past him.

Father Delaney wouldn't have been unnerved by the encounter. Father Delaney wouldn't have seen anything in her. He knows now there's nothing in him like Father Delaney. Seeing's not enough. He has to try and do something for the girl.

TWENTY
EIGHT

February continues. Paolo perseveres. He comes to understand in practice what he's only understood abstractly before: this, in its predictable repetitions, its boredoms and joys and small frustrations is his spiritualism. He had harboured a private fantasy that he now considers both arrogant and absurd. He had believed that forsaking a career in the Church hierarchy to concentrate on this would lead to a different, superior illumination. He saw this as a path to a spiritual distinction rarer and more important than the kind of decisions he chose to leave to others. He saw himself becoming some kind of spiritual aristocrat. That was the phrase he had even said to himself, an ambition that now strikes him as sinful in its lack of humility. He isn't a mystic, he's a foot soldier. There won't be any Damascus. It was crass arrogance to hope. It's the continuity of the cycle, of baptising and marrying and burying them that gives it its dignity. This is his consolation. And he finds the less time he has for contemplation the happier he becomes.

He draws strength from the lengthening mornings. He can stand on the church steps after early service and watch his breath evaporate in a world coming to light. The freeze lifts and suddenly everything appears less brittle. He feels everything's wakening up. The first two days of March are blustery and settle into bright mornings with a dusting of decorative frost that disappears by nine, and clear nights of star-studded skies, rendered more visible by the blackout.

Danny's escape route via the pipe has been effectively blocked. He's taken to sitting alone on the top of the communal bin-shed in the back court, ignoring his mother's summons to come in, called down from above into the well of darkness. His sense of disappointment is only eclipsed by his sense of wonder as he looks at the distant points of light. Are there other worlds? Other Gigs? If there are other Gigs there must be other Dannys. Do those lucky bastards have pubic hair? Do they get the girl like in the films? His mother's calling him again. He can gauge her tone to perfection, balancing insubordination to the point where it will incur consequences. That last shout had the edge of ultimatum to it. He stirs, reluctantly.

The clear nights continue. The city huddles, muffling its lights. The sheen of the estuary, dull aluminium in the bright moonlight, gives their camouflage the lie. The wardens are anxious. On the night of the 13th Paolo is still reading against a nagging insistence at the back of his mind telling him to go to bed. It's late and he has an early start. He tuts at the siren and goes to the bottom of the stairwell, awaiting Mrs Quigley. When she doesn't come he climbs the stairs, taking the torch from the hall stand as he goes. He can hear her snores from the half landing. He knocks, diplomatically at first and then with more insistence. The snoring stops with a sudden glottal splutter. He doesn't hear her cross the room but the door is suddenly opened. She has already put on her housecoat. She's wearing a kind of bandana, from the forehead to the nape of her neck, and the shock of her silver hair sticks out the top electrically, like the crown of a pineapple. Her face looks nacreous in the torchlight. He takes a step back until he realises she's applied some kind of night cream.

'We'll have to go to the shelter.'

She nods. They talked about it earlier. Given the number of false alarms, they both feel safe enough remaining in bed but he feels hypocritical, asking his parishioners to take to the shelters if he doesn't do so himself. He explained this and she accepted without question. He takes her arm, directing the beam on to the top stair. There's something different about her other than the strange colour and bizarre appearance. She looks much older. She stops, twitches his arm and says something he doesn't understand. He's obliged to shine the light in her face. She blinks in the dazzling cone.

'What?'

'Teef.' She repeats and nods her head back towards her bed. He realises what's made the difference. The bottom half of her face has lost structure and folded in on itself. Her mouth looks like a shucked clam. He stands at the door, shining the light inside, looking away as she crouches over her bedside cabinet. She straightens and turns.

'Bloody Germans.'

The transformation's like a conjurer's trick. She's already impatient for the all clear to sound. It's not just the upheaval, it's the prospect of socialising in the wee small hours. The church shelter was constructed on the instructions of a zealous sub-committee of the parish council. It numbers a builder among its members. He saw it as his chance to shine. It's large enough to house adjacent families. All this was already seen to by the time Father Bernacchi arrived. It's all but monopolised the garden. He has the Notre Dame of bomb shelters resting in the lee of his squat urban church. He turns off the torch for the thirty foot walk from the back door to the shelter. It's a clear night and they can navigate by the crunch of their steps on the gravel path. Her muttering is more comprehensible with her teeth in. He knows as soon as she sees the others, especially the children, she'll rally. Her grip on his arm has tightened in the darkness and it tightens still further when they hear the unmistakable drone of the engines. He hurries her forward to the steps descending to the half-buried shelter. She's at the top step when they hear the first detonation.

'Dear God!' This is from him. He can hear a shriek behind them in the darkness and knows there are others seeking the shelter. He risks the torch, directs Mrs Quigley down the stairs and shepherds the Wilsons after her. There are already people in the shelter. He doesn't know how many. He can hear the welcome. He closes the door on them, ignoring Mrs Quigley's entreaty to come in, and stands in the darkened garden, fanning it with his torch, checking for latecomers. Timing, in this case, might be everything. He can hear the crump of falling bombs as the patterned explosions approach. His view is constrained by the surrounding buildings but he can already see a glow in the sky, over towards the West, and he can imagine the people, just like them, scrambling beneath the canopy of flames as the inferno descends. He blesses himself, scans one last time and moves quickly towards the shelter. The torch picks out two retinas in the compost pile and he whistles loudly in the darkness. It's a small dog, a mongrel. He doesn't know who it belongs to but it's got a collar and as much chance of having a home tomorrow morning as the rest of them. If any of them live to see it. Besides, he thinks, as he bundles it down the steps, it'll provide a culprit for Mrs Quigley's farting.

Up the hill, Stephen has assembled everything well in advance. They're sitting in the shelter with flasks, food and gas masks, him, Deborah and Michael. He did the lion's share of the work in building this. He thinks it can withstand anything but a direct hit. He hasn't said so and doesn't want his theory tested. Deborah's sitting clutching Michael, rigid with worry for her mother. Stephen's debating with himself how foolhardy it would be to try and get her. It's not fear. At least not for himself. His only fear in dying is fear of abandoning them. They've talked over various scenarios. He raised each in turn and she sat on the other side of the kitchen table, staring fixedly at the oilcloth, trying to come to terms with drastic possibilities. They finally agree: they'll stick together, see it through or be annihilated as a family. The worst scenario he can conceive is retrieving her mother and returning to a crater. Still, it goes against the grain, sitting here, while an old lady half a mile away might be paralyzed with confusion. Deborah can see enough through her own agitation to know what he's thinking. In the gloom she squeezes his hand. Gig and Campbell tumble in, dilatory, breathless. Stephen lets go of Deborah's hand and automatically offers Campbell a sandwich. They sit in silence for ten minutes, listening to Campbell methodically eat, while the firestorm approaches. The door opens and Alan bolts in, smoking a cigarette.

'If they get the yards there'll be no work tomorrow.'

Stephen's thinking: your help towards the construction of this shelter was the square root of fuck all, and you've got the fucking nerve to come in here and expect a conversation while folk are dying.

Deborah, sensing, takes Stephen's hand again. With his free hand, Stephen reaches across, takes the cigarette out of Alan's mouth, throws it to the earth floor and crushes it with his heel.

Michael sleeps throughout.

Across the way, Danny is playing animal snap with his little brother in his shelter, supervised by Irene. She's concentrating very hard on the cards, lest her imagination wanders to Thomas, on night shift, working furiously at the intended epicentre of all this. Both boys are gleeful at the novelty of being allowed to be awake at this hour. And there's that earthy subterranean smell to savour. She's talking levelly to Paul. 'Cat not rat. Donkey doesn't make a match – ' and stops at the nearness of that last one, dislodging a small mantle of dust that drifts down, setting the younger one sneezing. 'Parrot and... another parrot. Snap! You're both going to have to be a bit quicker.'

Heather Cunningham has made it to the Underground with Dougal. There's a smell of food and bodies and an undertow of chat punctured with children crying. There's a half-hearted attempt at a sing-song, inspired by a sense of camaraderie with those irrepressible Londoners, those cockney salamanders so beloved of the Pathé news reports. Eventually it takes, and the tiled walls give them back their melody, echoing defiantly down the darkened tunnels in waves that peter out between stations.

'Now you take the high road and I'll take the low road...'

The suspended lights above them dance, swivelling the shadows. A piece of plaster falls on the track and fragments to dust. A defiant pub singer perseveres and they compose themselves to take up the end of the refrain.

'Where me and my true love will never meet again,
On the bonny, bonny banks of Loch Lomond.'

'Maybe it would be better to sing a song that wasn't about loss,' Dougal whispers to his mother. She's thinking about him without looking at him and now turns and looks. How did she make this thing, this precious, thoughtful, beautiful boy? She's under no delusions about herself. And his father, God rest his soul, was no more exceptional than her. How have their base materials compounded something finer than either? Her love is so intently directed at him that for a moment she forgets his brother. She gathers him to her as she used to, when he was of an age to play animal snap, and in the anonymity of the half-darkness, he lets her.

The first explosion finds Miss Herne at the bay window of her flat, opening the black-out blinds, defiant of the Luftwaffe, scornful of the flying debris that will kill hundreds. Her heart is already lacerated with joy at the prospect of the test to come. The street below is abandoned. Were anyone to loiter as contemptuous of danger as she is, they'd see her framed in her window, intermittently illuminated as the bombs detonate, like a pantomime genie. The falling bombs are like a series of giant destructive footsteps, igniting and pulverising everything in their path. She takes her place, kneeling beneath the crucifix, and is suddenly stilled in a transport of rapture as the maelstrom rages all around. As she's said to Gig before, Our Lord will not despise a sacrifice so willingly made. She whispers to Him, sibilantly, against the shriek of the approaching firestorm. And then the windows implode.

TWENTY
NINE

It's almost morning before the all clear sounds. Paolo insists they stay where they are until he can assess the situation. He clambers out. Dawn is coming up through the smoke. He takes inventory, like a motorist in the aftershock of a collision, patting vital areas to ensure they're still intact. The squat church emerges first, although many of the windows are put in and the surrounding areas strewn with fragments of someone else's rubble. He goes out the gate and into the street. The yard next to the church is completely untouched, although there's no sound of industry at the moment. He looks up the hill. A gable end is simply not there, removed as effectively as a pulled tooth. The revealed cross-section seems somehow indecent in its domestic intimacy: a hanging toilet chain and cistern lacking a toilet bowl on what would have been a half landing; an ostentatious oblong of Regency stripe wallpaper; a teetering iron range balancing the ubiquitous soup pot. But the rest of the street is mercifully unscathed, as is the school, frowning down from the hill's summit.

He goes back to the shelter and helps them all out, one at a time.

Mrs Quigley emerges pale as a geisha. He'd forgotten about her night cream. He asks Mrs Quigley if she might be good enough to feed them, given what might be the privilege of an intact kitchen.

'Aren't you coming with us, Father?'

'They didn't drop all that ordnance to do as little damage as this. There must be other places needing me.'

'What if they come looking for you?'

'Feed them, Mrs Quigley. Feed them all. I'll be back as soon as I can.'

He climbs the hill to the school, to try and get some wider perspective on the extent of the destruction. The general drifting smoke is lifting but one or two spots are still burning fiercely. The landscape looks arbitrarily chequered with ruins and defiantly upright tenements. The light treatment this street received isn't the norm. People are beginning to emerge from all over. An acrid column of black smoke rises vertically nearer the river, perhaps a mile downstream. He begins to make his way towards that.

Stephen has never issued instructions to Deborah in his life, but after he's satisfied himself that the surrounding buildings aren't going to tumble, and that their flat is structurally sound, and in fact habitable, with running water and lights that miraculously work, he does exactly that.

'Stay here.'

'No.'

'I'm going to your mother's.'

'I'm coming.'

'How will you react if she's not there?'

'Where else will she be?'

The colossal naivety of the question disqualifies her. He throws up his hands to indicate heaven, the ether, dust... Worry has temporarily unhinged her.

'The building might not be there.'

Her hands fly to her mouth.

'Stay here.'

'No!'

'I don't want you to see it!' For the first time in this flat he's shouting.

'She's my mother!'

'You'd have to bring Michael. He might see it. He might remember.'

He goes out and slams the door behind. She snatches up Michael and follows. The boy starts to cry in the stairwell, the sound of his distress magnified by the ceramic echo. She's crying too by the time she makes the street, running after him, blurting, 'I'm coming too! I'm coming too!' between sobs. She can't narrow the gap and loses a shoe, shouting in her exasperation. He turns and stands transfixed by the sight of her with one shoe, dishevelled, her face blotched and running, clutching the boy. He runs back, encircles them both with his arms. Someone comes up with the shoe. It's cheap, make do and mend, like everything else fabricated or salvaged on this island since the U-boats isolated it. The heel has come off.

Her mother is sitting on the stairs to a close across the road from her own flat. A man with a helmet is staring at the entrance to her flat. The helmet appears to wobble as he shakes his head, dubiously. Aside from this the sole indication of his official status is an armband, difficult to distinguish from the rest of his clothing as he's powdered with dust. So is Myra. Her grey hair looks as artificial as a Regency wig, and as she turns and sees her daughter a light cloud, like dislodged pollen, lifts from her. She half stands and a punctured sound escapes her. But Deborah's already there, with Michael, and he temporarily disappears between the two of them. Deborah's softly kneading her mother's creased cheek, like dough. She needs this tangible corroboration. Stephen goes across to his mother-in-law then joins the man at the close entrance. There's a crack in the lintel, above the close entrance, that extends in a deviating fissure to the roof.

'How did you get here so quickly?' Stephen asks.

'I live... lived here.'

Stephen moves to the steps. The man raises his hand to prevent him. Stephen turns.

'We're taking her,' nodding towards Myra, 'with us. She's lived here forty years and buried her man from this flat. It might be the last time she sees it never mind live in it again. I want her to be given the chance to take something away.'

The man steps back.

'Do it before they come and cordon off the building. I don't doubt that the rest of the street will have to come down too.'

He crosses to Deborah, crouches in front of her mother who's sitting again and patiently explains the situation. Myra extends her hand for him to take and he helps her upright. As the two of them cross the road Deborah rises to follow and sits down again at a backward glance from her mother. For a moment they revert to their old relations of required permission. He goes first, ascending one step at a time, testing the integrity, pulling her incrementally up. At the first ominous creak he's prepared to forego any deference for her dignity, put her over his shoulder and run out. But they make the second floor without mishap and she produces jingling keys, sparking metallically in the bright stairwell. She unlocks the storm door, and the inner door and he advances into the small hall, where he first stood over ten years ago, awaiting Deborah on their first publicly acknowledged date. His arm bars her way until he's sure, rocking forward on the balls of his feet, testing each forward step like ice on the canal, taking the weight with the secure foot until he's confident enough to transfer it. If it will take him it can take her. He's never been able to disentangle this interior in his mind from his fledgling wife, the place he helped her leave. Her father wasn't long dead and it was a sense of love, and duty, that clipped her wings to a short journey and settled her within a convenient radius, where she could see her mother daily. As he walks further in, listening for protests, he has a sense of intruding on cracked nostalgia. There's a patina of usage to everything. The old lady, compliant, waits until he waives her forward and she stands in the hall, momentarily taking his hand. Her children were conceived and born in that small bedroom over there. Stephen stood in the front room, over there, still an apprentice, beside Deborah, as her father's coffin rested on the catafalque while friends and neighbours filtered past to pay last respects, or sat on the edge of borrowed dining room chairs in the kitchen, making subdued small talk, while this heroic old lady made endless tea and robbed the holiday money to distribute sittings of corned beef sandwiches and bought Battenberg cake, because baking wouldn't have been seemly. He recalls her exactly, when they came up the stairs for Deborah's father. She produced a comb from nowhere and arranged his flaccid hair, then kissed him just once more, rubbed his inert cheeks as Deborah just kneaded hers, stood back and nodded, crossed herself while they screwed down the lid.

Memories are cascading down around him, like falling roof slates. He can only begin to guess what she's feeling.

'Towels,' she says.

'What?'

'Towels. We should take some.'

'We've got lots of towels.'

'No. You can never have too many towels.' He's wondering if she's grasped the finality of the situation when she says, 'Would you like a cup of tea?'

'Myra, this is it. We're not coming back. I want you to take something for yourself.'

She frowns down and some of the life seems to leak from her at the acceptance. And now there's the problem of selection. What to take when everything's emblematic? They're only things, but somehow the years of their handling deserve more fidelity than this.

'All right.'

She gestures towards the kitchen. She's spent most of her waking hours there, as they do in theirs. He wasn't allowed to see, but Deborah told him her wedding dress was suspended from the pulley that morning, to hang out the creases once Myra had gone over it with an iron one last time, an elongated bell of lace suspended like a levitating angel. She got dressed standing on a stool under mother's supervision. Her father thought to make kippers – their last breakfast as an intact family. Myra rounded on him. Did he want his daughter going down the aisle with her dress smelling like the apron of a herring wife? They settled for scrambled egg. Deborah couldn't eat a thing.

He pushes open the door. The ceiling has collapsed and the upstairs kitchen has descended into hers. There's soot everywhere and the broken flue stands exposed. The integrity of the building, viewed from the front, is a façade. Part of the back wall is missing and has tumbled down into the back court since she left the shelter there. Neither the flat nor shelter are safe now. She stands in the hall, craning to see over his shoulder. He moves to one side of the doorway without allowing enough space to admit her. She stands, blinking, and points at some cheap figurine he's never even noticed before, incongruous in its fragile intactness. It has no conceivable utility, besides what it can invoke. He can reach without stepping further into the kitchen. She wraps it in one of the towels. He retrieves a battered suitcase from above her wardrobe and she begins to fill it methodically until his sense of urgency communicates itself and she piles in the clothes pell mell. He takes the case and holds her hand down the stairs. When they get to the street Deborah's shifting her weight in agitation. Michael's back on her hip. She throws her vacant arm round her mother, as if the old woman has surfaced from a dangerous plunge into deep water. Myra, suddenly exhausted, rests her head against her daughter. Relations have reversed again.

Across the street, two doors up from where they first found Myra sitting, a group is working frantically. Stephen crosses and comes back, takes his jacket off and drapes it round Myra's shoulders. He makes Michael stand, links his hand in his grandmother's and steers Deborah a few feet from both.

'There's someone buried over there. The older man says he can recognize his daughter's hand by the engagement ring. I'm staying. Take your mother home. Leave the case and I'll bring it when I come.'

But Myra clings to it with the tenacity of a guardian of the artefacts, keeping a vestige alive. They ignore Michael's protests and make him walk, hauling the case in turns between them. Deborah lists towards the absent heel.

The Gildeas, minus Thomas, emerge to what appears to Paul to be a smouldering new playground. From a quick survey of the back court all the buildings look intact. She doesn't risk walking through her close until she's sure of the integrity of her building. Instead she reaches the street with Danny and Paul via the pend, the vehicle entrance from the street to the communal back courts. Ever since they left the shelter, Danny's been repeating his request like a chanted mantra: 'Can I go and see the Neavies?' She knows Michael's too young to command Danny's attention and that he really wants to go because Campbell and Gig share the shelter with them. She's staring at the pall of smoke and suspended dust in a kind of dejected awe, projecting the same thing in her mind for the yards and imagining Thomas lying under collapsed superstructure, when she's suddenly, disproportionately, irritated.

'Go!' she bellows. His litany immediately stops with the initial surprise, then he turns, cheerful, and runs off. She's young enough herself to remember the complete selfishness of a child's preoccupation. Then she thinks of all the latent hazards. She's immediately sorry and calls him back, but he's accelerating with the joy of being alive and either doesn't hear or pretends not to. It doesn't occur to him that anyone he knows or cares for might actually be hurt.

She pats down her little boy, composes herself, picks him up and begins walking towards the river. When she turns the corner to the sight of the miraculously intact yard, her first thought is to go and give thanks in the miraculously intact church next door. She had half imagined herself rabidly throwing aside fallen masonry, and the flood of relief has left her indecisive. The whole church like that next to the whole yard. Isn't that why God spared them? Shouldn't she give thanks now? Mightn't that seem a bit premature, given she hasn't actually seen Thomas? On the other hand, if she doesn't, won't that seem ungrateful?

She realises she's wandering. She puts a stop to her indecision by ordering herself to the yard and promises a novena for doubting the divine credentials.

When she gets to the entrance there's a man in a boiler suit loitering there, posted to dispense news. He's only ten years older than Danny.

'There's no point, missus. I'm guessing you came here looking for your man. No one here's hurt, at least not as far as I know. Not unless they ran home and got bombed. Soon as the all clear sounded they all ran out to their families. Fucked off, the lot of 'em. He's probably out there looking for you and the wee one there.'

She runs up and kisses him, turns back and begins resolutely walking back up the street. Back again within sight of the flat she sees Thomas coming out the close entrance. If she hadn't come via the pend she might have spared herself that fraught trip to the river and the novena. He hasn't seen her yet. She shouts his name and waves. The very matter of factness of his everyday appearance seems somehow strangely exotic in these charged surroundings, and her heart is flooded. His reaction takes her by surprise. When he sees her she's anticipating the collision of relief, as he runs towards her and throws his arms round her and Paul. But he doesn't do this. He stops, frowns at them both from the distance and seems suddenly to want to sit down, patting the wall to steady himself. She suddenly realises he's done a head count and come up with one short. She starts shouting as she runs towards him.

'It's all right! It's all right! Danny's gone to the Neavies.'

He draws a grubby hand across a grubby face and wipes away his discomposure. The very economy of the gesture is too much for her. She's surfeit, to bursting. Every emotion she's ever felt seems to have come back for a reunion. She doesn't hug him but hands him the baby and sits on the steps, crouches forward and buries her face in the hem of her uplifted skirt.

Heather and Dougal have returned through a mosaic of destruction. Their street and their flat, like the majority that populate the slope from school to church and yard, are intact. They stayed in the Underground until well after the all clear sounded. Almost everything flammable has been consumed. Dougal notices the flitting of rats and points it out to his mother. She never thought of vermin as refugees before. They were just something on the farm they shot or trapped and then hung up. They pass a crater in the main road in which a car sits perfectly, as if placed, like a ship in a glass bottle. Once they've reached the flat he asks his mother if he can go and check on his friends. Every instinct screams to her to cling to him.

'All right. Don't go into any building roped off and don't go beyond the street.'

She thinks about her other son. For all she knows he could be near the Arctic circle, snaking his way between icebergs towards safe harbour south of the Grand Banks, in the Eastern seaboard of the United States. She thinks about chance and the aggregate of suffering this war has created and is yet to mete out. Can her diminished family command a sufficient portion of luck? All she's asking for is survival, no more. And not even for herself. And yes, for herself, but just to see them through. Is it too much to ask? She knows it's everything.

Stephen works until the light starts to fade. People have come and gone in relays, but he's stayed. In some way he can't begin to describe, he feels he's making atonement. People have come out of adjacent houses and shared what food they have. A young man, younger than him, gave them some hard-boiled eggs and said he wanted nothing for himself. Word circulated his eighteen month-old daughter was dead and his wife missing. The owner of the engagement ring was excavated. It took five hours. Her father wrapped her in his coat. As darkness falls she is still at the side of the road, awaiting collection. They found two more and unearthed a pram, filled with rubble, mercifully empty.

As the day wore on people seemed to return, defiantly setting up what makeshift shelter they could. And now he's on his way home, numb, exhausted. He meets Paolo, who looks as tired as he is. They fall in with one another in the brief walk home and exchange stories. Stephen tells him about the owner of the engagement ring and the persistence of her father. Paolo has witnessed similar occurrences since this morning and heard about worse.

'I'm told there's a pub... there was a pub, between the yards and the borough hall...' He stops. He can't walk and say this at the same time. Stephen waits. 'I met a warden. He says there were people, I think he means men, I hope to God he means men, in there, in the basement...'

'They'll have wanted a lock-in. Probably thought they could out drink the Luftwaffe.'

'It was a direct hit. The warden said they couldn't distinguish anything. That's exactly what he said. Anything. Rubble and bits of people. They couldn't begin to...'

'They'll just bury them,' Stephen says. 'All of them. Everything.'

'That's what he said. He said when he left they were shovelling quicklime into the crater before they fill it.' He's thinking about the privilege of being dead in his bed, of individual benediction. It's hard to find evidence of grace when two dozen people disintegrate among beer kegs. How do you bless debris? Stephen steers him round and they begin walking again. There's a weary camaraderie. When they turn into the street Stephen shakes his hand.

'Just in case,' he jokes.

'Don't wait for the sirens tonight. Get to the shelter early. Tell the others. I'm telling everyone I can.'

'You think they'll be back?'

'Do you see any clouds?'

'No.'

'They didn't touch the yards. Any of them. I've spoken to a few officials. They think they'll be back to finish what they started. Did you get your mother-in-law?'

'Yes.'

'Good. Goodbye. Good luck.'

'Good luck to you too, Father.'

THIRTY

The earthy novelty of the shelters has worn off for the children. Those who stayed behind assembled more quickly when the sirens sounded than they had last night.

Their parents' demeanour has subdued many of the children. There's no animal snap in the Gildea shelter. Thomas has gone back to his last night shift of a fortnight. Irene didn't ask him to stay. If she had she knows what he'd have said: that it would be like letting them win; that others face worse every day; that you don't see London shutting up shop. She closed the door on him and timed his footfalls on the stairwell to go to the front room and peer from the window at his retreating back, the less dark patch that merges into surrounding darkness. She's already in the shelter with the boys when the siren sounds. The older couple from upstairs join them. They have two sons obliquely referred to as, 'in the fighting'. They've had the threat of telegrams, not just bombs, to contend with. And telegrams discriminate. They nail your kids to history. It's beyond Irene how Mrs McCluskey copes with the strain. She's feeling compelled to touch her sons, intermittently, all night, despite the fact that they're not away in the fighting. Mr McCluskey likes playing with the boys. He's showing them how the top of his thumb bloodlessly detaches and then, just when you've run out of awe or suspicion, restores itself.

Deborah Neavie's also bedded down early in the shelter with the whole family. Stephen's shifts are providential: he's not back on nights for a week and who knows what can happen in that time. There might not be any yard for him to go back to. There might be a yard and no Stephen to help populate it. One thing is certain: they'll see it out or perish together. She's got Michael on her lap, her mother on one side and husband on the other. They're so tightly congregated it's going to take a direct hit on the nucleus of her family. Before they went down to the shelter Stephen went upstairs and banged on the Renton's door. He persisted until there was no mistake. He even knelt on the landing, staring through the letterbox into the vacant flat. He joined them in the shelter and shrugged at Deborah's questions. Inwardly he's smouldering. 'Perhaps,' says Deborah, 'they've gone to the Underground. I know a lot of people did. Heather Cunningham said she was there with Dougal last night. She said it was almost like a party. They're going again tonight.'

Heather and Dougal are there tonight but none of the Rentons join them. This time they're better provisioned, as are most of the others, expecting to make a night of it. The singing is better too, more defiant. Even Dougal would have to concede the choice is more suitable. The pub singer, who's decided that this is his destined forum, belts out 'On the Sunny Side of the Street', forgets the second verse and is applauded for the compensating gusto of his chorus. He even produces spoons to accompany himself on 'Skip to My Lou'. If he survives this then the rest of his war, perhaps the rest of his life, will be an anticlimax.

They're lilting in unison through the first verse of 'You Made Me Love You' when the first of the distant explosions are felt.

'...And all the time you knew it
I guess you always knew it

You made me happy sometimes
You made me glad
But there were times
You made me feel so bad...'

One or two falter. The pub singer, with a Churchillian sense of the hour, jumps up and proceeds to conduct them with an imaginary baton.

'... Give me, give me, give me what I cry for'

That one was almost overhead. Some children are crying.

'You know that you got the brand of kisses, that I'd die for
You know you made me love you.'

'ONE – MORE – TIME,' he bawls. The final chorus is repeated. Another explosion, further away. They've passed. There may be another wave but this one's passed.

'Give me, give me, give me what I cry for
You know that you got the brand of kisses, that I'd die for
You know you made me love you.'

Rabid applause. Right now, everyone loves everyone.

Back in the Gildea's shelter, Mr McCluskey realises he's got to up his game if he wants to distract Danny and Paul from the rattling explosions that seem to be peppering them from all sides. If there's any compensation in this it's the lack of the bombers' apparent method. He's found a coin behind Danny's ear and transformed his handkerchief into a cloth rabbit. He's dredging his repertoire of parlour tricks he used to perform for his boys, and swallowing back the recurrent bile of sheer fear, when the door bursts open. Campbell tumbles in and stares around.

'Is Gig here?'

It's obvious to everyone, including him before he gets out the last syllable, that Gig isn't here.

'Sit down, son,' Mr McCluskey says. He's never seen him before and doesn't know whether Gig is a boy, girl or household pet. Mrs McCluskey moves two feet and pats the vacated spot.

'I've kept it warm for you,' she says, and adds, 'We've got tea.'

Campbell coughs, from street inhalation and casts another frantic look around. His face is streaked. There's a look of desperate entreaty on his face that Danny can imagine being easily replaced if they produce Gig from behind a curtain and all guffaw at the joke, the humour proportionate to the reprieve.

But they don't, and no one laughs, and Campbell rushes out banging the door behind in panic. They all sit momentarily stunned. Danny's imagination has been sucked into the vortex on the other side of the door where Gig, in some form or another, circulates. He shatters the collective inertia by jumping up, as if spring loaded, and rushing out after Campbell. Mr McCluskey shoots out an arm to try and bar his way but his amateur magician's reactions aren't up to it. He runs after the boy as far as the threshold. He's nearly sucked off his feet by a searing gust from the firestorm and shades his eyes just long enough to see Danny dodge into the close entrance from the back court. The very air seems on fire, and he can feel it scorch his windpipe. Irene Gildea's at his immediate back, screaming something he can't hear into the maelstrom. His reactions are up to this. He pushes her back inside, wedges the door and points to Paul. She covers her face with her hands and screams into her palms. Mrs McCluskey gathers her into the space she just made for Campbell.

The reason Gig isn't in the Neavie's shelter and with Campbell is because in the course of this afternoon, as Stephen was helping to extricate the dead owner of the engagement ring, Miss Herne threaded her way through the smouldering rubble and past confused people to find her. And when she did find her she told Gig that they, separately surviving in separate immune pockets among wholesale destruction, had been separately handpicked for a reason. And Gig had asked if that's the same reason they, gesturing towards those in their visible radius, bewildered with grief or doggedly salvaging, had come through it too. And Miss Herne declines to answer because she believes Gig isn't yet old enough to understand the portentousness of the fact that she can stand among the ruins and frame a question, that she's still among the quick. Because Miss Herne views these other survivors as mere stage props for the culmination of a drama being acted out for the benefit of the elect. The only people she perceives as real are herself and her immediates, and at the moment that's restricted to Georgina.

The calves of Miss Herne's legs are lacerated. They were the only part unshielded by the bureau when the windows collapsed. She'd been kneeling before the crucifix and had bent forward in a final act of penitence when the glass blew in. Much of it was embedded in the wall to her left, at precisely the level her head had been before she bowed, and she construed this act of supernatural mercy as a sign of her immunity. Through the swirling dust she can see a glass fragment protruding from the wooden ribcage of the hanging figure and she interprets this as another sign, that He has been pierced again to reprieve her.

She has cleaned the wounds with undiluted antiseptic, bound her legs and now wears the marks lightly. The flesh is cut, but only superficially, and she doesn't think there's any glass lodged there. It's a badge. He did not intend this to stop her, so she refuses to convalesce. Once the air settles she piles the debris in a corner. The water's still on and she sprinkles the air to dampen the dust, lays moist tea leaves on top of the powdery pile and sweeps it up. She uses her select patronage again and co-opts an ex-pupil, and his father, from the flat across the street, to knock out the remaining glass and cover the gaping windows with salvaged doors. It appears there's no shortage of salvage.

'Come with me, Georgina.'

It's been a day of fluctuating emotions: relief at survival; elation at recognized faces; an unmistakable undercurrent of public misery for the majority of undiscovered dead; defiance with which people try to recolonise ruins. Miss Herne's serenity disturbs Gig. It's a calm of complete disengagement. She doesn't appear in the least disturbed by what she sees. In fact, she seems to have become more tranquil at each new discovery as they pull out another one. And there's another thing: the seesaw of emotion and lack of food has left everyone exhausted. In contrast Miss Herne seems galvanised by the surrounding distress.

'I think I'll go to the Underground tonight, Miss Herne.'

'Nonsense, child. We haven't found one another for you to perish like some grubby buried animal.'

Gig doesn't tell her that they didn't find one another. She came and found her. For the first time the intensity of Miss Herne's fervour comes home to her, silhouetted against the grief and rubble that doesn't touch the older woman. For the first time she's frightened, not inspired.

They return to Miss Herne's flat, now perpetually gloomy with the boarded windows. Miss Herne improvises a meal for Gig but takes nothing herself. The gloom deepens as the light outside fades. People head for the shelters early. Gig feels the embattled fear welling up from the street below. Miss Herne prays, whispering the entire Rosary, ignoring her calves as she kneels before the crucifix. Gig casts around with growing unease that ratchets up to repressed panic. She's never seen Miss Herne like this before. In the past she's at least tried to observe the social norms.

'I want to go and check my brother's all right.'

Miss Herne concludes her prayers without haste and rises softly.

'Have you had enough to eat?'

'Yes, thank you. I'm worried about my brother.'

Miss Herne doesn't respond but goes instead to the perforated bureau that saved her and retrieves a large bunch of keys that Gig's never seen before. She holds the front door open for Gig and locks it behind her with a separate key Gig has seen her use on every other occasion. In the darkness she takes Gig's hand. Normally the girl's very proximity is sufficient for her. There's no sense of coercion intended.

'Where are we going?'

It would be difficult for Miss Herne to frame a reply Gig could understand. She's following a prescribed path with the person ordained to accompany her. Instead she simply points, up the hill. They walk in silence to the school gates. In the darkness Miss Herne's choice of key is unerring. She closes the gate behind but leaves it unlocked. They cross the deserted playground to the sandstone mass of the school, looming intact beneath the starlight. Gig's astute enough to know what clear conditions mean. Sure enough, as they stand in the lee of the main doorway she hears the sirens sound. Miss Herne gives no indication of having heard anything as she again selects the correct key. The door is large and takes effort to open and close. They stand in the entrance hall. The stratum of institutional smells that both are familiar with seem to Gig wildly incongruous in the silent darkness. There are rhomboids of quicksilver light cast on the floor from the high windows, and in the shaft of one of these milky diagonals Miss Herne investigates the enormous bunch of keys. They tinkle in the silence and glisten like swerving fish as their shadows on the floor are fingered by the shadows of Miss Herne's fingers.

'Where did you get them?'

'I collected them... gradually.'

It occurs to Gig that she's done this before, been here before, in circumstances like these, without company and the imminence of destruction. She has more keys than any of the rooms she has taught in. She has more keys than legitimate purposes. She's interrogated these rooms, alone, at night, dipped into desks, surveyed others' work without compunction because she believes it to be part of her legitimate vigilance. And the fact that she's allowing Gig to see her now, here, like this, is a concession that Gig believes was never granted to any of her predecessors. This frightens her even more.

'Come.'

She navigates without faltering in the darkness. They make the central stairwell, where filtered moonlight from the curious cupola falls vertically, like luminescent plankton, sinking into the void. Beyond the twin echoes of their footfalls Gig can again hear the distant crump of falling bombs, and the stuttering flack. They ascend past Miss Herne's classroom to the top floor, a place of incidental rooms too small for classes, where the occasional paraphernalia of gym and archived paperwork are consigned. But there's one more stairwell Gig has never seen. A tight spiral that curves out of sight to a small door recessed into the ceiling. Miss Herne climbs up these and in the darkness above her Gig can hear the obscure key grate.

'Come.'

They're in an attic that must occupy all of the space from the gable end to the cupola that sits centrally and interrupts the roof line. Two spaced windows admit light, projecting the flicker of detonated incendiaries onto the back wall that follows the slope of the roof.

Miss Herne walks to the nearest window and throws it wide. She looks across at Gig and gestures to her to come and share the spectacle. There's enough space for them to stand side by side. The low sill admits on to the sloping roof that extends downwards for ten feet towards the gutters, falling off to the raging vista. Before them spreads a flaming mosaic curtailed at one extremity by the dark strip of the river. An exclamation mark of flame shoots up a mile or so distant, higher than them. Even at this distance, suspended above the inferno, Gig can feel the heat. She feels this building has outlived its luck after last night. And now this. She turns and looks. There's a monumental quality to Miss Herne's immobile face, like a stamped coin, the profile rendered alternately dim and fiercely bright from the pulsed light coming up from below. And there's something inexorable in her determination to occupy this space, at this time, keeping an appointment she believes has been ordained before this city was a settlement clustered round a ford. This is her test, standing above destruction. Like the singer in the Underground she has her sense of the hour. She's keeping faith with history.

'I have to go to the toilet.' Gig says. Miss Herne turns and looks at her. The nearest toilet is on the level with her classroom. The girl's physical need is a disappointment to her. This moment should transcend such claims. To bring it to the level of evacuation is debasing.

clergy of various denominations, not there to officiate but to lend it something: solidarity, recognition, something that, if asked, no words he might find could hope to approximate.

Representatives of the great and good are officiating. The Secretary of State for Scotland is here, as is the Lord Lieutenant of Dunbartonshire and the Clydebank Provost. But he doesn't sense any perception of privilege. The grief – colossal, numbing, civic, is a leveller. Looking around there are many faces of private anguish, those unmistakably trapped in their own misery, but he also senses a defiant social cohesion. Until now the losses, sustained elsewhere, have only been immediate to the relatives. For the rest it's been like second-hand news of an equatorial landslip, sad but remote, another person's tragedy. But now it's as intensely personal as it's possible to be.

There's a single huge hole, a clay trench that resembles an open wound, its edges red and ragged. The bodies, the majority unidentified, some, he suspects loose aggregate of parts, are muffled in canvas, wound in serge, wrapped in whatever comes to hand and laid like parallel railway sleepers, nudged into closer proximity to putrefy in tandem. He experiences a sense of complete unreality at the thought of this post-mortal intimacy. He's brought up short by the sight of a pair of feet, in children's shoes, protruding from a man's loden coat.

He makes his way back towards the church, nodding wordlessly to the familiar faces in the crowd's dispersal. The church is still there, despite the best endeavours of the Luftwaffe, the apathy of dwindling congregations, the cynicism of the atheists. Some think it divine intervention, which raises the question why this protection wasn't afforded elsewhere. Some think it the proximity of the yards, of good luck rubbing off. Most of the windows have collapsed in, either directly from the force of the blast or the ferocity of the surrounding heat. And he's permitted himself a small measure of private grief at their disappearance. Even if the funds are found to replace them, he doubts that the reverential skills that fashioned and fixed colour in glass in a display of faith, still exist. He expects, in the fullness of time, something utilitarian, serviceable, more easily cleaned. They'll do what the previous ones did, exclude the elements, admit light, but without the prismatic filter of faith. He feels his sadness at their disappearance is almost a venial sin. They were just coloured pieces of glass. To be sad about windows in the midst of all this, to lament the loss of something inorganic after what he's just seen, is plainly wrong. But there it is, nevertheless, this little quarantined regret.

Paolo's sorrow is premature. He's as wrong as he can be. The windows will be replaced, in the fullness of time, not with some utilitarian panes but with ochres, ambers, turquoises, violets, blood reds, dazzling greens, emphatic purples, leaded and fixed with the finest skills that money can buy. The skills that go into the fitting out of state rooms of glorious liners fabricated on the Clyde will be deployed on Paolo's church windows. And the money for this won't come from the diocese or public subscription. It will come from Mrs Quigley.

Mr Quigley is twenty-five years dead. Mrs Quigley's daughters are long ago settled in Canada, married off to different scions of those first families driven across the Atlantic by the Highland Clearances. Her daughters are the genuine article, genuine Scots among the counterfeits, the ceremonially kilted who pine for a Celtic twilight that never was. Mrs Quigley saw her girls off one at a time from the Clydeside, consigning her heart in three instalments, to sail down the estuary and follow in the wake of the earlier Diaspora. With her youngest, and last, the contingent waving farewell from the disappearing quay had dwindled to one: her. She walked back from the waterfront to a flat of phantoms, the ghost of her husband having to contend with those not yet dead, her girls in their raucous instalments of childhood and teens and adolescence. She withstood the tumultuous silence for two days and decided that this wouldn't do, this simply wouldn't do. A woman who has struggled to bring up three children in the aftermath of a husband taken early isn't the type to succumb to self-pity. She marched down the hill to interview the young Father Delaney, a man in a house in dire need of domestic supervision if ever there was one. The next week she surreptitiously sublet her flat at a modest profit and moved her personal effects eight hundred yards, where they've remained ever since. Her bedroom is a shrine to absent daughters and grandchildren she has yet to see in the flesh. Photographs festoon every surface. She's scrupulous about birthdays and exact in the distribution of her attentions. Each grandchild is repeatedly remembered in a novena, the cycle is continuous as long as there's breath to give it utterance, like a nudged prayer wheel. Her latest thanks are offered up for God's foresight in installing her kin beyond the reach of the Luftwaffe.

Her needs are modest, her thrift effective. She pockets her salary against a rainy day, manages the domestic accounts and hoards on the priests' behalf. The years of illicit rental accumulate. Mrs Quigley doesn't think there's anything wrong with this. She hasn't been transparent in her dealings with the Factor, who is probably equally opaque in his dealing with the owner. The Lord gives and the Lord takes away. She's not comfortably off, she's only a conduit. The windows are a case in point. But that act of generosity has yet to manifest itself. In the meantime Paolo can only stand back and marvel.

The fact that the church is still standing isn't as extraordinary as Mrs Quigley may want to believe, given the reprieve of several surrounding streets. Nevertheless, she sees it as totemic among the ruins. She's not alone. Others have begun to congregate, and not just bombed out parishioners reluctant to leave the only place they've ever known. There are other intact buildings, civic buildings commandeered for the purpose. But still they come to the church. Paolo has told Mrs Quigley that the place has become a Mecca, and Mrs Quigley has responded by saying that she doesn't know about that, because the only religious thoughts Mrs Quigley has ever entertained have been Catholic.

Were any turbaned Muslim to arrive looking for help he wouldn't find her wanting. They're sleeping in the church hall. They're sleeping in the pews. The doors are never locked. They're billeted on her living room floor. She's expanded to the occasion like a liberated genie. She's thrown open her antiseptic bathroom for public use. She cooks heroically, shift after shift, everything fried, everything eaten. She plunders the hoarded reserves, dumps down piles of fritters, mounds of corned beef hash, troughs of baked beans and gestures them all to dive in. She disappears into her sublet flat, now deserted beneath its tottering chimneys, and returns with armful after armful of girls' clothes, mothballed, fifteen years out of fashion, patched but clean. She distributes these with the same largesse. She farts and grunts at the same volume and frequency but now almost always in a crowd. She isn't keeping an appointment with history, she doesn't have a Churchillian sense of the arrival of her moment, but in a week she's become a force of nature. All that love, for absent daughters and unseen grandchildren has accumulated with the illicit rent. The Luftwaffe lanced something. The only thing that has matched her growth is Paolo's admiration of it. He thinks she's become operatic, a Valkyrie.

She's the one thing he looks forward to seeing, walking back from the funeral. He's bone weary, the lines on his face etched by dust of pulverised matter. Like everyone else he's been breathing smoke and brick dust for days. He's a caricature of a young man with prematurely stamped authority. The last time he looked in the mirror he felt he looked like some pantomime character. He's aged ten years in three days and hopes to shed some of this in the year to come, grow younger as the fatigue and grief disperse and their numerous house guests find other accommodation. No one who has lived through this will ever be young again.

This morning he listened to the roll-call in the shipyard. There was a delay of five seconds or so at each failure to respond. The name was called again. If the silence was repeated the name was struck through. The register moved on. There are the wounded, the no-shows who were damaged or perished while off shift. It's ironic that the intended target was the safest place to be. He saw Stephen at the roll-call. There was a sense coming off the assembled men, like breath from herded cattle on frosty mornings: sheer relief at survival; guilt felt for the same reason; grief; camaraderie. More than anything else there's a barely repressed determination to mock their efforts; to out-produce them; to launch tonnage down the Clyde that will sink theirs; to give voice to those who aren't there to answer the register by silencing those who silenced them. In the half-light and the crowd Paolo prays for them, those unmolested people in sleeping towns and cities on the other side who had nothing to do with this but will bear the brunt of its expiation.

Thomas Gildea's still intact but not at work. He's not at work because he can't leave the flat. He can't leave the flat because he's looking after Danny's brother in Irene's absence. Irene isn't there because she's looking for Danny.

Irene's barely recognizable. At the first sound of the all clear she hands Paul to Mrs McCluskey and plunges out. There's no method in her search. Initially it consists of rushing to the now desolate places he might be and repeatedly screaming his name. When this elicits no response she runs to a random mound of rubble near the close entrance to her flat and begins throwing aside broken bits of masonry. When nothing is disclosed she moves to another mound. She goes further afield and keeps this up for a few hours until her manic search is interrupted by instantaneous exhaustion and she lies down among the ruins she's standing in and falls asleep. She's only out for two hours and is roused by wardens, who initially think she's an intact corpse amidst the destruction. When she's animated into twitchy life and starts shouting Danny's name they realise they have another problem. They explain she can't stay here. The Germans dropped landmines by parachute, some with delayed reaction fuses. They handle her with the circumspection of a charge that might still detonate. One attempts to put his jacket round her shoulders but she shrugs this off and bolts like a skittish mare, stumbling on the rubble until she's out of sight beyond the collapsed gable.

She stumbles back towards the flat, repeating the prayer underneath her breath in a desperate chant. 'Let it all be a mistake. Let it not be him. Let him be there when I get back. Let it all be a mistake. Let it all be a mistake.' She's rehearsing in her mind their reunion when she will fall on him and tell him never, never, NEVER do that to her again. But when she gets within minutes of her street she finds searchers looking for her. There's no reprieve in their approaching faces and she covers her face with her hands and suddenly sits in the middle of the glass-strewn road. They help her up. Suddenly rejuvenated by not wanting to hear what they say she runs on. When she turns into the street Deborah is there and she rushes towards Irene, throwing her arms around her. Irene wonders for a moment if this is restraint, or ballast. Does Deborah know she feels as if she will simply float away?

'Thomas is in the flat – with the baby.' Deborah says this very deliberately. It doesn't work.

'What time is it?'

'Gone six o'clock. It'll be dark soon. You have to go home, Irene. You have to.'

She's doing a calculation. Six o'clock. Six o'clock on the evening following the night he ran out. He must be hungry. She's not but he must be. He's of that age when they're always hungry. Especially boys. He's an eating machine. He's around here, somewhere, under this. She pulls out of Deborah's embrace and pushes aside a broken ashlar block, or this, the shredded end of a sash window frame. Deborah goes in and comes back with Thomas and Paul. They call to her. She stops foraging for a moment and comes across to kiss all three, then turns and resumes with a more intense preoccupation.

There's a kind of order beginning to assert itself. Bodies are being stacked in the pend, awaiting collection, shrouded for decency as best they can manage. That rebellious persistence that manifested itself yesterday, after the first wave, to stay, to make a fist of it, has gone with most of the flammable material after last night. There isn't anything for most of them to live among.

They're clearing the main roads of debris, working in shifts, to get the buses through and the people out. Wardens circulate with news that a refugee area has been set up in the Vale of Leven, and there will be others, in Kirkintilloch, Milngavie and further afield. They'll run special trains to Helensburgh when arrangements are made. Irene hears this and says to herself that she's not leaving. They can come back again and pulverise this place until there aren't two atoms to stick together but she's not leaving.

Because there are things that can't be admitted. They just can't.

Even to consider them gives them a kind of provisional existence she can't afford. She's her imagination to give credibility to pitiable odds. But postponed facts are hovering. They're circling closer with increasing persistence. They dart forward. They inflict possibilities. They say that Danny, *her* Danny, is vapour, blown back to the same stellar dust that we and all that we see are compounded of. They say he's not going to totter round the corner, all bravado gone. They say he's nothing, or he's here, somewhere. They say he's not sitting in some little cave somewhere, miraculously groined by masonry that just happened to fall into a protective arch. They say he's not awaiting the breakthrough shaft of light and the reprieving shout, to be carried on a stretcher, sitting bolt upright like some comic potentate, drinking sweet tea. They say he's deformed into the shape that the dynamics of falling rubble admit; his bones, shattered; his organs, paste; the chalice of his skull, brimming with delicate intelligence, caved.

She swats these thoughts away and runs to the pend and with surprising logic discounts the bundles that are too big. And then she begins systematically to go through the smaller ones, without reverence or qualms. She's not horrified at what she sees, just incrementally relieved each time the blanket doesn't give her his face. She senses the people around are beginning to approach. Perhaps they're officials who put the bundles here. Perhaps they're relatives. There's a hand on her shoulder that she brushes away. And now there's another, more forceful. And now Deborah has caught her up.

'It's all right. I'll take her. I'll take her.'

And this time Irene doesn't run away but sinks.

'Come home. It's still standing. Stephen can... can look here. Come home. Come home. Come with me.'

She can't articulate what it means to leave, to give up, to admit the possibility, to cease to deny, to conclude the sustained act of imagination that's keeping him alive. It's abandonment.

She kneels down, blocking the pend, and Deborah kneels beside her.

THIRTY
TWO

Deborah joins Stephen and Paolo in the blustery March sunshine, gazing down the hill. And now she wishes she hadn't. Apart from the acknowledgement that civility demands, neither has said anything to her. She came down for some relief and has only confronted this silent bond that she feels her sex, or her pragmatism, or one of the countless other things she doesn't know about, excludes her from. She's about to leave when she reflects that it was on this very spot, a thousand years ago, with Michael perched on her hip that they watched the launch and Father Delaney hove into sight. Perhaps there's a significance to the moment that's caused it to be emblazoned, but if so, she can't distil what it is. She's about to try and explain her dilemma to both of them but decides not to bother. It's beyond her powers of articulation. And what interest would it be anyway, to know a past moment of no perceived significance has assumed a gravity in someone else's mind simply because they remember it? She goes back inside.

They're not trying to exclude her. They unintentionally give the impression of unity but each is locked within his own preoccupation, posed like parallel Easter Island figures with uncharged air between.

'The cats.' Paolo says, and breaks the spell of inactivity by actually pointing.

'What?'

'The cats. Look. They're famished. They're all over the place.'

He never saw cats as victims before, just as Heather Cunningham never thought of vermin as refugees. They're not all over the place. He realises he's exaggerating but at the moment he can see two, and he's seen others this morning. And those that he has seen look as if their proverbial resilience is all used up, large headed, matted, concave in the flanks. It occurs to him they've been domesticated to exactly the wrong extent. They lack the initiative of the migrating vermin. The rats left when the bodies were removed. These cats are tied to what they know, circling a non-existent hearth. 'Aren't we all?' he says to himself and realised he's inadvertently said it aloud as Stephen looks down at him, and then goes back to looking back down the street. Paolo makes a mental note to do something. What? They're only cats. What would Saint Francis of Assisi have done? But he didn't have a parish ravaged by the Luftwaffe to attend to. It's all very well being a spiritual genius, but now isn't the time to advocate poverty to these burned out people who have mostly lost what little they had. He might have taken off his clothes, but he didn't have a March wind coming in off the estuary to contend with. They're only cats. Still. He'll see what he can do.

Stephen returns to what he was mulling over before the distraction. The cacophony of the shipyards is floating up to them in waves with the smell from the river. This combination is so deeply ingrained in him it's almost genetic, a comforting backdrop to the name he's mulling over with slow metronomic regularity.

Kinloch Rannoch. Kinloch Rannoch. Kinloch Rannoch.

It's the nearest they ever had to a honeymoon, Myra Neavie calling in a favour of her dead husband's sister to give them something other than a single night in the Central Hotel. They'd had their night there, their first together, and afterwards she'd said to him, 'That's that then,' and laughed aloud, just for him, private, raucous, and that's when their compact had been truly made. They'd taken the early train with their new-found intimacy to the Highlands. And in his mind the train's cryptic rhythm had whispered their destination: Kinloch Rannoch, Kinloch Rannoch, and he wondered if it would be too juvenile to say to her.

The train deposited them at Rannoch station and then dwindled, glinting in the autumn brightness, towards Mallaig. They climbed the steps to the walkway over the tracks, he with their creaking new luggage. And when he got half way he put down the bags and simply looked.

The basin of moorland was fringed with distant mountains and the light seemed to pour down on all sides from an overarching sky. He felt as if he was standing in the centre of a colossal bowl of purples and russets, capped by a luminous dome that sucked up the dispersing vapours into infinity. Until now his world has been encompassed by tenements, an industrial river and shipyards. As he continues to breathe, his circumscribed spirit soars. She becomes embarrassed by his preoccupation. She's been here before. She arrived too young for awe. She tells him their luggage is blocking the walkway, although the truth is that there's no one to impede. She snaps him out of it by saying they're being rude and keeping their lift waiting, although she doesn't know if it's waiting for them at all.

There's a single track road that services the station and terminates there. A middle aged man stands chatting to a uniformed station official. Stephen sits in the back with luggage and various miscellaneous supplies while Deborah sits beside the driver, who chats to her, amicably, asking questions, elucidating for his own benefit the network of kinship with her aunt. They snake down the north bank of Loch Rannoch and the van stops at every other settlement, sometimes lone houses, sometimes clusters, where the driver hands things out, or takes things on, or both. Stephen wonders if this is his job, or is this just the way commerce is conducted up here? When they get to Kinloch Rannoch he's embarrassed by their indebtedness, and attempts to put his hand in his pocket to give the driver something for his trouble. She stops him in time.

'That's not how they do things up here,' is all she says.

With the exception of an obelisk to celebrate a long-dead local poet and clergyman, everything, the church, the hotel, the houses, the dry dykes dividing the fields, is made of local stone. Everything's local. It takes him a few days to work out that it has to be.

Deborah's aunt looks like a healthy older female version of her father. It takes him aback, since he never knew the man in a consecutive week of health. And here's a woman surfeit with it. She came up here to be married and, like Myra, outlived her husband. The locals have taken to her, but he knows that if she lives to be a hundred and fifty she'll still be the widow from Glasgow. The house is the gable end of a small stone terrace of six, the end chimneys symmetrically smoking in a picturesque effect that looks put on for their arrival. She's given them her room and takes him out, on the pretext of showing him her small home, to allow Deborah to unpack their things and make the room temporarily their own. The end location gives her an additional strip of garden and she shows him her vegetable patch, an oblong of netting and parallel cultivation.

'But the winters are fierce,' she says, replying to an unasked question. And anticipating another she says: 'No, I couldn't ever go back.' And by way of explanation she gestures round to all this, the susurrating trees, the lichen-covered stones, the luminous air and water cascading off the hillside in peaty torrents the colour of stewed tea, thundering down carved recesses into incremental foamy pools. And he looks at her and marvels, the way he marvels at Myra, to come here and bury a husband and carve out a life among these people and this landscape – these woman and their vitality.

The village nestles in the lee of Schiehallion, a mountain of improbable regularity, of intersecting diagonals like a child's drawing of an Indian tepee. Its very uniformity has made it amenable for calculation. It's piece of local history disclosed to them in the bar on the third night, as Deborah sips her first ever dry sherry and feels sophisticated. In 1774 the Astronomer Royal, the Reverend Nevil

Maskelyne, calculated the weight of the mountain and from that inferred the mass of the Earth. Neither Stephen nor the local pretend to understand how it was done. Remembering that fireside conversation, Stephen knows it's one of the things Jacek would have understood. Failing Jacek. Housebound Jacek. He wished now he'd told him, not to want to understand but just to have given him the pleasure of explaining. It was one of his few comforts, the gift of unfolding the complicated, of bringing it into understandable compass, that stayed with him almost to the last. Dying Jacek. His atoms would now be more widely dispersed than his books had he lain on his ottoman this past week. Birds now fly through the space his bookish little niche once occupied.

Kinloch Rannoch. Kinloch Rannoch.

That calculation, centuries old, intended to make the world explicable, and that human gloss of occupation, centuries older, didn't begin to touch the place. It felt ancient, raw, scraped by glaciation. Ice has deposited single stones larger than tenement blocks to sit like sentinels and ignore millennia. Being there gave him a comforting sense of insignificance. Kinloch Rannoch. It's not what it is, it's that the Germans would never get there. And if they did, if darkness won out, this brief period of human colonisation deserves to conclude.

Kinloch Rannoch. Kinloch Rannoch.

Going through the bundles in the pend, because Deborah asked him to. Excusing himself to the hovering relatives and moving on to the next pend, the next bundle. Some of them unrecognizable, identified by clothes and artefacts. None of them the Gildea boy. Not that his absence was any reprieve. Not after all this time.

Every time someone meets someone they didn't expect to see there's the relief and the unspoken mutual congratulation. So you're still among the quick. But the surprise rendezvous have now all petered out. There are hundreds of stories of fortuitous survival but none that bear Danny's name. He's pieced together the story that does bear Danny's name and it says that a besotted schoolboy ran after a girl who wasn't there and was never seen again. There's a story-book finality to this. The girl was seen again, crouching petrified in a school toilet. And her brother was seen again, broken but breathing, among the glass and shop debris the blast had thrown him through. But it took someone other than their father to locate both. Finding his flat standing Alan had waited there with a bottle, reasoning that to be a better tactic than the three of them wandering round with the possibility of their paths not crossing.

Stephen thinks that had their father been in the locating business, Alan might also have been in the protecting business, and there wouldn't be two renegade children to find. Stephen thinks that had that fucking little parasite shown one iota of care for his children, Irene Gildea wouldn't now be wearing a face so creased with grief that it looks as if pulled in by a drawstring. Stephen felt so strongly about it that yesterday afternoon he walked to Alan Renton's booth. The cigarette end didn't get the opportunity to describe eloquent circles. It was still in Alan's mouth when abruptly extinguished in a flurry of ash, by the force of a blow that dislocated Alan's jaw and liberated four carious teeth.

Kinloch Rannoch. Kinloch Rannoch.

He's always harboured a little fantasy of them being there. The only snag is that he doesn't have an exportable skill, and they don't make ships there. If they did he wouldn't want to go. And he can't see him successfully knitting himself into the landscape and the community the way Deborah's aunt has. He's always been conspicuous, although he never tried to be. Still, there's no harm in dreaming. He could see Michael there. There's a primary school. It probably comprises only one classroom and probably only one teacher for the whole place. It's probably a woman. What if she's no good? Still, can't be worse than that maniac the Gildea boy and Renton's kids had to suffer, dragging that terrified girl up to the roof in the midst of a firestorm, to tempt providence or keep some kind of rendezvous none of them can imagine.

Deborah's looking down from the window at him. He can feel it. When she came down a few minutes ago he couldn't find anything consoling to say and he doesn't trust himself to say anything, just as he doesn't trust himself to look up and meet her glance head on. She left the house of her mother to manage the house of her and her husband. They've never known any kind of separation. He feels as if he's being physically cloven and he knows she feels it worse than he does. At least she'll have Michael. And her mother. And the girl. Four females in a small house in the lee of Schiehallion and probably a female schoolteacher too. He hopes Michael doesn't become effeminate. He'll take the train to Rannoch station as often as their finances permit, travel down the bank of that shining loch and arrive to surprise his son with a model spitfire and blasts of masculine bonhomie. He'll pretend to wrestle and hold him tight for embarrassingly long interludes, just to make up for the accumulated contact he's forfeiting. He'll send his pay packet North. But it's not just the money. The skill of those spared is needed now more than it ever was. Even if he had the money he couldn't run up there and hide. The fantasy will have to wait.

She didn't take much persuasion. And if the risk to the boy staying here wasn't enough he tipped the balance by pointing out the luxury of voluntary separation.

'Look at Irene Gildea...'

She stared at the linoleum. He wanted to shout, to rail – this fucking war! They've contaminated a hemisphere. Fucking bastards. He wants to break plates. But he doesn't.

She goes to pack.

Their honeymoon luggage, minus his things, sits to bursting on the steps between him and Paolo.

Deborah knows she won't have to go and look for Irene Gildea because Irene is observing the whole scene from her window across the street. Her best and oldest friend, Deborah, is leaving with her breathing son and she doesn't trust herself to come down. She retreats from the window into the shadowy recesses of the room and is replaced by Thomas, with Danny's brother hanging round his neck. The boy's taken to clinging, in the increasing tension of his brother's absence, of crying spontaneously at the relentless silences. From the perspective of his living-room window Thomas has seen something that the observers on the ground haven't. He makes his way down, still holding Paul, and crosses the street to join Stephen and Paolo just as the van crests the hill. Another favour. Paolo called it in this time. Thomas nods to each of them in turn. Stephen doesn't know what to say to him. He tried thinking himself into the other man's position, but couldn't. The hypothesis of a world without Michael was too distressing. He thinks that Father Delaney would have made some cack-handed attempt to relegate it to the context of eternity, and congratulate himself on a job well done. Paolo seems to be as lost for words of consolation as he is. Thomas' face isn't creased like a dried chamois the way Irene's is, but there's the trembling crust of an assumed expression that's being sustained at who knows what cost.

The van draws up opposite the luggage. The driver gets out. He's young, early twenties, and all business. He's surprised at the integrity of the street.

'You've had it easy round here then.' The others take their cue from Thomas and say nothing. 'You want me to take the luggage, Father?'

Paolo looks at Stephen who answers.

'No thanks.'

He wants something to occupy his hands when the time comes.

'Few streets across,' the driver continues, impervious to the mood, 'saw a family, washing themselves at a burst water main. A whole family. Fancy.'

No one knows if it's a question. Paolo coughs. He imagines his lungs powdered with brick dust.

'Just goes to show,' the driver says.

Paolo's tempted to ask what it goes to show. That destitute people are resourceful, or just desperate? Couldn't they have sent someone older? Again he reprimands himself. They're doing him a favour. High spirits might be out of kilter here, but it's in dire shortage just now and it's what they need to see them through. He's young. They need that too. People who aren't going to be defined by the past few days.

'Where's the Renton boy?' Thomas asks, turning his full attention to Stephen.

'Vale of Leven hospital. Nothing permanent. He'll get back. Heather Cunningham's agreed to take him.'

'The girl?'

Stephen nods towards his stairwell.

Paolo's done this too. He'll deny any credit. All he's done is facilitate, match two of the numerous needs to the best available offers. And these are good offers. He doesn't know what official channels would be in circumstances like this but there's a glaringly obvious higher good. He simply walked into Alan Renton's booth and announced he'd forfeited his children. He left before Alan began to practice the effect of culminating parental ire. Paolo's timing was fortuitous. Stephen called in two hours later and put a stop to the performance. Any thought Alan might have had of starting the 'proceedings' he'd been shouting to himself about, whatever they might be in a bombed out parish of haphazard facilities and a fair proportion of them dead, stopped suddenly and disappeared with his liberated teeth. When the swelling subsides, and his tongue becomes accustomed to the cavities, he'll cultivate a new persona: the dispossessed parent. But he'll be careful only to practice it when Stephen Neavie isn't there.

Paolo's mulling over Stephen's evaluation of the damage to Campbell being nothing permanent. What else is he supposed to say to Thomas? Nothing permanent. Paolo doubts that. He'll walk and talk again. He'll come out and convalesce with a woman who will feed and care for her son's best surviving friend. But he'll be without Gig.

Stephen's thinking of the brother and sister too. It's bad enough to have a useless little prick like Alan for a father, but now there's the stigma of the Gildea boy's death waiting to stick. No one's said anything. No one's had to. But there's the unspoken fact that Danny ran out after the brother and he, not Campbell, paid the shocking price for the sister's absence. It doesn't matter that the girl was coerced by that insane woman. It doesn't matter that Campbell was activated by love of his sister. They're still among the living. And to be alive in circumstances like these, when Danny isn't, is, to some, somehow blameworthy.

Knowing that the girl's in their house Irene can't bring herself to come down and see her best friend off. And Stephen reflects that his isn't the only family that's being broken up. The brother and sister have never been separated and now she's going to Kinloch Rannoch, to stretch the scant resources there, and he's going with Heather Cunningham and her son once he's mended enough. Heather's got country relatives too. Who knows, perhaps he'll even collect the boy on one of his trips north, effect a double reunion, fly kites at the foot of Schiehallion. Anything's possible.

Paolo's got his own hopes. There isn't much of a population in the parish to sustain rumours. Of those left, most are leaving. Like just now. Some of the few intact buildings are going to have to come down. He's looking forward to the time his church is more than just a dormitory. He harbours a cosy fantasy of a rebuilt parish, like one of those architectural models of the ideal community, with boulevards and green spaces and municipal happiness, repopulated with people as ebullient as the young driver, who'll walk around and wish one another good morning, all the misery disappeared with the cleared rubble. And in the more immediate future, Campbell restored to full health and reunited with his sister. He imagines himself standing at a discreet distance to witness this, just as he'll keep to the periphery of the action when another van deposits Deborah and Michael Neavie back on these steps where the luggage now squats, and he'll watch Stephen come down the stairs and put his arms round them.

Deborah comes out with Myra on her arm. Her mother has aged visibly in the last three days. That last rally has sapped her. Every novelty costs. She looks as if air has leaked out. She didn't carry much weight but this slow puncture of her vitality has revealed the structure beneath her visible parts. She glances out from her skull. The hand, along Deborah's forearm linked in hers, is an articulation of joints, sinew and vessels, peppered with liver spots. In the past seventy-two hours Stephen has watched her deflate. He hopes Kinloch Rannoch will insinuate its beauty and blow some life into her. It's either that or six feet of Perthshire because they've run out of room to bury folk down here.

Gig follows, leading Michael. This has been sold to him as a holiday to a magical land he's never visited before, and there's an old lady there who apparently loves him despite no effort on his part. He's so happy he looks as if he's filled with helium. He's hungry to get the adventure started. He wants to leave, right now, in this van. And then there's a train. He's never been on a train. He's trotting on the spot, keeping up with his elusive dream. His charged happiness throws the mood of the others into starker relief. For an instant there's a flicker of something imploring on Stephen's face, and then he musters. He wouldn't have the boy understand otherwise, he helped manufacture this fiction, but somehow Michael's excitement at the wrench makes it harder to take. Thomas looks at Michael intently, for half a sustained unblinking minute, and is suddenly absorbed with his own son's buttons. Stephen sees, and picks up the luggage.

With no forewarning, Miss Herne emerges into their little arena. Her approach has been obscured by the van. Her movements are stiff. The lacerations on her calves must be telling. Her appearance lacks her normal finish, performing her toilet in the half dark with doors for windows, intermittent water and no electricity. But she's still the best groomed person in the street. The suddenness of her appearance and the public knowledge of her behaviour gives her an assumed gravity. They all fall silent. Even Michael. She doesn't say anything but transfers her bag to her left hand and extends her right towards Gig. The girl looks at her with an expression of sheer fear and then turns to Deborah. Her young face cracks. There's a momentary tableaux. Stephen's about to put a stop to it when there's a scuttling of feet brushing past. Irene Gildea launches into the charged space and slaps Miss Herne on the face with a pendulum force that resounds like a pistol shot down the canyon of ruined tenements. Miss Herne is displaced by the sheer force of the blow and falls to her knees. She gasps for breath on all fours and tries to regain her equilibrium. Irene Gildea stands over her. Her face is distorted. Stephen drops the bag and moves between them, his back to Miss Herne. In all his life, in the violence of the yards, he has never seen an expression like Irene Gildea's. Thomas moves towards her, nodding to Stephen. He puts an arm on his wife's shoulder, his other still supporting Paul. She leans towards him incrementally, a ratcheted descent, and buries her face in the gap between him and the child. There's a stifled blurt, louder than the slap, even though it's suppressed. She suddenly leans back. Her face is a tormented smudge. She takes a screeching breath. Paolo makes a move towards her but is intercepted by Deborah. She has left her mother and put her arms around Irene. They shuffle in an ungainly little tripod towards her close entrance. Half-way across the street they unravel and Irene allows herself to be led on either side. They make the stairs and disappear into the tiled passageway.

Paolo helps Miss Herne up. Her hair has come untethered. A stray tendril falls over her face and she tucks this behind her ear. Her stockings are badly torn. One knee is bleeding. There's a large welt on her cheek and a cut where the wedding ring made contact.

'In the van,' Stephen orders, snatching up first Michael then Gig and stowing them like luggage. He next helps Myra to the back seat.

'Suitcases,' he says, to the driver. The younger man's watching the exchange like an astonished tennis spectator and is suddenly galvanised by Stephen's order. Stephen thinks the only good thing to come out of this is that the pretence of being preoccupied with the luggage isn't needed anymore.

'You're bleeding' Paolo says. 'Come down to the church house.'

She looks at him, as if from a great distance, with the disinterest of scrutinising a statue in a foreign city.

'I still have my school,' she says.

'No.'

'What do you mean? It's intact.'

'It's closed.' He gestures to the unpopulated spaces beyond the intense little group. 'They're all gone. And it's coming down.'

She bows her head and stays quite rigidly still for a minute. She turns and begins to walk slowly uphill.

Deborah returns from Irene Gildea's flat. Her mouth is twisted. It can't twin Stephen's as he kisses her. The air is escaping from Michael too as he looks around, perplexed. Everybody's suddenly no fun anymore. Stephen leans over Myra and lifts his son bodily from the back seat. He kisses him. They make the gesture on the side of the van of a bottle launching a ship, their little private pact. He produces a box from his hip pocket. It's a small mouth organ, wrapped in opaque tissue. Michael blows out a discordant note and sucks in another. Stephen rewraps it, replaces it in the box and puts this in the boy's jacket pocket. Michael's back to being elated.

He puts the boy back, slams the door, throws a shilling to the driver through the open window. He holds the front passenger door for Deborah and closes it behind her. The reflection of the tenements is superimposed on her upward glance towards him, her mouth still twisted. The engine rattles to life. Michael's already standing on the seat waving to his father through the back window. They overtake Miss Herne before the brow.